COURTING SEASON

Also by Jo Anne Cassity . . .
Don't miss her critically acclaimed
Diamond Homespun Romance *Tender Wishes*:

Diamond Books by Jo Anne Cassity

TENDER WISHES
COURTING SEASON

COURTING SEASON

JO ANNE CASSITY

DIAMOND BOOKS, NEW YORK

This book is a Diamond original edition,
and has never been previously published.

COURTING SEASON

A Diamond Book / published by arrangement with
the author

PRINTING HISTORY
Diamond edition / August 1994

All rights reserved.
Copyright © 1994 by Jo Anne Cassity.
Cover appliqué illustration by Kathy Lengyel.
This book may not be reproduced in whole or in part,
by mimeograph or any other means, without permission.
For information address: The Berkley Publishing Group,
200 Madison Avenue, New York, NY 10016.

ISBN: 0-7865-0023-9

Diamond Books are published by The Berkley Publishing Group,
200 Madison Avenue, New York, NY 10016.
DIAMOND and the "D" design
are trademarks belonging to Charter Communications, Inc.

PRINTED IN THE UNITED STATES OF AMERICA

10 9 8 7 6 5 4 3 2 1

For the boys—my brothers: Jim, Don, and Chuck, with love.

ACKNOWLEDGMENTS

With deepest appreciation to the following people and organizations:

Once again, Dr. Dianne C. Eddie, D.V.M.: my favorite veterinarian.

Pat Jackson: from the Boonville Area Chamber of Commerce.

The Friends of Historic Boonville: for all the wonderful information about old Boonville.

The Boonville Public Library.

Judith Stern, my editor: Judy, thanks for everything, especially for allowing me to continue the Hawkins's family story.

Carole, Paulette, Tammy, and Jolene: I'd be lost without you guys.

Debbie and Dee: I love you both.

And to all of you out there—the rest of my family, my dear friends, my readers: my encouragers. Thank you does not nearly say it eloquently enough.

Jo Anne Cassity
August 19, 1993
Niles, Ohio

PROLOGUE

May 1892, Poplar Bluff, Missouri

"Ouch!" The blow caught him in the left eye, knocking his head backward. His vision blurred, and his eye began to throb immediately.

Yessiree, he acknowledged silently without anger, *it'll be purple by evenin'.* Through his undamaged eye he watched his attacker spring to her feet and stomp off across the tree-shaded banks of the Black River, her skirts hiked up to her knees, revealing the patched, faded britches she wore beneath.

James Gordan Lawson grinned. "Whewee, Meg! Ya still know how to pop one!" His fourteen-year-old voice echoed his admiration and respect.

Megan Hawkins turned and angled him a fiery, blue-eyed glare that said she thought him a mindless fool. Then she bent and retrieved a short branch from the dew-stained grass. She shook it at him in a threatening manner and affected her most admonishing tone. "You try any more of that fancy smoochin' stuff on me, Gordie Lawson, and I'll bean ya brainless. I thought we was gonna study some this mornin', but I shoulda known better!" She anchored one hand on a girlishly slender hip and cocked her head. "What in Sam Hill has gotten into you lately?" She tossed her long mane of blond hair over her shoulder and eyed him with every ounce of disgust her twelve-year-old face could muster. "You're tetched, I swear! All ya wanna do anymore is get a peek under my skirts and slobber all over me!"

Still nursing his throbbing eye, Gordie lifted his lanky frame off the damp riverbank and closed the distance between them. He stopped before her where she stood beneath the branches of a large poplar tree. "Well, hell, Meg. I couldn't get a peek of anythin' anyway with you always wearing those darned britches."

She tipped forward at the waist and bellowed, "Say damn, dammit! How many times do I gotta tell ya, if you're gonna cuss, do it proper! 'Darn' ain't a proper cussword!" Reminding him of that fact brought to mind the old childhood fantasy they'd once shared. "It's a damn good thing we didn't run off and become outlaws like we'd planned, 'cause you shore woulda made a sorry one. You'da caused any 'real' outlaw shame and humiliation!"

Unaffected by her harsh words, he grinned again, a lazy, lopsided one this time, infuriating her all the more. He had long ago outgrown the fantasy she still harbored, but he humored her just the same with a loud, heartfelt "Damn!"

"That's better," she acknowledged begrudgingly, then dropped the branch, deciding to forgive him for his earlier misconduct. After all, he was a poop-head and really didn't know any better.

He stepped closer, his hand still shielding his injured eye. "Everybody does it." His voice was quiet, his young face very serious now.

"Does what?" she asked, though she knew the answer.

"Kiss and stuff."

She snorted her disbelief and studied him from beneath short thick lashes. It irritated her that in the space of a few months his shoulders had broadened considerably, and he'd outgrown her by several inches. And somehow his nose, which used to look flatter than an inside-out mushroom, was now very nicely shaped, while his face, which was once homelier than any critter this side of the Missouri, was becoming something akin to handsome. "Not everybody," she muttered, then looked off across the river, wondering what the hell was going on with him.

Too many things were changing.

Her gaze came back to him. Oh, he still adored her, that much she knew. His sleepy brown eyes never failed to reveal that fact. But a very big change had occurred between them, and somehow things were different. He no longer repeated everything she said; he no longer jumped to do her bidding; he no longer followed her lead, but fought to lead on his own. His gaze was entirely new, expressing something she couldn't quite discern or control. That something annoyed her as much as it challenged her.

"What do you think your sister and Doc Randolph do? What do you think they did to get that baby she's carryin'?" he asked bluntly, dropping his hand from his swollen eye.

Megan blushed and averted her gaze. She tossed her head to cover her embarrassment. "I know what they did. They got married!" She took two steps away from him and abandoned the cool shade of the poplar for the glory of the bright morning sunshine. Her hair caught the light and glistened with highlights.

"Did ya ever think about that with you an' me?" Gordie asked, all the while thinking she was the most beautiful girl in Missouri.

She threw him an impatient glance. "Think about what?"

"You and me," he repeated, "gettin' married."

Her eyes rounded, and her chin jutted forward. "Humph!"

She felt her cheeks burn even hotter. "I wouldn't marry you, Gordie Lawson! I wouldn't marry you if you were the last man left in Poplar Bluff. I wouldn't marry you if you were the last man left on this earth! I'm goin' East to school to be an animal doctor, just like my brother-in-law, the doc. Then I'm comin' home to marry someone like my pa, or my Uncle Chester, or . . . or . . ." She tipped her chin up high, while her eyes took on a defiant sparkle. "Maybe I'll even marry me an outlaw!"

Gordie decided to make his move. Forgetting his injury, throwing caution to the wind, he grabbed her arms, pulled her close, and awkwardly locked his lips on hers.

For a second she grew still, allowing the different sensations to sweep through her adolescent body. Then, without warning, indignation flared within, and she bit his lower lip. Hard.

He yelped and wrenched away. Seizing her opportunity, she made a fist, drew back her arm, and slugged him hard in his good eye.

He yelped again.

She nodded her satisfaction at the sound of his pain, then turned and stalked off in a heated huff, leaving him to squint after her.

He sucked in his damaged lip and tasted blood. Then he grinned and hollered, "You're still the prettiest girl in Missouri, Meggie. And you'll want me someday! You just wait and see!"

CHAPTER
1

Late May 1898, Poplar Bluff, Missouri
As the train slowly ground to a hissing halt, a long, loud whistle blew, announcing the Iron Mountain's arrival.

"Poplar Bluff!" Hurley Baker, the conductor, bawled, as he'd done for the last twenty-odd years. He peeked his head around the corner of the doorway to wink at the pretty young woman who occupied the front seat. "All off who's gittin' off! That means you, Miss Megan." His somber expression immediately disappeared into a wrinkled wreath of smiles.

Megan Hawkins chuckled and stood, then smoothed the wrinkles from her skirt. She was clothed most elegantly in a high-necked, fitted traveling dress of green satin, over which she wore a pretty cape. Perched most stylishly upon her piled, pale hair was a matching hat topped with feathers.

She was the perfect picture of propriety and looked every inch the lady.

But everyone in Poplar Bluff knew her and knew better, and they loved her just the same. She was, after all, one of their own.

5

She retrieved her bags from the compartment above her head, then made her way to the door. Setting the bags down, she gave Hurley a big hug, then lapsed easily into the accent of most locals, quickly abandoning the articulate verbiage she'd adopted during her stay in the East. "I've missed you somethin' fierce, Hurley."

Hurley flushed with pleasure and rolled back on his heels. "It's good to have ya home, Miss Meg."

"It's good to be here." She made her way past him and down the steps to stand on the hard-packed ground. She inhaled deeply and gazed out at all the familiar sights that looked exactly the same as they had when she'd left five years ago. Nostalgia swept her so sharply, so sweetly, she had to blink back tears.

In the distance she saw a wagon coming her way and knew it carried her pa and her three big, blond brothers, Matthew, Mark, and Luke. Though the distance was too great for her to make out the expressions on their faces, she could sense their wide, happy smiles.

She blinked again. She'd missed her people. She'd even missed Gordie Lawson.

She'd missed him far more in the past few years than she ever would have imagined. Far more than she ever would admit to anyone, even him.

"Think you'll be stayin'?" Hurley asked her from behind. He came down the steps carrying her bags.

She turned, shrugged, and offered him an uncertain grin. "Well, now, that depends. . . ."

"What do you mean, he's gone?" Megan frowned, trying hard to hide her disappointment. She continued to stroke the head of the huge black tomcat sprawled in her lap.

"Jist what I said. He's gone," her sister Johnnie answered matter-of-factly and rose from her chair. She picked up the empty platter from the table, then carried it over to the stove, where she busied herself heaping it high with another pile of cookies. "He moved on up to Boonville last year. Took a job there as deputy sheriff."

"Deputy sheriff!" Megan's voice was so shrill her cat, Willy, gave her a disgruntled glare and quickly abandoned her lap.

"That's what I said. Deputy sheriff. I didn't stutter."

"He'll get his fool head blown off! He never could shoot straight!" Megan tried to picture Gordie as an adult, competent enough to wear a badge, tote a gun, and keep the peace like her Uncle Chester had done in Poplar Bluff for so many years.

But try as she might, the image just wouldn't form.

"What did his folks say?" Megan rose from the table and joined her sister at the stove, plucking a large cookie from the nearly full platter.

"Seems to me they couldn't say much. After all, Jim's a grown man now."

"Jim!" Megan made a face. "Since when did Gordie become Jim?"

"He started usin' his first name about a year after you left." Johnnie angled Megan a glance. "It suits him a sight better'n Gordie does now." She was silent a moment, then quietly added, "He's changed some since you last saw him five years ago, Meg. He's full-grown. Ya might say he's become a real looker."

"Nobody changes that much!" But in all honesty Megan knew the change had begun long before she'd left.

"Jim did."

Bemused, Megan turned and crossed the room to stare out the window at her sister's orderly front yard. A trio of goats grazed on a new patch of grass, while a lone chicken pecked aimlessly at the ground. Megan watched Willy slink across the grass, readying himself for a surprise attack on the hapless chicken, then watched him abandon the attempt for the more challenging prospect of a small field mouse out near the old milk house her brother-in-law used as an office and animal hospital.

When she spoke, there was a wistful note in her voice. "I remember a time when he didn't so much as spit without checkin' how far with me first." She turned and gave Johnnie a slow smile. "Do you remember how he insisted he was gonna marry me, even when I said he'd be the last person on earth I'd marry?"

"I remember." Johnnie joined her sister at the window and wrapped an arm around her waist. She laughed. "It used to make your blood boil."

Mellowed by the memory, Megan's smile hovered for a moment, then disappeared. "I wrote him a long time ago and told him I expected to be home some time in May this year." She slid her hands into the front pockets of her faded britches. She hadn't been home ten minutes when she'd abandoned her fancy proper dress in favor of the preferred garment. "Seems to me he could've waited till I came home 'fore he up and took off that way."

"A man can't wait forever," Johnnie said quietly, her blue eyes reflecting wisdom far beyond her years. " 'Specially once he gets grown."

The back door slammed open, interrupting the reflective moment, and in strode Adam, Poplar Bluff's first and up until now only school-taught veterinarian. Behind him trailed two little boys, one who looked to be about seven years old, the other only about five. Behind them came Matthew, Mark, and Luke Hawkins.

For a moment Megan forgot Jim Lawson. Going down on one knee, she held out her arms to the two dark-haired boys who looked so very much like their handsome father. "Come on over here, boys, and give your Aunt Meg a hug."

They shuffled their feet a bit hesitantly, for neither boy remembered her.

"Go on," their Uncle Matt said, and gave each boy a gentle shove from behind. "She don't bite hard."

Not to be outdone, Luke snorted and rolled his eyes to the ceiling. "Don't lie to the boys, Matt. She don't bite at all. She jist sort of chews on ya a mite, that's all."

Mark chuckled, then said, "Don't listen to them two. They got corn husks for brains. Why, you boys got nothin' to be afraid of. She's pretty tame now that she's got some learnin'."

The boys hung back a moment longer, then finally honored Megan's request. She grabbed one in each arm and squeezed tightly until they giggled with delight. "Blue," she said to the oldest boy, whom his father had named after the deep color of his mother's eyes, "you were just a little tadpole when I went off to school, and you, Toby," she said to the youngest, "weren't even a serious thought yet." She threw back her head and let loose with a loud "Wheweeee, what I could teach you boys!" She arched her sister a wicked glance.

"Now, Meg," Johnnie warned, crossing the room to plant a kiss on her husband's jaw. "You teach them boys any of yer bad doin's, and you'll be reapin' what you sow in a few years when ya have your own young 'uns."

"Humph!" Megan rose and playfully swatted the boys on their behinds. "I sincerely doubt it. An' why would I want my own young 'uns when I can enjoy yours?"

Johnnie's eyes softened, and her gaze lifted to her husband. "When you fall in love, you'll want your man's babies. It's only natural. It's a sharin' of the finest kind. You'll want everything that's his, and you'll want to give him everything that's yours. It's like two halves comin' together into one bein'. You'll understand someday."

The brothers looked embarrassed, while Megan snorted her disbelief. "Who in Sam Hill is gonna father my young 'uns? There's nobody left in Poplar Bluff!" But even as she said the words, she knew they weren't true. It was her way of saying she didn't know a man in Poplar Bluff she would accept.

"There's plenty of young fellas still here in Butler County," Luke insisted, looking totally confused as usual. "I'm here."

Matthew arched him a look of scorn. "Not you, barkbrain. You're her brother."

Mark gave Matthew a grin. "If none of them is to your likin', Poplar Bluff ain't the only town in Missouri."

"You suggesting I take my doctorin' elsewhere?" She raised her chin in pretended indignation.

"No," Adam answered truthfully for all of them. "But you know very well this town won't keep two veterinarians busy for long. If your family hadn't taught me how to farm this land, I'd have a hard time of it feeding my family." He crossed the room and gave his sister-in-law a big hug. "Lord knows we missed you, squirt. We're glad to have you home." He grew silent a moment, then said, "It's a shame, though, you didn't get to see Jim Lawson 'fore he left. He's quite a fella. I'm real fond of him. We all are." He hesitated a moment, then offered, "Far as I know, he ain't married up yet. But it's not for the lack of several young ladies' efforts here in Butler County."

Megan frowned hard. "What in tarnation are you suggestin'?" But the ornery glint in his eye told her exactly what he was suggesting. "Me and Gordie?" she asked, planting her palm flat against her chest. Her gaze swept the faces of all present. She snorted and drew herself up to her full height. "Why, I wouldn't have ol' Gordie Lawson if he was the last man on earth, even if he did start callin' himself Jim. Humph!" she huffed and glared. "Jim, my eye!"

That same day, in the quiet little town of Boonville, Missouri, Jim Lawson yawned and tipped his chair back to rest the heels of his dusty boots on the edge of his desk.

He pushed his Stetson back on his head, continued polishing the barrel of his gun, and contemplated the wide stretch of mid-afternoon sunshine glaring in through the open office door of the Cooper County Jail.

He sighed and yawned again, wishing the day was over and nightfall would come, so he could get on with some real work.

He was bored with his new job. It wasn't that he didn't enjoy his position as deputy of Boonville. It was more that the job required very little of him.

The most he'd had to do since his arrival was settle a few squabbles between some of the more troublesome boys over at the schoolhouse and lock up ol' Sam Sweeney, the town drunk, every now and then. Of course, he reminded himself, he had to smooth down the feathers of Sheriff Jasper Johnson's wife whenever Jasper drank a few too many licks of whiskey over at the Old Tavern on his way home.

Jim hoped Jasper would make it home on time today. He'd left early, saying he had business to attend to, but Jim suspected that business was, as usual, to be settled between Jasper and a few hearty swigs of whiskey.

Jim smiled. He couldn't blame the man. If he were Sheriff Johnson, he'd need a few good swigs before headin' home to Gladys, too. Wrestling with that woman verbally or any other way was enough to drive any man to drinking. She was as mean as a spooked porcupine and just about as ugly. Jim shivered, grateful for once to be so bored.

He glanced around at the walls of his office, which were papered with many "Most Wanted" posters. As he listened to the echo of quiet resounding within the limestone walls of the large two-story building, he thought about the many vacant iron box cells and remembered the jail in his hometown of Poplar Bluff.

It seemed Chester Hawkins, Megan's uncle and the

sheriff of Poplar Bluff, rarely wanted for an occupant for his jail. In fact, on some particularly active evenings when there were some really bad doings in town, there was hardly room enough to hold all the boisterous hooligans who could be rounded up.

Not so in Sheriff Johnson's jail. At least not anymore. But, Jim reminded himself, Boonville was hardly Poplar Bluff. Things were different here. Quieter, more civilized . . .

Maybe a bit too civilized.

Just the same, things hadn't always been so quiet in this town. Why, in April of 1884 the notorious Frank James had been brought to this same jail to answer a warrant for his arrest for a train robbery that had taken place back in 1876. Surprisingly enough, however, the sympathetic citizens of Boonville had raised his bond in a matter of hours, believing him innocent of that particular charge. The case was later dismissed for lack of evidence.

Jim chuckled and thought, *Imagine that! Megan Hawkins would have enjoyed that little bit of news.*

Memories of her swept through his mind. God, she was somethin' else. Spunky! Yes, sirree. The spunkiest girl he'd ever known. He wondered if she'd changed much over the years. He supposed she had. No one stayed the same forever. The thought saddened him. He tamped down a feeling of nostalgia. It had been quite a while since he'd thought of her so intently, especially since he'd grown so fond of a local young lady he'd been courting for the past several months. Still, he supposed, he would always harbor a certain affection for Megan Hawkins. After all, for many years she had been the only girl in the whole world for him, and up until a few years ago he'd been sure she was the only one he would ever marry.

He wondered if she'd made it home like she'd planned. It would have been nice to see her, but he would have hated to miss the opportunity of this job.

After all, he thought, as he gazed through the front door to see Gladys Johnson waddling his way, Boonville needed him desperately.

Four weeks later, on a stage bound for Boonville, Megan Hawkins sat with her hands in her lap, her heart in her throat.

As she reflected on where she was going and why, she wondered if maybe she'd suffered some sort of serious brain damage the day she'd fallen out of that big oak tree ten years ago, when she was showing off in front of Gordie.

Yep, she decided, 'course she had. Why else would she have put herself in such a predicament? Why else would she have let that fool brother-in-law of hers send a letter off to Boonville, offering her services to the town as an educated veterinarian?

But she knew why.

She wanted to practice medicine as she'd been trained to do. And . . . she wanted to see Gordie Lawson. It was as plain and simple as that.

She was female enough to be curious about him, as well as woman enough to be mad as hell that he'd thrown her over without so much as a second thought. In the years they'd been apart, she'd come to realize that he'd been a very significant part of her past.

So she'd allowed Adam to send the damned letter. She'd been more than a little surprised when Mr. Tidwell, Boonville's postman and the town council's secretary, replied so quickly, saying that Boonville's townsfolk would be proud to have a real, qualified veterinarian of their own. They asked if Dr. Hawkins would come at once.

And so she did.

Yep, she was brain-damaged all right.

She turned her attention to the window, to stare at the

passing scenery. The sky was faultless, bluer than an artist could paint it. The passing scenery was rich with the various colors of wildflowers in full early-summer bloom.

She'd been uncharacteristically silent during most of her journey, though she'd met all three of her fellow passengers when the stagecoach had stopped at a post along the way to pick them up.

There was a pleasant older gentleman, who'd introduced himself as Mr. George Pribble. He had long, bushy sideburns that curved over his cheeks and connected with his equally bushy mustache. With him was his short, stocky wife, Edith, who frowned incessantly and whose huge breasts rested like mountains above her ample stomach.

Also aboard was a young woman very close to Megan's own age. Her name was Clarissa Westfield. She had shiny hair the color of dark honey, and big lovely eyes exactly the same shade. She also had a voice as soft and smooth as velvet. Judging from the little bit of conversion she and Megan had exchanged, Megan decided she was not only beautiful, but a real nice person as well.

They rode on for the space of an hour or so before Mrs. Pribble decided to voice her thoughts. "I certainly hope we aren't accosted by any of those horrible outlaws who've been rustling our neighbor's cattle."

Mr. Pribble patted his wife's hand. "I doubt we'll have to worry about that, dear. So far as anyone knows, they've never hurt anyone."

Mrs. Pribble sniffed and said, "Can you imagine, they even stole Maxwell Fletcher's dog. Now, isn't that a despicable thing to do?"

"Yes, dear," Mr. Pribble agreed obediently.

"Well," Mrs. Pribble said, and her second chin flapped as she nodded her head in indignation, "if a man will steal another man's dog, there's no limit to what else he'll take or what else he'll do."

"True, true." Mr. Pribble was not about to argue with his wife.

The carpetbag at Megan's feet rocked and jerked. She reached down, opened it a slice, and patted the occupant's head. "Now, you just settle down in there, Willy," she said, keeping her voice low and stern. Pushing the cat aside, she withdrew a large, gleaming pistol and placed it in her lap. She nailed Mrs. Pribble with a steady, blue-eyed gaze and told her, "You needn't worry none, ma'am. Any fool who bothers this stage will have a chunk of lead added to his anatomy."

Instead of being grateful, Mrs. Pribble's eyes widened with surprise. Then she slowly frowned her disapproval of the brash young woman.

Across from Megan, Mr. Pribble caught Megan's eye, offering her a questioning glance.

Megan smiled at him. "The gun is a gift from my pa, and that down there making all the noise," she said, gesturing to the rocking carpetbag, "is Willy. My cat."

"I see," said the gentleman, thoroughly charmed.

"A cat!" said his wife, not charmed at all. She abhorred guns. But even more than she abhorred guns, she abhorred cats. Not more than two seconds passed before she sneezed. She nailed Megan with her sharp gaze. "I insist you put the creature off immediately!"

"Off?" Megan's eyes grew round with disbelief.

"Yes! Off!" Mrs. Pribble repeated in a tone that indicated she wasn't used to people questioning her commands. Edith Pribble was a very important person in her hometown of Boonville. She was president of the ladies' quilting club, head of the Presbyterian ladies' circle, and chief organizer for all social and charitable events. No one, except Flora Fletcher, the pompously arrogant, wealthy wife of Maxwell Fletcher, dared challenge her importance and authority. Not if the townspeople wanted to live peaceably in Boonville.

But even if Megan had known of Mrs. Pribble's lofty stature, she wouldn't have been impressed and certainly not afraid. Her cheeks flushed with anger. "I beg your pardon, ma'am?" she ventured.

"I said you simply must put the animal off the stage! I can't travel with such a creature at my feet." Her cultured voice echoed her contempt. "Cats make my eyes water. They make me sneeze. I itch. I wheeze—"

As though he knew he was the prime topic of discussion, Willy stuck his head out of the carpetbag, looked directly at Mrs. Pribble, laid his ears back flat, and hissed fiercely enough to make any mountain lion envious.

Affronted, Mrs. Pribble nearly choked. "If you don't put him off, I'll put him off myself!"

"Now, is that a fact?" Megan drawled, pretending intense interest. She felt the heat rise within. "I don't think so, ma'am," Megan said quietly, her voice slipping into her accent. "You see, me and Willy, well, we sorta belong to each other. I've had him ever since I was ten years old. Why, I'd no sooner put him off this stage than I would you. Truth be told, you'd go first." She hefted her six-shooter quite expertly, twirled it around her finger a few rounds, then laid it carefully in her lap once again.

Mrs. Pribble's eyes nearly popped from their sockets. Her gaze went from the gun to Megan's face at least five times before she sputtered, "Are you threatening me, young woman?" Her full cheeks grew a very dark shade of purple, looking every bit like two large ripe plums about to explode.

Megan lifted her brows and considered the thought for a moment. "Might be that I am. If you think you can get away with touchin' one hair on that critter's body, you're dead wrong. You might find yourself singin' with the angels 'fore you can count to ten."

"Why, I never!" The older woman turned her haughty

gaze on her husband, who remained quietly subdued at her side.

"I bet you don't, either," Megan said matter-of-factly, cocking her head, "an' if you don't learn to be a little nicer, you never will. Isn't that right, Mr. Pribble?"

Mr. Pribble coughed and covered his mouth. Mrs. Pribble made a strange garbled sound.

Thoroughly impressed with the young woman beside her, Clarissa Westfield giggled discreetly.

"George, are you going to let this, this . . ." The older woman searched her mind for an appropriate term to use to describe the impertinent young woman seated across from her. Finding it, she squawked, "Are you going to let this *hoyden* talk to me in such a disgusting and disrespectful manner?"

"Now, Edith, I'm sure the young lady meant no harm." Mr. Pribble patted his wife's hand to calm her, while he worked hard to hide his smile, enjoying how his wife was being put down.

Mrs. Pribble pursed her lips into a tight, wrinkled bud and glared. When she finally found her voice, she shook a short chubby finger under Megan's nose and delivered a threat of her own. "When we get to Boonville, I'm turning you over to Sheriff Johnson, young woman. Decent folks do not tolerate verbal attacks and threats to their bodily person."

Megan didn't move an eyelash. "You do what you gotta do, ma'am."

The four remained silent for quite some time after that, and the morning drew on into a warm afternoon. Eventually Mr. Pribble dozed off and began to snore. It wasn't long before his wife joined him.

Clarissa leaned in toward Megan. Her voice hardly above a whisper, she asked, "Are you staying in Boonville or just passing through?"

"Staying." Megan smiled. "At least, I plan to."

"It won't be easy for you, I'm afraid. You've made a formidable enemy in Mrs. Pribble."

Megan nodded and grinned, not at all affected by Clarissa's grim warning. "I don't doubt it for a minute."

Megan's nonchalant mood was infectious. Clarissa smiled, relaxing. "Well, I'll look forward to seeing more of you, then. Boonville is my home, too. I'm returning from visiting one of my aunts in Springfield."

Megan turned to the other woman. "You like Boonville, do you?"

"Oh, yes," Clarissa answered easily, speaking louder so she could be heard over the Pribbles' snoring. "It's a lovely little town. The river bluffs are especially beautiful. You must go out to see them. And Thespian Hall offers our residents a bit of entertainment. I give readings there." At Megan's look of confusion, Clarissa explained. "You know, Shakespeare and the like."

"I see," Megan replied, understanding. "You have a beautiful voice. I imagine you're very good at what you do."

"I enjoy it. It keeps me busy for now. Once I marry and have children to care for, I doubt I'll have time for such things."

"You have a beau, do you?" Megan asked, having sensed that Clarissa was hoping she would.

"Yes, I do." Silence, then, "Do you?"

A hint of a smile touched Megan's lips. "I used to. I'm not sure anymore." She shrugged. "I kinda doubt it."

Clarissa discreetly changed the subject. "Well, I think you'll like our town. It's very quiet and peaceful."

Megan eyed her sideways. "Humph. Sounds a mite boring," she replied honestly, not bothering to hide the true nature of her thoughts.

Clarissa considered Megan's statement, then laughed. "I'd never thought of it that way," she said, a hint of surprise in her voice, "but I suppose it could seem boring to some." She studied Megan silently for the space of several seconds while she fanned herself with a lace-embroidered handkerchief. Miss Megan Hawkins was indeed an original. She was straightforward and unpretentious, and Clarissa had never met anyone quite like her. Clarissa decided she liked her immensely. "Are you planning on a long stay?" she asked, hoping she was.

"I s'pose you could say that. I'm taking on a position in Boonville as the new veterinarian."

Clarissa's eyes rounded with surprise. "Indeed!" She couldn't, in her wildest dreams, imagine the staunch, stuffy gentlemen of Boonville hiring a woman for such a position. She would have to see this to believe it. Their arrival was going to be a very interesting event! She remembered Mrs. Pribble's threat and thought it best to remind her new friend of its seriousness. "She means it, you know. She'll turn you over to Sheriff Johnson. She's rich enough and powerful enough to get her way. She was rich before she met Mr. Pribble, and she never lets him forget it, even though Mr. Pribble does well enough on his own with his mercantile store.

"It's not uncommon for her to make a fuss about nothing at all, and although the sheriff would like to put her in her place, he's married to her daughter, who's every bit as cranky, so he tries to pacify Mrs. Pribble to keep the peace."

Megan shrugged. "It won't be the first time."

"The first time for what?" Clarissa ventured, half-afraid to ask, but thoroughly intrigued.

"The first time I've been turned over to the law and set a spell in jail. I sincerely doubt it'll be the last."

At that statement, Clarissa's brows shot upward. She thought about her beau and suppressed a giggle. Poor Jim. He certainly had his work cut out for him.

CHAPTER
2

"Boonville!" the stagecoach driver bellowed and slowed the coach to a halt in front of a tidy little depot on High Street.

"Finally." Mrs. Pribble sniffed and tipped her pudgy nose into the air. She pressed her handkerchief against her swollen nostrils in an exaggerated effort to let everyone know exactly how miserable she truly was.

Unaffected, Megan lifted an eyebrow, while Clarissa stifled a chuckle.

Mr. Pribble sighed wearily and stepped down from the stage. His wife followed, clucking her complaints as she went.

Behind them came the two young women.

It was dusk. The town was draped in the hazy afterglow of the sunny day's warmth. In the distance the sky dripped pink ribbons into the horizon. Today was Sunday, and the streets were empty of activity, although a small group of men could be seen over on Morgan Street, huddled together in quiet conversation around a building that boasted a sign that read, *Cooper County Jail*. The air was laced with the low hum of their talk, which blended musically with the night sounds coming in off the river that bordered the little town. From a church down the street came the unified resonance of voices raised in song.

It was a peaceful place indeed, Megan thought. "So what do you think, Willy?" she asked softly, more to herself than her cat. "You think you can learn to like it here?" She clutched her carpetbag with both hands and gazed around at her surroundings, impressed with the orderliness of the streets, the planked sidewalks, the elegant Victorian design of many of the houses, and the tidy row of merchants' shops with their neat displays of merchandise arranged in huge glass windows. She turned to Clarissa, smiled, and decided her new friend most appropriately belonged in a town such as this one. At the same time she wondered how a girl like herself would ever manage to fit in. For all her outward trimmings of refinement, she was at heart a simple being who still liked critters better than she did most folks. "You have a real nice town here, Miss Westfield," she said to Clarissa. "I can see why you're so partial to it."

Noting the arrival of the stage, the small group of men dispersed, and two of them set off to greet the newly arrived group.

Clarissa waved off the formality of her name. "You're going to like it, too, Megan. And please call me Clarissa. After all, we're friends, aren't we?" She spun and pointed down the street. "Down there, on the corner of Main and Vine, is Thespian Hall. In the past several years, it hasn't been used for such grand events as it was in the past, but we still hold many of our social functions there, and of course some of us still give readings from time to time. I'd love it if you'd come sometime. I could show you through—"

Her offer was rudely interrupted by Mrs. Pribble. "You'll do nothing of the kind, Clarissa Westfield. Why, your mother would simply drown in her tears if she knew you were keeping company with this coarse young woman! I simply cannot allow—"

"George! Edith! Hello!" the smaller of the two men called out. He was string-bean skinny and looked to be about thirty-five years old. The most noticeable things about him were his large ears and the wide smile he wore. On his vest was a badge that read, *Sheriff.*

Watching him approach, Megan thought him an even less formidable figure as a law-enforcement officer than her Uncle Chester was. At his side strode a younger, much taller man. His face was marked by a lazy grin.

"Jasper," George Pribble said to the sheriff and waved a greeting. "Good to see you."

Mrs. Pribble's greeting was not quite so amiable. "How's my daughter?" she barked.

"Gladys is fine, just fine." The words were spoken cheerfully enough, but the smile he'd sported so naturally instantly dropped from his face and was replaced by a look of accustomed long suffering.

Satisfied by his answer, Edith Pribble turned her cold gaze on Megan and gave her a look that told her she was in one heap of trouble.

"Uh-oh," Clarissa mumbled, feeling sorry for her friend. She elbowed Megan to get her attention, hoping to prepare her for the coming wrath of Mrs. Edith Pribble.

But Megan was not worried. Never one to be cowed, she met Mrs. Pribble's gaze with a challenging one of her own.

Her concentration was broken, however, when the man beside Jasper lengthened his stride, drawing her attention away from the waspish woman.

Megan's gaze found the young man's face. His smile broadened, and her heart skipped a beat. Her eyes went to the badge he wore on his chest, then back to his face once again, and her heart broke into an excited gallop as recognition dawned. She might not have seen him in five years, but she would have known those sleepy eyes and that crooked grin anywhere, even when that grin was partially hidden beneath the cover of a very dark mustache.

Johnnie was right. James Gordan Lawson had indeed grown into quite a looker: His face was tan, his shoulders broad, his eyes as warm and dark as she remembered. Joy swelled within her.

He stopped before the two young women. As his name was about to escape Megan's lips, Clarissa said, "Hello, Jim."

Megan's heart gave a queer little lurch, and she realized he had not been smiling at her.

He had not come to greet *her*.

In fact, he hadn't even noticed her. That smile—the one she remembered so well—was for Clarissa Westfield alone.

Jim Lawson gazed down into Clarissa's eyes, and his smile grew. It grew into the smile of one smitten, the smile of one welcoming home the one who held the key to his heart. "Clarissa," he said, his voice deep and earnest. He whipped off his hat, tucked it under his arm, and took her tiny hands into his own. "Welcome home. I've missed you."

The pretty young woman gazed up at him, her honey-colored eyes reflecting mutual affection. "I've missed you, too, Jim."

Megan felt as if her lungs had been trampled. She held her breath, afraid to breathe, as disappointment like none she'd ever known gripped her. She gazed up at Jim Lawson and realized that the Gordie she remembered, the boy whose loyalty and affection she had always taken for granted, was gone, replaced by this man with an easy swagger and a handsome face. She felt the loss of her young friend as keenly as though he'd been stolen right out from under her nose.

"Jasper!" Mrs. Pribble snapped, interrupting Megan's thoughts. She pointed a thick finger at the younger woman. "I insist you incarcerate this young woman!"

All heads swung in Megan's direction. She felt her cheeks heat with self-consciousness. She dropped her gaze. Normally she would have gone head-to-head with Edith Pribble. But today was different. Today, her fighting spirit had been momentarily squelched.

"Edith?" Jasper questioned, wondering what in tarnation the old bat could hold against the pretty young woman.

"Don't 'Edith' me, Jasper Johnson! You're supposed to protect the people of this town and uphold the peace! Now, do so and arrest this young woman! She threatened my life with a gun she keeps hidden in that bag of hers!"

"Now, Edith," George Pribble began. "The girl did no harm—"

Edith whirled on him. "Shut up, George Pribble!" She swung around to face the sheriff. "You lock her up, or I'll make sure the next time this town holds an election for a sheriff, you won't even be a consideration. And," she said as she pointed to Megan's carpetbag, "when you lock her up, make sure you dispose of that evil creature she has stuffed in that bag along with her gun! I'm quite sure it's rabid!"

Megan's temper flared. She clutched her bag a little tighter to her skirts, and her fighting spirit surged to life. She reached into the bag, shoved Willy's head out of the way, and hauled out her gun. Batting her lashes innocently, she affected a drawl. "Oh, you mean this little ol' thing?" She held the gun awkwardly by the barrel a moment, then in the instant of a heartbeat she flipped it up into the air, caught it deftly by the stock, and pointed it dead center at Sheriff Jasper Johnson's chest. She nailed him with a zealous, blue-eyed gaze that would have done the Hawkins family proud. "My cat's no more rabid than you are, Sheriff. You touch him and you'll have your own space in tomorrow's obituary section of your local newspaper."

Jasper paled visibly.

Mrs. Pribble gasped and swooned.

Mr. Pribble tried to catch her on the way down and ended up beneath her.

Jim momentarily forgot all about Clarissa Westfield.

Up until that moment he had barely given the fashionably dressed young woman beside Clarissa a glance. He'd been listening to the commotion around him with half an ear, however, just in case he was needed. Now, hearing the young woman's voice—the threat along with the name "Willy"—he decided he'd better take a closer look. As he did, he felt as though she'd popped him in the eye once again.

A whirlwind of memories hit him. She was no longer a child, but a full-grown woman. Her blond hair was swept up into a puffy style that many of the modern young women of the day now sported. Her eyes were much bluer than he remembered. She was slightly taller than she'd been five years ago, and having filled out in all the right places, she appeared not quite so thin. She was dressed most respectably in a becoming blue traveling dress, and on her carefully coiffed golden head she wore a matching hat in the latest fashion.

She looked every inch the lady.

But as the people of Poplar Bluff did, Jim Lawson knew her and was not so easily convinced. "Megan?" he said, his tone incredulous.

Megan's gaze lifted and connected with his. For a moment she read nothing but confusion and surprise in his eyes, but as he stared down at her, she watched the surprise become full-blown as recognition became complete.

Their eyes locked for several silent seconds as each realized that time had indeed wrought changes in them.

His dark brows knitted into a perplexed frown. The years swept away. He struggled with the memory of the old affection he had held for her, while she struggled with a new awareness of him.

"Megan?" he whispered again.

"Hello, Gordie," she answered softly.

"Is it really you, Meg?" His expression was still confused.

"In the flesh." She forgot about Mrs. Pribble, the sheriff, and Clarissa, and lifted her arms at her sides, gun in hand. An uncertain grin caught at one side of her mouth.

"You know each other?" Clarissa asked, astonished, yet pleased at the thought that her new friend and her beau were already acquainted.

Megan's gaze was glued to Jim's. "You could say we do."

Meanwhile, down the street, people filed out of the gaping double doors of the pretty Presbyterian church. Drawn by the ruckus, a sizable crowd of curious onlookers gathered around the small group.

"Get the doctor!" someone yelled, seeing Edith pinning her husband beneath her on the ground.

Stumped, Jim reached up and ran his hands through his hair. "Well, I'll be . . ." He shook his head, unsure of the wave of emotions storming him. He stood face-to-face with the girl he once thought he'd marry, while beside him stood the girl he'd begun to think of marrying. At that moment he didn't know how he felt about either one, and he decided that no man deserved to be in such a hellish predicament. "Jesus," he whispered, stunned. He paused a moment, realizing he'd taken the peaceful serenity of this town for granted all these months. "What the hell are you doing here?" he asked Megan more harshly than he had intended.

Megan's heart heaved painfully, but instead of giving in to the pain, she got mad. "What the hell do you mean?" she asked, rocking her head from side to side, mocking him. She gestured wildly toward him with her gun.

The crowd gasped and backed away.

"I could ask you the same question, Gordie!"

Jim's face reddened at hearing her repeat his nickname. The first time he could overlook but, by God, he'd get her for this one!

Still, as irritated as he was, he answered her question. "I work here. I'm Boonville's deputy sheriff! I belong here!"

"Well . . ." She made a face and drew herself up to her full height. "So do I, Mr. Deputy Sheriff." She made sure to emphasize his title with appropriate sarcasm. "I'm this town's new veterinarian!" She delivered the words with the power of a well-aimed blow.

The crowd gasped once again, then went as silent as a cornfield full of scarecrows. The silence was so complete that a body could just about hear the great Missouri River lapping against the riverbank.

Then the murmurs began, and from out of the midst of the crowd came an elderly, very round gentleman, whose girth revealed a great affection for the dinner table. "Dr. Hawkins?" he inquired almost timidly, as though he sincerely hoped she wouldn't answer to the name.

"That's me!" Megan said, then turned a brief, satisfied smile on Jim. "Who's askin'?"

"Why, my name is Tid . . . Tidwell," the poor man stuttered, his forehead beading with sweat. "I run the town's post office. But I'm also the secretary for our town council. I hired you." His mouth worked silently for a moment, until finally he managed to say, "You can't possibly be him."

Megan was every bit as surprised as he at the situation, never having stopped to think that Adam would neglect to inform them of her gender. Nevertheless, when she answered him, her voice was strong and confident. "That's right. I'm not him. I'm *her*. Howdy!"

Mr. Tidwell pulled a handkerchief from his vest pocket and mopped his forehead frantically. "Oh, Lord. Oh my, oh my, oh my . . ." He turned to the crowd, his expression pained.

Another man stepped forward. He was tall, middle-aged, and dressed most elegantly in the finest of suits. He was a handsome man, with an especially attractive head of thick, dark hair. But there was a hardness to his face and a coldness to his eyes that took away from his appearance. "Tidwell!" he barked. "How could you make such a ridiculous mistake?"

Mr. Tidwell clucked his tongue, shook his head, and continued to say, "Oh my, oh my . . ." Finally he managed to get out, "I assumed Dr. Adam Randolph was offering the services of another man." Tidwell held out his hands in supplication. "I never thought to think otherwise. Why"—his gaze swept the crowd—"who ever heard of a woman animal doctor, for pity's sake?"

Listening to the conversation, Megan's temper escalated. "Well, you sure as hell have now! An' I'm as real as they get! I'm good, too! An' I plan on stayin' a spell whether you like it or not. I have it on paper that you hired me, an' I expect you to stand by your word."

"But, but . . ." Tidwell floundered, wondering how to remedy the difficult situation.

"It's your fault, Tidwell!" the well-dressed man accused. "We should have known better than to leave the situation in your incompetent hands. It's amazing how you manage to handle your job as postman!" He turned to Megan and burned her with a look of scorn. "A woman, for God's sake!"

Jim Lawson bristled. Maxwell Fletcher was not his favorite person, regardless of the circumstances. Fletcher was not particularly favored by any of the townsfolk. He was a vain man who seemed to love only three things—gambling, his hair, and his prize bull Beauregard. As for his wife, well . . . he loved her money.

Although he was not well liked by his neighbors, he was feared. His wife, Flora, was wealthy enough to buy her way into society's highest circles, and Maxwell had a name that had been part of Boonville from its birth. Those who dared cross him soon felt his wrath one way or another. Few ever dared.

Just the same, Maxwell's name and Flora's money meant nothing to Jim. Hearing Fletcher attack Megan only served to fan the flame of his antagonism toward the man. It also ignited within him a familiar protective instinct.

He watched her absorb the man's look without flinching, her blue eyes steady, her head held high. Jim took a step forward. "Now just a goddamn minute, Fletcher—"

But the normally timid Mr. Tidwell was ahead of him, having had enough of Fletcher's browbeating. "Listen here, Fletcher—"

"Gentlemen, gentlemen, please," another man reproved gently. As Boonville's banker, Silas Goldman was a fair but extremely shrewd man. He sized up Megan's feminine form and decided nature would soon enough remedy the situation. He'd yet to meet a woman who could handle such a demanding job as veterinarian. "Gentlemen. Dr. Hawkins is correct. We hired her, and she came in good faith. She must have the opportunity to prove she can handle the job. Fletcher. Tidwell. She deserves her chance."

"But, Silas," Maxwell Fletcher began. "We can't allow a woman . . ."

"Why not?" A large black man stepped out of the crowd. His onyx eyes were steady and calm. He met Maxwell Fletcher's gaze squarely. "If a Negro man can be this town's blacksmith, why can't a woman be the town's veterinarian?" His voice was smooth and cultured; the words he spoke were spoken clearly, with schooled precision.

His statement was followed by a low hum of agreement from several of the bystanders at the rear of the crowd.

Maxwell Fletcher's face reddened. Being reproved by anyone, let alone a Negro, in the presence of neighbors was not an affront he was likely to forget. But he responded with the only words he could think of to salvage his dignity. "You've earned your position in this town, Zach."

Zach nodded. "So maybe she'll earn hers."

Another hum lifted into the air.

Silas stepped forward and held his hands out in supplication. "Maxwell, I think we should all go home and let the sheriff do his job."

In the meantime, Edith had recovered and had been helped to her feet. "See there!" she announced, her expression one of malicious satisfaction. "This young woman is nothing but trouble! Not only has she threatened my life and the life of my son-in-law"—not that she truly cared a fig about Jasper Johnson's scrawny hide—"but she has disturbed the peace as well! I insist you lock her up immediately!"

From a short distance away, outside the carefully cultivated grounds of his parents' immaculate home, young Daniel Kincaid watched the scene with breathless anticipation. His ears strained to hear every word spoken by the pretty blond-haired woman, as his eyes took in every gesture she made. He thought she was without a doubt the most beautiful woman he'd ever seen. When she flipped that gun up in the air and fixed it squarely on Sheriff Johnson's chest, my, oh my, how Daniel's tender, eight-year-old heart had swelled with admiration. He was in love for the first time in his life, and he was almost weak with the joy of it.

Jasper sighed heavily and faced his mother-in-law. He paused several moments, considering the wisdom of refusing her demands, for he truly had no desire to hold the young woman in a cell for the night. The price he would pay for disobedience would be high, however. Gladys would be hell to live with for a month. Not that she wasn't hell to live with anyway. But with her fueled by her mother's wrath at him, he'd be lucky to have a moment's peace. Sighing once again, he turned beleaguered eyes on his deputy. "Lock her up for the night, Jim."

Jim's eyes bugged. "You gotta be kiddin', Jasper!"

Jasper blushed but held his ground. "Lock 'er up. She can't go round sportin' a gun like that, and you know it."

Frustrated, Jim shook his head but silently acknowledged that Jasper was right. He felt his blood heat. He didn't know whom he was angrier at: Jasper, Edith Pribble, the bigoted townspeople, or Megan Hawkins. He turned and faced her. "Let's go," he said, his tone clipped, his jaw tight. He surprised her by deftly snatching the gun from her hand before she could even blink an eye. He turned to Clarissa. "I'll drop by and see you in the morning."

With that, he took Megan's arm and led her toward the jail. After a few steps Megan's senses returned. She jerked her arm away from him and snapped, "You go to hell, Gordie Lawson!"

His face reddened, and his jaw bulged. He leaned in close to her ear and, in a very low, very dangerous voice, said, "You either come with me peaceably, Meg, or I'll throw you over my shoulder and haul you into that jail. And once I get you in there, I'm gonna whup the livin' daylights outta your skinny hide. I'm deputy here, and I intend to keep my job and the respect of these people. An' I sure as hell don't need you comin' here and messin' things up for me. Now, come on!"

Looking up into his dark, unwavering gaze, Megan's eyes widened. She'd been right in her assumption that this man certainly wasn't the Gordie she remembered. She considered popping him one, just to show him who was still boss, but somehow he must have read her mind.

"Don't even think about it," he warned. "I ain't fourteen anymore."

Caught off guard by his remark, she snorted her disgust, then whirled and stomped off toward the jail. "Well, fine, then! I needed a place to sleep tonight anyhow!" Jostled beyond his endurance, Willy howled a complaint. Over her shoulder Megan snapped, "What about Willy? He's hungry and needs to take care of a few of nature's necessities!"

"I'll take care of him," Jim growled right behind her. He didn't trust her for so much as a minute. The girl he remembered would not have taken this insult lightly. Retaliation would be forthcoming, and God only knew what form it would take. It was a scary thought. The scariest one he'd had in years.

Well into the early hours of the next morning, Megan lay on her cot, stewing. She was angrier than she'd ever been in her life. In fact, she was foot-stompin', bull-chargin' mad.

She was hurt, too.

How could he replace her so quickly? And with someone so entirely different. The ache grew as she realized that she couldn't blame him. Clarissa seemed to be a wonderful person. It was only natural he would be so taken with her.

He used to be taken with you, too, a voice within reminded her.

Yeah, well, it didn't take him long to forget all about that. Five years had passed, but she hadn't forgotten him. Well, she had to admit she hadn't wanted him when she had him.

Stubbornly she set her jaw and decided her anger was, by far, more comforting than her pain.

She got up off her cot for the tenth time that night, took the tin cup from the rickety piece of scarred wood masquerading as a table, and ran it across the bars, creating a hellish racket. Her face set with malevolent determination, she kept up the clatter until she heard the satisfying bellow. "Dammit, Meg! Will you knock it off! I gotta get some sleep!"

Smiling with satisfaction, she yelled back, "I see you don't have any problem sayin' cusswords now, Gordie Lawson!"

"You're damn right I don't," he hollered. "Now, go to sleep before I come out there and tie you up and stuff a gag in that mouth of yours!"

Humph! she thought, thinking he wouldn't dare. But she held her tongue, no longer so sure of anything concerning him. Instead she retreated to her cot once more, deriving immense pleasure from the fact that Jim Lawson would have bags as big as cow udders under his eyes by morning. *So how do you like them apples, Mr. Deputy Sheriff?*

In her state of heightened aggravation, she almost wished she had access to a good dose of Granny Grady's potion. Granny was especially good at revenge hexes. If anybody knew how to hex a body, Granny sure did.

But Granny's cabin, nestled in the hills outside of Poplar Bluff, was a long way from Boonville. So Megan decided she'd have to figure out a way to exact her revenge on her own.

She just had to decide what would rile Jim the most.

Meanwhile, in the adjoining sheriff's residence at the back of the building, Jim Lawson lay wide awake. Flat on his back, his forehead creased into a deep frown, his arms crossed over his chest, he contemplated the pleasure of running Megan Hawkins out of his town.

It seemed hard to believe that a month ago he had thought that given the chance he would be glad to see her again.

He'd been wrong.

Too much time had passed. What he had felt for her all those years, he reasoned, had been nothing more than childish infatuation.

How 'bout that, Lawson? he said to himself. *All this time you carried a torch for that hellcat, and it was nothing more than puppy love. You even thought you wanted to marry her. Well, you'da been as miserable as Jasper. Yes, sir! Maybe worse! Now, aren't you glad you grew outta that idea?*

He reached down at his side and stroked Willy's furry head. Willy responded with a garbled meow. Surprisingly enough, the cat remembered him. Or maybe, Jim thought, he was just real happy to get out of that carpetbag. A carpetbag, for God's sake! "Jeez, Willy," Jim said, "you'd think as much as she loves you she coulda made you better travelin' arrangements."

He thought about the irony of Clarissa and Megan being on the same stage. He wondered what Clarissa must think of all this ruckus. He decided that her quiet ways and her genuine air of refinement were much more suited to him than fiery Megan Hawkins's temper was.

The clattering began again. He groaned and covered his ears with his hands. God only knew what he'd do with her in the morning. That is, he decided, if she lived long enough to see it.

CHAPTER
3

Morning came, but not nearly soon enough to suit either of the jail's two human occupants.

As the rosy light of dawn seeped in through his window, Jim decided it was time to face the fire.

He rose, shaved, and dressed with a little more haste than usual, half expecting the clattering to begin at any moment. It had been only about an hour since the last round of hellish noise.

After he had strapped on his gun and gone over and patted Willy, who remained curled in a ball in the center of Jim's bed, he took the huge ring of jailer's keys from his nightstand and made his way toward the front of the building to greet his prisoner.

He stomped down the hall, making as much noise as possible, spitefully hoping to wake her as she'd woken him so often throughout the night. But when he reached her cell, instead of creating more of a clamor, he stopped and stood staring at her, his anger dissipating.

Memories surfaced.

He decided she looked much more like the young girl he remembered than the respectably dressed woman who'd stepped down off the stage last evening. She lay on her side on the cot, facing the wall. Her hair, without the fancy hat, lay over her shoulders and down her back in a disorderly mass of golden tangles. Her traveling dress, no longer neat and tidy, was wrinkled and hiked to her knees. Her feet and calves were bare. Despite himself, a grin threatened. He'd have been willing to bet it hadn't taken her long to abandon her shoes and stockings. He'd seen her do so many times to run free and unhampered through the silky spring grass along the banks of the Black River.

He felt a swift, unexpected rush of affection for her, and from out of the past came another memory—this one of them standing outside Chester Hawkins's jailhouse in Poplar Bluff. He was twelve, she ten, and they were plotting Adam Randolph's escape on the memorable day when he'd been unjustly accused of poisoning Harley Baker's cattle.

"We came to break ya out!" Megan had yelled out to a questioning Adam, while brandishing her gun high in the air.

Jim's smile grew, remembering his own words. "Yeah! We came to break ya out!"

"We're outlaws!" Megan had affected her most fearsome glare.

"Yeah, outlaws!"

"Real bad outlaws," Megan assured Adam.

"Yeah, real bad," Jim repeated after her.

"Like the James gang."

"Yeah, like the James gang."

"Maybe worse." Megan cocked her head, considering the delicious possibility.

"Yeah, worse . . ."

So lost was he in his thoughts, Jim didn't see the tin cup coming.

Clang! It hit the bars directly before his face, startling him. He jumped like a spooked cat, his memories fleeing to the past.

He swore expansively and glared his hardest through the bars at the woman sitting up on the cot. "What the hell is the matter with you, Meg?" he roared.

She sprang to her feet and, hands on hips, sashayed across the floor to confront him face-to-face. She found it difficult, however, since he now topped her by a full head. Instead of dissuading her, that fact only managed to fan the flames of her anger. She tipped her chin up and let him have it. "Well, I just reckon I don't know what's wrong with me! I suppose there isn't nothing at all for me to be upset about, bein' as you locked me up in this here jail for the night. 'Specially since it's my first night in town an' all, and I didn't have any previous arrangements made for other accommodations."

"Now, Meg." He shifted his weight onto his other foot, his expression still set. "It's my job—"

She cut him off. "After all, bein' we're such good friends an' all, it was mighty kind of you to look after me that way." She grinned maliciously and drawled, "Gorrrrdieee."

"Now, dammit, Meg—" His cheeks took on a ruddy glow.

She tipped forward, cocking her head to the side. "What's the matter, Deputy? That name ain't good enough for you anymore? Gordie! Gordie! Gordie!" she chanted like an obnoxious child.

The color of his face deepened. Tiring of her antics, he looked her up and down and said in a low, very firm voice, "Meg, you call me by that name one more time, and I'll tie you to the saddle of a mule and ship you back to your pa so fast your eyeballs will spin circles in that empty head of yours."

"Humph!" She crossed her arms over her chest.

"Humph!" He did the same.

Deadlocked, they eyed each other with unconcealed venom, while silence stood between them like a wall, every bit as thick and impenetrable as those surrounding them.

In time, Jim gave in. Weary of the bickering, he sighed and unfolded his arms. His expression pained, he raised his hands in entreaty. "This isn't home, Meg. Things are different here. Folks don't go round aimin' pistols at each other." He ran both hands through his dark hair. "They don't take on the way folks do back home." At least not during daylight hours, he thought to himself.

Shifting her gaze to a safer place beyond his shoulder, she felt the betrayal of a huge lump forming in her throat. Suddenly she felt very homesick, very lonely. More homesick and lonely than she'd felt in all the years she'd been away at school. Despite what folks back east had thought of her, she'd always known she was going home eventually. It hadn't mattered whether the easterners accepted or approved of her. She still had her home, her family.

She realized she had hoped that in taking the position here in Boonville, this town might become her home.

After all, Jim was here, and he was practically family. Well, he used to be, she reminded herself.

But the people of this town didn't want her. Neither did he.

Her subdued countenance unsettled him more than he cared to admit. His tone gentler, he went on. "The people of this town aren't used to women like you—"

Blinking back the burn in her eyes, she turned on him, her blue eyes blazing. "I guess not! Seems folks in this town don't like women unless they're sourer than rhubarb like that awful Mrs. Pribble, or sweeter than sugar like Miss Clarissa Westfield!"

No sooner were the words off her lips than she wished she could call them back.

She dropped her gaze and studied her bare toes, feeling very small and mean-spirited. She truly liked Clarissa and had no desire to say anything wicked against her. "I'm sorry," she whispered sincerely. She lifted shamed eyes to his. "I didn't mean that. Clarissa Westfield seems like a fine person."

"She is," Jim agreed, surprised at Megan's apology. The old Meg would have choked on such a humble concession.

She stared up into his familiar brown eyes and felt her animosity toward him die, as she acknowledged that she had indeed lost her admirer, her beau. It was a painful realization, but one she knew she must face. Despite the pain she felt, she squared her shoulders and accepted the truth for what it was. Somewhere along the way, while she had taken Gordie's love as her due, someone else had bested her by returning his affection in a way she never had. She had no one to blame but herself.

She felt the urge to move close against his chest and ask him to hold her, as she'd done the day she'd gone off to school. But Johnnie was right. Things were different. This man was different. Looking at him now through fresh eyes, she had to agree the name Jim suited him far better than the name Gordie that she and his family had favored in the past.

She swallowed and drew in a deep breath. At least she still had her pride. He didn't know she had come to Boonville expecting him to feel the same for her as he had those many years ago. He would never know the depth of her disappointment. Not ever. She took comfort in that truth.

She still had a job to do. She had a purpose. That would have to be enough for now. She lifted her chin a notch and announced, "I'm not sorry about what I said about Mrs. Pribble, though. That old woman needs a lesson in good manners. I'd stuff her full of Granny's revenge potion if I could."

Jim didn't doubt it for a minute. He nodded. "Edith Pribble would try the patience of a saint."

United in that one thought, they felt the silence fall around them once more. Neither was quite sure how to continue the conversation. They felt awkward, like two strangers searching for common ground when there was none to be found.

"How's your family?" he finally asked.

"Fine."

Silence.

"Did you see mine while you were home?"

"Yes." She hesitated a moment, then added, "They're fine, too."

"Good . . . good."

The silence grew again. He noticed how very blue her eyes still were. She noticed that his hair was darker, thicker, a bit more wavy than it used to be.

He was relieved to remember the keys hooked to his side. He reached for them, unlocked the cell door, and swung it open. "You're free to go. I have Willy out back. He's waiting for you."

Megan nodded and pushed her hair from her face. Not waiting for him to change his mind, she turned, crossed the room, and gathered her belongings. "I appreciate you seein' to Willy. If that ol' crow had her way about things, he'd be dead by now." Guilelessly, as though they were children once again, she sat down on the cot and donned her stockings, securing them well above her knees, then slipped on her shoes. She took a handful of hairpins from her pocket and haphazardly pinned her hair up into something only vaguely resembling the pretty hairstyle she'd worn the day before.

He watched her perform the familiar feminine rituals, heedless of his presence. Suddenly uncomfortable with the intimate picture she presented, he looked away.

"Willy's not rabid, and you know it," she went on conversationally.

"I know it."

"I can't believe anyone would be so wicked."

"I wouldn't have let anyone hurt him, Meg." His voice was quiet and earnest.

When she heard the sincerity in his statement, her gaze came up to meet his. She felt the lump return to her throat. Determined not to show any further weakness before him, she fought it back and snorted, "Humph!" Her eyes clouded with doubt. "I wonder."

He shrugged, deciding to forgo her new challenge. "Come on. I'll take you to Willy."

He led her down the narrow hall, past a long row of identical cells that boasted the varied carvings of their many past occupants.

"I had the rest of your belongings sent over to Habel Habershaw's boardinghouse."

"Oh?" she said absently. Behind him, she studied the impressive width of his shoulders, then allowed her gaze to ride down to his tight backside, where her eyes lingered for what seemed like quite some time. Her eyebrows rose in appreciation, and she grinned, thinking Preacher Mosely would have dunked her several extra dips in that ol' Black River on baptism day had he known what she would now be wonderin' about.

"Habel has a nice place over on Main Street." When she didn't answer, he went on, "The nicest in town. You'll like it."

"Mmmm," she said absently, her thoughts not on Habel Habershaw at all.

"Habel's a spinster lady, but a fine woman."

"I don't doubt it for a minute." What else would a spinster be but a fine woman?

"This is where I live," he told her when they reached his quarters.

"Where does the sheriff live?"

"He lives over on Walnut Street, in a house more suited to his wife's liking." He turned and gave her a sheepish grin. "Gladys would never agree to live in a jail."

Megan turned in a slow circle, taking in the condition of the rooms. They were spacious and furnished well enough, but clothes were strewn everywhere, unwashed dishes sat on the table, and footprints marked the floors. The rooms were the picture of untidiness, very much in need of a thorough cleaning. And though she'd have been the last person to lay a claim to being a spotless housekeeper, Megan couldn't help but exclaim, "Can't say as I blame her. Criminy, Jim! How do you live in this pigsty? Your mother and sisters would croak if they could see this shambles."

Affronted, he frowned. "I'm comfortable enough."

"Well, so are pigs in mud," she said and shook her head in disgust. Megan wondered if Clarissa Westfield had ever seen his rooms. She decided that if she had, Clarissa would be probably even more appalled than she was. "Jim Lawson," she said, finding that the name came quite easily to her lips now that she'd accepted it, "you'd put our old sow Hilda to shame." From the farthest room in the back, she heard Willy call her. "All right, Willy. I'm coming." She disappeared into Jim's bedroom for a moment. When she came out, she was carrying the big tomcat pinned securely beneath her arm. He howled a complaint and flattened his ears at her treatment of him. "Well, I can't say as I blame you, Willy. This isn't the most comfortable way to travel, but unless you want me to stuff you inside the carpetbag again, this'll have to do."

She turned to Jim and went silent a moment as the past rose up to meet the present. "Who would have thought you'd grow up to be a man of the law." Her eyes mirrored her amazement and, surprisingly enough, a certain measure of respect.

He controlled his grin, but his brown eyes grew mischievous. "What'd you think I'd grow up to be, an outlaw or somethin'?"

She snorted, scoffing. "Hell, no! You'da made a sorry outlaw."

He raised an eyebrow. "Folks can surprise you. You never know anyone as well as you think."

"I thought I knew you."

"You did." He fell silent a second. "Then."

She nodded, succumbing to the truth of his words. "Well." She sighed, sensing she shouldn't linger any longer. "I'll be on my way."

He led her outside his door, into the dewy morning air, and pointed down the street toward a huge barnlike building. "Just so you know, that's the livery straight down on Morgan. I figure you'll be needin' a horse and buggy soon enough. Zach Davis owns it. He's the man who stood up for you last night. You'll like him."

"I like him already," Megan said, meaning it.

Jim changed the direction of his arm. "Habel's house is down that way. Keep going till you get to Main, then take a left and go on for a spell. You can't miss it. She has a sign out front." He went silent for a moment, then added, "Aw, hell. I'll walk you over." He felt an odd reluctance to let her go.

But she seemed to feel no such diffidence about leaving his company. "No need. I'll do fine on my own." She took off down the steps, forgoing the discomfort of a prolonged good-bye.

"You're plannin' on stayin', then?" he called after her.

She turned and over her shoulder angled him a grin that made his insides quiver. "Did you doubt I would? Thanks for the hospitality, Deputy. I'll be seein' you 'round." She turned on her heel and hefted her cat under her arm. "Willy, I think we'll go over and meet Habel, then when we're settled in, we'll head on over to the livery and buy us a rig. It's time we went to work."

She left Jim looking after her, feeling confused. As he watched her walk away from him, he couldn't help but wonder what would become of Boonville, Missouri, now that Megan Hawkins had come to town.

Megan met the Reverend Steven Dunmire on her way over to Habel's. She'd followed Jim's directions, setting off onto Morgan Street then taking a left onto Main. So engrossed was she in holding onto Willy and her carpetbag, and gazing around at the awakening town, that she didn't see the reverend until she was almost on top of him. When the toes of his meticulously polished shoes came into view, she halted her steps so quickly she rocked backward, almost losing her balance.

He caught her arms firmly and righted her. "Pardon me, miss," he said quite politely, as though he were the one at fault.

Their eyes met and held. He was about two inches taller than she, and she guessed he was a few years older than Jim. His eyes were a very light shade of blue, his hair a nondescript brown. A lock of it fell forward onto his forehead, giving him a decidedly boyish appearance. He was dressed in a neat black suit, and he wore a spanking white shirt with a meticulously knotted bowtie.

Since he was the most polite person she'd met in town other than Clarissa, Megan decided she owed him the apology. "No, please excuse me," she said in her most schooled tone.

He smiled. He had a very nice smile. "There's nothing to excuse. I'm afraid I wasn't watching where I was going. I was on my way over to the jail."

Megan lifted one blond brow in curiosity. "I see."

"It seems, according to the morning edition of the *Boon-*

ville Advertiser, that a certain young lady has come to town, threatening murder and mayhem."

Megan lifted her other brow. "How terribly dreadful."

"Yes." He feigned a great sigh and shook his head. "It's been said she's quite a fearsome creature."

"Is that a fact?"

He nodded. "It's said by some of our residents that they're afraid they'll be murdered in their beds."

"Indeed!" Megan's eyes sparkled with mirth.

"Yes, indeed. Especially Edith Pribble."

"You don't say" was Megan's only comment.

"She woke me herself this morning, insisting I get myself and my Bible up and over to the jail to save the poor young woman's soul."

Not able to resist the temptation, Megan leaned in toward him and whispered, "Maybe the wicked young woman doesn't have a soul to save." But she knew very well that her soul had been well taken care of many years ago by the very best pulpit-pounding Baptist preacher this side of the Missouri. What Preacher Mosely couldn't save didn't need saving.

"I suppose we'll know soon enough." The young reverend's mouth twitched with humor. "I don't imagine you've seen her?"

"Could be that I have. Did she have a whole mess of untidy blond hair?"

"So I'm told."

"And wild, crazy blue eyes?"

"I believe so."

"And was she hauling around a cat that foams at the mouth?" She hefted Willy in her arms and held him out toward the reverend. "A big black one like this one?"

"Sounds like the lady."

"Then I guess you've found her." Megan smiled, knowing she'd made another friend.

He chuckled his amusement. "It would seem I have." His blue eyes rested on her with unconcealed admiration. "Allow me to introduce myself. I'm the Reverend Steven Dunmire. And you must be . . ."

"Megan Hawkins. Dr. Megan Hawkins," she added. "The new veterinarian."

"It's a pleasure, Doctor." He reached out for her carpet-bag. "Let me help you with that."

She allowed him to take her bag. They fell into step, side by side. "I'm looking for Habel Habershaw's boardinghouse."

"A fine choice of residence for a proper young lady. Allow me to show you the way."

She slid him a glance, her sky-blue eyes winking mischief. "Let me warn you, Reverend." Her accent returned with force. "I ain't so proper."

He chuckled again. "I think I've already figured that out."

She nodded. "Just so you know."

"I do."

"You're not going to preach hell and damnation to me along the way, are you?"

He laughed out loud and shook his head. "No, Dr. Hawkins. I believe I'll save that for next Sunday." As he lengthened his stride to keep up with hers, he decided Megan Hawkins was a much needed, most welcome breath of fresh air.

Habel Habershaw was a tiny bird of a woman. She was every bit of thirty years old and barely five feet tall. She was modest and plain, unassuming and unpretentious. In fact, she was so meek and subdued that many people said she made a corpse look lively. Her hair, pulled back into a tight knot, was an unremarkable brown, but her eyes, oddly enough, were a most serene and lovely shade of gray.

Most folks in town rarely noticed her presence at all. Her only claim to recognition was that she provided Boonville with a very respectable boarding establishment, one of its best.

But for all her staunch Presbyterian propriety, Habel prided herself on being an open-minded woman.

Although the gossip about Megan Hawkins had torn through the town before the roosters could crow in the morning, Habel decided to reserve her judgment of the young lady until a later date. After all, that nice Deputy Lawson had brought the young woman's belongings to her door, asking that Habel look after her.

And so she would.

As for the grim warnings about the visitor's evil cat, well, Habel didn't find cats so evil. They were sleek, sensuous, uninhibited creatures that conformed to no rules but nature's own. As a matter of fact, cats, along with most animals, had always held her admiration and respect.

She had often wished to be so free.

But her fate had long ago been sealed by the opinion of others who thought she was far too shy, far too homely to ever hook herself a husband. She hadn't proved them wrong. She'd fulfilled their prophecy. She never tried to find a husband. Other than old Samuel Sweeney, the town drunk, no suitor had ever darkened her doorstep. Sometimes Habel thought Sam had only done so because he was drunk, had gotten lost, and thought he'd found Merilee's establishment instead of her boardinghouse. Habel had sent him on his way.

She'd spent her years alone, turning the house her father and mother had left her into a boardinghouse. When she allowed herself a few minutes of enjoyment, she read. At night when she went to sleep she dreamed that someday someone would come and rescue her from the lonely sentence of mundane respectability that had shackled her existence for as long as she could remember.

So when Megan Hawkins knocked at her door that morning, Habel Habershaw was more than ready to welcome her into her home . . . and into her life. "Miss Hawkins," she said so softly she could barely be heard. She opened the door wide. "Do come in."

CHAPTER

4

The good reverend left Megan at Habel's door with a request to see both her and Habel at Sunday's services.

Megan told him she'd think about it, and she meant to.

"This way, please, Miss Hawkins," Habel said after the reverend had taken his leave. "I've been expecting you." She led Megan over the slick, gleaming floors of the foyer and on through the meticulously clean and polished dining room, finally halting at the foot of a lovely walnut staircase.

Her thoughts still on the young minister, Megan asked, "What kind of reverend is he?"

"Who?" Habel blinked her confusion.

"The Reverend Dunmire."

"Oh, Presbyterian, of course," Habel said as though it were the only respectable denomination in the world.

"Humph!" Megan paused a moment before continuing. "He certainly isn't anything like Preacher Mosely."

"Preacher Mosely?" Habel's curiosity having been stoked, a feeble light lit in her beautiful gray gaze.

"Yes, ma'am. Preacher Mosely is a Baptist preacher down in Poplar Bluff." Megan grinned. "Nobody pounds a pulpit better."

"Pounds a pulpit?" Habel queried, confused further. Her brows rose. Her little beak lifted into the air.

"Yes, ma'am. You know, squashes sin."

"Hmmm." Habel tipped her head to the side, considering the idea. "I can't say as I've ever seen it done. Baptist, you say?"

"Oh, Lordy!" Megan rolled her eyes toward Habel's spotless white ceiling, then back to the little woman, as though she couldn't believe anyone had been so sheltered. "You mean to say you've never attended a Baptist revival?"

Habel thought a moment. "No, I can't say that I have. Of course," she added hastily, while inwardly wondering if she might have missed something significantly important in her Christian tutelage, "we do have a Baptist church here in Boonville."

"Well, hell, Miss Habershaw, take yourself on over there some Sunday morning."

Habel visibly flinched at Megan's use of profanity.

"You just might like it. It's an awesome thing to behold!" Megan sighed, feeling a little homesick again. "Why, there's hardly a dry eye left in our congregation when Preacher Mosely's done preachin'. He could move Gabriel himself to repentance. Someday you'll have to go on down to Poplar Bluff for a visit. You haven't seen anything till you've seen Preacher Mosely go at it."

"Indeed!" Habel bobbed her little head, thoroughly intrigued. Her mind clicking with excitement, she turned and led the way up the carefully preserved staircase. She felt a bit winded. Megan Hawkins's exuberance was contagious. Just listening to the young woman talk made Habel's heart beat faster. "I hope you'll like your room."

"I'm sure I will," Megan responded amiably. "I'll only need it till I can find a place to set up on my own."

"Oh." Habel felt vaguely disappointed, though she wasn't sure why.

"I'm hoping to find a house with a little speck of land so I can get to work."

"Will you be practicing here, then?"

"I sure as hell hope to."

Again Habel flinched at the young woman's choice of words, but she continued down the hall, past several closed doors, until she reached one that stood open. She laced her hands before the skirt of her severely plain gray dress. "Last night when Deputy Lawson stopped to say you'd be needing accommodations, he told me a little about you."

"Oh." Megan made a disgusted face, expecting the worst.

"He said you liked wildflowers."

Abashed, Megan felt her mouth go lax; her eyes softened. Who would have thought he'd remember such a thing. "He did?"

"Yes," Habel continued, leading her into the room. "So I sent one of my neighbor boys to pick you a bouquet early this morning."

Touched, Megan swept the perimeters of the neat little room with her eyes. It was plain in a simple, rather virtuous way. White lace curtains framed the large floor-length window, and on the bed a lovely white crocheted coverlet waited invitingly. The oak floor was bare, but varnished to a high gloss. And on the bureau stood a large vase, filled with a variety of colorful flowers.

Megan turned, and, without giving the action a second thought, she hugged the tiny woman, almost breaking her frail, tiny bones in the process. "Thank you, Miss Habershaw."

Habel held herself stiff as a broom handle while embarrassment burned a path through her. Having had very few close friends, and no living relatives, she was unused to such a spontaneous demonstration of affection. When finally Megan released her, she tried to hide her discomfort by chattering, "He also told me about your cat." Habel noted

the sudden, defensive lift of the younger woman's chin.
Habel reached out a hand to stroke Willy's head. "He's
very beautiful. I don't have any of my own, but I'm very
fond of animals."

"Then you oughta get some." Megan relaxed once again.

"Oh . . ." Habel shook her head. "I wouldn't think of it.
I wouldn't want to offend any of my boarders."

"Well, criminy! It's your house, isn't it?"

"Yes. I suppose it is at that."

Megan frowned, confused by the strange little woman's
attitude. "Habel, where have you been all your life?"

Habel's eyes clouded over as she thought about that
question. "Right here," she finally said, as though she just
now realized it. "I've been right here all of my life."

Megan set her chin and made an instant decision. "We-
e-e-ll, we're gonna have to do somethin' 'bout that. An'
about you, too, Habel!" She grinned. "You say you like
cats?"

"Oh . . . yes, I do."

Megan held Willy out. "Then you might as well hold
him. He's friendly enough, most of the time. 'Course he
gave Mrs. Pribble what for soon enough."

Hearing that, Habel swallowed her smile before it could
even begin, afraid of what it might unleash within her. As
though she weren't sure she should, she accepted Megan's
offer, awkwardly taking the huge cat into her arms. She
stroked him lovingly and allowed a wisp of that almost
smile to crease her usually emotionless face. "Hello, Willy," she said after several silent moments. Her eyes lifted
and connected with Megan's. "I'm very glad you came to
Boonville."

"Hurry, Daniel!" Lucy Kincaid called up the stairs to her
young son. Her hands gripped the oiled, curved banister.
"You're going to be late again, and Professor Lewis will be

most displeased. You'll get another demerit for certain."

Sitting on the bed in his richly furnished bedroom, Daniel listened to his mother's grim warning. He set his small chin, flopped back onto the bed, and began to hum a little ditty he'd learned while hiding behind Merilee's House of Entertainment.

"Da-a-a-niel!"

He continued humming, ignoring her.

Merilee's house sat on the far end of Water Street. Mother said Merilee's was a sinful, dreadful place—nothing more than a cheap dancing hall and a place to gamble away money. But Daniel liked Merilee and her girls anyway. Every time they caught him peeking around, they pulled him into the kitchen and plied him with treats. He smiled, remembering. Sometimes he had wonderful fantasies about living in that sinful, dreadful place.

"Your father will be so disappointed, Daniel!"

That one got his attention. He stopped humming and sat up like a sprung mousetrap.

Father would not take kindly to the disappointment of another demerit. After all, having once been Kemper Military Academy's prize pupil, his father found it a hard pill to swallow that his only son did so poorly in the school from which he had graduated with top honors.

Daniel sighed and remained on the bed a few more moments, purely for the sake of defiance.

When Lucy heard no movement coming from his room, her voice rose two more octaves, revealing her growing frustration with her beloved only son. "Ple-e-e-ase hurry and be a good little soldier, darling."

Soldier! Daniel made a stubborn face and wrinkled his freckled nose. Reluctantly he stood and buttoned the shiny buttons of his crisp miniature military uniform, from his chin all the way down to his hips, while he indulged himself in yet another fantasy. He imagined himself jumping the train over at the Missouri Pacific Depot, just as it was about to pull out of Boonville. Yes, sir! He'd ride that train to hell if he had to, where Kemper Military Academy and Professor Lewis would never find him. Then he'd be whatever he wanted to be. Maybe he'd be a cowpoke, an outlaw, or maybe even a deputy like Mr. Lawson or a blacksmith like his friend Zach.

But one thing Daniel would not be was a soldier.

Still, he was smart enough to know that eight-year-old boys had little choice in deciding such matters, so he finished dressing and met his mother downstairs. A few minutes later he was on his way to school.

The morning air was slightly cool, but the sun beat down on his bright red head with the tempting promise of a balmy day. The birds sang above him, and he heard the winsome whistle of a steamboat call out to him as it passed on its way down the great muddy river.

Little by little his footsteps began to falter, and his pace slowed. It wasn't very long before he wasn't thinking about school, demerits, his father, or Professor Lewis, but rather about those great big fish just waiting down at the river to be caught by him alone. So when he got to Third Street, instead of taking a left and heading toward the academy, he took a right and headed on down toward the riverfront, where fantasies were spun and freedom waited, along with a carefully hidden fishing pole. . . .

Since it was still quite early, Jim Lawson moped around the jail for a while, unsure of what he wanted to do with the start of his day. He felt out of sorts and wasn't quite sure why, but he supposed it had more than a little to do with Megan's arrival.

It had unnerved him more than he cared to admit.

When Jasper came in to relieve him, he took himself over to the local gathering spot, which was a small, homey restaurant owned and operated by Big John and Beulah Franklin.

Big John was anything but big.

But someone had tagged him with the name years ago, and it had stuck tighter than a tick. His wife Beulah bested him in size at least twice over, but Big John didn't seem to mind. He loved her wholeheartedly and didn't bother to hide the fact. She was, without doubt, the best cook in town. Everyone knew it, and no one was more appreciative of that fact than Jim, who ate almost every meal at the Franklin establishment.

"What'll you have, Deputy?" Beulah asked, coming out of the kitchen, her ample arms laden with muffins and pastries that had been baked fresh that morning.

"The regular," Jim answered and took his customary place at the little table by the window, overlooking Main Street.

With coffeepot in hand, John ambled over to Jim's table. He turned Jim's cup over and filled it to the brim. "What did you make of all that ruckus last evening, Deputy?"

Jim shook his head and gave Big John a crooked grin. "I don't hardly know what to make of it."

"Well, I'll tell you what I make of it." Big John decided to offer his opinion, as he was prone to do whether anybody cared to hear it or not. "That girl is just what this town needs, that's what I think. I'd be willin' to bet that not only can she take care of our animals right proper, but she can also put some of those stuffed shirts in their places while she's at it. Did ya see the look on ol' Fletcher's face?" Big John chuckled, nearly choking himself. "Yes, sir, it sure was somethin' to see."

Jim almost chuckled himself, remembering how incensed Fletcher had been at the thought of a woman caring for his stock.

"Did you have any problems gettin' the young lady settled in?"

Jim thought about the question and decided to lie. "Not in the least."

"Well . . ." Big John heaved a great sigh. "That's good. She looked to be a real spitfire if she had a mind to."

"She has a mind to," Jim put in matter-of-factly. "But she's over at Habel's right now. I doubt she can get into too much trouble there."

"Do ya think the town council will keep her on?"

Jim smiled, thinking of Megan's stubborn nature. "I don't think anyone will have much of a choice."

After he'd downed a huge plate of ham, three eggs, and a mess of fried potatoes, he paid and thanked the Franklins, then headed over to see Zachary Davis.

He knew he should be on his way to see Clarissa, and part of him wanted to be, but for some strange reason another part of him just didn't feel up to it yet.

So instead he headed for the livery.

The livery was the home of the town's only blacksmith as well as the favorite boardinghouse for many of the locals' horses. It was a huge, whitewashed, barnlike structure that boasted an impressive sign that read, *Boonville Livery. Rigs and Stock for Sale or Hire. Blacksmith Available.*

The sign was a great source of pride to Zachary Davis, the town's blacksmith and sole proprietor of the successful business. After all, he had painted each bright red word on the sign himself two years ago when he'd taken over operation of the establishment. To be able to read and write was no insignificant thing for the son of two Georgia field slaves who'd never learned how to write their own names.

With the morning sun gentle on his neck, Jim approached the gaping double doors. *Pang! Pang! Pang!* The sound of Zach's hammer rang out through the still morning air. It was a comforting sound to the townspeople. It meant that life was going on as usual. Those who hadn't yet motivated themselves to begin their daily chores knew it was now time: Zachary Davis was at work.

Pang! Pang! Pang!

Jim walked through the doors into the shadowed building, past a long row of stalls occupied by several horses. He gravitated toward the sound, which came from the far end of the building.

Reaching his destination, he stuck his head into the smithy. The hammering ceased. A blast of heat hit him like a hot slap in the face. The room was shadowed and dark, except for a ruddy glow that radiated from the forge, where Zach stood working. Hung neatly around the skirt of the brick fireplace were tools: tongs, chisels, hammers—all ready and waiting for the master's hand. Oblivious to Jim's presence, Zach continued to work the bellows, his powerful arms pumping out a steady rhythm, to which he softly hummed an old spiritual his mother had taught him.

Watching the man at his work, Jim felt respect and admiration for him rise anew. Although Zach was only three years older than Jim, he was one of the most skilled craftsman Jim had ever met.

As the sole apprentice to Nathaniel Wells, who'd been Boonville's blacksmith for over thirty years, Zach had little competition in expertise. When Nathaniel died, leaving his livery and all that was in it to his young Negro apprentice, many may have thought it inappropriate, but few could question his decision. Nathaniel had no children of his own, and his wife had died several years before him. Though it was difficult for some to accept Zach as an equal in the community, especially since Missouri had once been a slave state and old opinions and customs die hard, there were many who knew his worth, both professionally and personally, and they accepted him for what he was: a good man.

The new deputy was one of the many.

"Hey, Zach!" Jim finally called out as he entered the room.

Zach looked up. He'd been expecting Jim. Especially after the commotion he'd witnessed last night. His movements slowed, and he flashed a white smile that seemed to beam out from his black face. "Jim, hello!" He swiped a forearm across his glistening forehead and stopped working.

Noting that, Jim felt guilty about interrupting his day, especially since Zach had the forge all set and ready to go. After all, he didn't have anything all that important to discuss. He just felt the need to visit with someone. He couldn't think of anyone he felt more comfortable with than Zach. "You don't have to quit working. I can talk just the same."

Zach pulled the soot-smudged leather apron over his head and tossed it onto a crude wooden table that was scattered with more tools. His bare torso gleamed with sweat, and his head glistened with countless droplets that winked like diamonds from his tightly coiled black hair. "I need a break anyway. I'm thirsty as a cactus." He ambled toward Jim. "How about you?"

Jim smiled. "Sounds good. It's hotter than hell in here. I don't know how you stand it day in and day out."

Zach led the way out of the smithy. "You get used to it. After a while you crave it."

They abandoned the closeness of the livery for the shady branches of an ancient oak that stood guard over a well just left of the livery doors.

Jim drew a fresh bucket of water up from the cool depths while Zach made himself comfortable on a grassy spot against the tree's trunk. He bent one knee, laid his head back, and sighed, enjoying the late morning breeze on his heated skin.

"Here." Jim held out a cup of water to his friend.

Zach accepted it and drank deeply. "Hmmm." Satisfied, Zach dumped the remainder of the water over his head, then shook it like a hounddog shedding water from his hide. "There isn't anything in the world like a good cool drink of water."

After getting himself a drink, Jim sat down beside Zach. "You're right 'bout that."

Side by side they sat, while time passed by in easy silence.

"So," Zach finally said and turned to Jim. "What's eating you?"

Jim's eyebrows rose. "Nothin'. Why?"

Zach's expression became thoughtful. "Well . . . seems to me when you come visiting me instead of that pretty little girl you been courting, something isn't quite right."

His eyes suddenly defensive, Jim snorted. "Can't I come over and jaw with you awhile without you thinkin' something's wrong?"

Zach shrugged. "Sure. But something's still eating you."

"Nothin's eatin' me! Jesus!" Jim turned and studied an old yellow-striped cat that was lazily making his way over to a sunny spot near the open doors of the livery.

His feelings injured, Zach got stubborn, his full bottom lip protruding more than normal. "Have it your way, then."

"Fine! I will!" Jim scowled, instantly sorry for his harshness, yet unable to curtail it. Zach's perceptiveness often unnerved him. Sometimes Jim wondered if he had some way of knowing things nobody else could, like Granny Grady always had.

Silence.

Simultaneously they stole a glance at each other, then hastily looked away, like two embarrassed children, neither wanting to be the one to give in.

"So . . . you want to talk about it?" Zach tried once again.

Even though he did, very much, want to talk about it, Jim remained stubborn. "No."

"All right, then. So what the hell are you doing here interrupting my day?"

Abashed, Jim shot him a look that said he wasn't quite sure what he was doing.

They fell into silence once more, this time for a long while.

A wagon clattered down the brick-paved road, filling the wordless void with much-needed noise. "Hey, Deputy! Hey, Zach!" the young driver called out to the sulking men.

Both Jim and Zach waved a greeting.

After a few more minutes Zach slid Jim a glance. "How'd things go with Dr. Hawkins?"

Jim glowered and slunk farther down against the tree.

"Ahhhh," Zach said, understanding "So that's it. I don't suppose you got much sleep."

"I don't suppose I did." Jim's voice was sarcastic.

"You look like you been trampled by a herd of buffalo."

"She's worse than a herd of buffalo. Them you can shoot."

"Hmmm . . ." Zach murmured his empathy.

Annoyed, Jim sat up a little straighter. "Well, say somethin'."

"I'd say that little girl put a burr the size of Kansas up your ass, boy, that's what I'd say," Zach told him bluntly. After a couple of seconds he asked, "Is she the one you told me about? The one from back home, with the sister and all the brothers?"

Jim nodded. "That's her."

"I thought so. So what are you going to do about her?"

Confused, Jim met Zach's eyes. "Do? Well, I'm gonna stay the hell away from her!"

"I see."

"She's a walkin' heap of trouble!"

Zach nodded his understanding. "I can see that she is. . . ."

"And there's Clarissa—"

"Of course."

Jim frowned and looked away. "I didn't ask her to come here."

"No, you didn't."

"Will you quit!" Jim barked.

Zach went silent for a few seconds, then quietly asked, "What do you think she'd say if she knew what we'd been up to at night?"

"Who? Clarissa or Megan?"

"Either."

"Well." Jim thought a few seconds. "Clarissa would be shocked as hell. She'd probably turn me in and throw me over so fast I'd be dizzy from the fall." As he thought about Megan, a grin threatened, and he chuckled softly. "But, Meg, hell, she'd probably kick in with us. In fact, before we knew what was happening, she'd probably take over and be ordering us around so fast we wouldn't know what direction we were headed. We'd have to bind her and drown her in the river to get us a moment's peace."

Zach chuckled, amused. After a while he said, "You shouldn't have stolen his dog, Jim."

Jim's head snapped around to stare at Zach. "What?"

"His dog. You know. That yellow pup you took the other night." Zach stared at Jim as though he had a few pegs loose. "You shouldn't have stolen him." He shook his head. "Jesus, Jim. That's worse than stealing a man's horse."

Jim's eyes registered understanding and grew defensive once again. "I only do what I gotta do, Zach. I never really planned on doin' any of this. You know that. He was abusin' that pup just like he does the rest of his animals."

Zach nodded, unable to deny Jim's words. "Don't you think I know that?"

"And I didn't steal him, I just removed him from the situation."

"Well, then," Zach said with mock seriousness, "I'm sure the judge will only hang you half-dead if you put it to him that way."

Jim grinned. "That's the way I figure it."

"What are you going to do with him, anyway?"

"I'm gonna keep him."

"Where?"

"Where we keep all the others."

Zach rolled his eyes to the sky, groaned his frustration, and lapsed into an exaggerated dialect. "Sweet Jesus have mercy on me, dis boy's gonna git me killed."

Jim's grin straightened out a bit. "I'm gonna catch him one day, Zach," he promised. "You just wait and see." His grin returned full force. "You worry too much."

"Somebody's got to."

"Didn't your mama ever teach you that worryin' was bad for you?"

"What my mama taught me was to stay away from white trash like you."

Jim chuckled. "Is that a fact, now?"

Zach nodded, then asked, "So . . . when we going back out?"

"I think we'd better lay low for a while. I wouldn't want to raise any unnecessary suspicion." He slid his friend a glance. "What do you think?"

Zach sighed with relief. "I think you're finally getting some brains in that wood head of yours."

They both laughed, and the easy camaraderie between them returned.

"So," Jim said, a mischievous grin climbing his cheek, "you still wanderin' on over to Arrow Rock to see Anna?"

"Whenever I get the chance."

"Her pa still shootin' at you?"

Zach nodded. "Every chance he gets." His gaze grew soft with longing. He thought of Anna's huge dark eyes and pretty dark skin. "Yep. He thinks his girl can do a sight better than a blacksmith."

"Well," Jim said thoughtfully, "we're gonna have to do somethin' 'bout that."

CHAPTER
5

Megan spent her first day in Boonville in the room Habel had prepared for her. She was tired and a little homesick and wanted some time to herself. She supposed her feelings were the result of a sleepless night in jail. But she also knew they had a lot to do with the fact that she was disappointed in her reception: the one she'd received from the townsfolk as well as the one she'd received from Jim.

So she took a nap to rest her body, and she wrote her family a letter to ease her mind and heart.

She knew they would be worried about her. After all, she was the baby. When her mother died during her birth, Pa, the boys, and Johnnie had made it their duty to make sure she wanted for nothing.

She hadn't. Johnnie made sure she never wanted for mothering; Pa and the boys made sure she never wanted for anything else. They loved her. They spoiled her. And she knew it. Sometimes, now that she was grown, she wondered if maybe they hadn't done her more harm than good in spoiling her in such a way, for it hadn't taken her long, once she'd gone off to school, to learn that life was not quite so simple. Just because a body wanted something didn't mean it was hers for the asking.

She'd grown up those years she'd been away at school. Now she was glad she had, because it made the town's rejection and the loss of Jim's affection a little easier to bear.

And she still had spirit. Yes, sir! She was a Hawkins: She might get down every now and then, but she'd never stay down for long. No sirree!

She awoke the next morning with that thought in mind. When she came down from her room, she felt ready to take on Jim Lawson and all of Boonville if need be.

As she stood at the entrance of the dining room, holding Willy in her arms, the first thing she observed about mealtime at Habel Habershaw's boardinghouse was that it was a solemn affair.

Habel and all eight of her boarders were seated at their respective places, some engaged in quiet conversation, others picking unenthusiastically at their food.

"Mornin'!" Megan boomed cheerfully to the group.

All heads turned her way. Eight pairs of eyebrows lifted. Habel's pale cheeks grew pink as the morning's dawn.

The gazes of all eight boarders fell upon the furred creature Megan held in her arms.

"This is Willy," she announced, holding him out toward the group, "and I'm Megan. Dr. Megan Hawkins. Nice to meet y'all."

A barely discernible hum rippled around the table, finally stopping when it reached Habel. Normally Habel would have wilted with embarrassment at her boarders' opinion of Megan's presence at her table. But today was no ordinary day. Something within her rose to defend the young woman.

Clearing her throat, Habel gathered her courage and replied, "Good morning, Megan." She lifted her pointed little chin into the air in a subtle act of defiance—one of her first. It was a most exhilarating experience. "Come," she said, her voice a little louder, a bit more confident, "join us." She gestured toward the kitchen door. "I set some milk and food out for Willy in the kitchen."

Megan grinned, her blue eyes sparking friendliness. "Well, thanks, Habel." She buzzed on by the table and released Willy into the kitchen. "Go on now, Willy!" She bent over and slapped her palms against her skirted bottom, shooing him on. "Habel's lookin' out for you, so you do a good job on that breakfast." Megan straightened, glanced over at the table of silent spectators, and made a face. "He just isn't as enthusiastic about gettin' to his vittles as he used to be when he was a young'un." She crossed the room and took a seat between Habel and an elderly gentleman, who cleared his throat and stared at her as though she'd stepped out of the pages of some dime-store Western novel.

"It don't look like you're too enthusiastic about gettin' to your vittles, either," she said to him, gesturing to his untouched plate of food. Her gaze shifted to the plate of hotcakes in the center of the table. "Criminy, I'm so hungry I could eat the ears off a hog!"

The gentleman almost choked.

One lady almost coughed up her coffee.

Habel felt faint.

Megan elbowed the man at her side. "Better jump into those eatin's or somebody's liable to beat you to it, Mr. . . ." She waited politely for him to offer his name.

His eyebrows rose another inch. "Higley," he huffed, blowing out his bushy white mustache.

"Nice to meet you, Mr. Higley." Not waiting for him to offer his services, she reached across his plate for the platter of hotcakes.

"Can I pass you something, young lady?" he finally managed to ask, totally appalled by her forward manner.

"Oh, no, I can get to it. You just go ahead and eat." She busied herself with "gettin' to it." She knew better than to waste time thinking about eating. It was one of those things you either did or didn't do at the Hawkins home. But if you were gonna do it, you got down to it right and proper. There was plenty of time for conversation later.

Habel's guests watched on in silent amazement as Megan heaped her plate high with hotcakes. She reached for the platter of sausages and piled them on, too, then slathered her hotcakes with butter and topped them with a generous amount of maple syrup.

Watching her newest guest, Habel began to relax. A tiny smile caught at her mouth. She couldn't remember when breakfast had been so entertaining.

Oblivious to the stares surrounding her, Megan attacked her plate of food. She picked up a hotcake, rolled it into a long log, and took a bite off each end, closing her eyes in pure enjoyment of the taste.

Another hum vibrated around the table.

After several minutes she looked up to find the boarders' gazes upon her. She glanced over at Habel, wiped her mouth, and smiled. "Habel, you sure know how to set a fine breakfast table."

Pleased, Habel blushed profusely and laid down her fork. Making a decision, she took her hotcake into her delicate little hands and rolled it as Megan had done. Then, with a smile, she took a tiny bite off one end.

The hum rippled again. Louder this time.

"Thatta way, Habel!" Megan said approvingly. "Don't it taste better that way?" Unconcerned with the shocked expressions surrounding them, Megan grinned and dove back into her breakfast, while she secretly contemplated Mr. Higley's untouched plate and decided she better not stay too long at this establishment, or Habel would lose all her boarders.

*   *   *

Megan felt that she had come to terms with the fact that Jim was Clarissa's beau.

That morning after breakfast, however, she learned another one of life's more difficult lessons: Feelings and emotions were not so easily set aside, no matter how logical it might be to do so. Deciding something and actually accepting it were two very different matters.

She was on her way over to the post office to mail her letter when she saw a buggy coming toward her. Not until it was almost upon her did she realize it carried Jim and Clarissa, who were seated side by side, smiling and talking, obviously on an outing of some kind.

She halted her steps and faced them head-on, her head held high.

"Megan, hello!" Clarissa called out, her lovely face bright with sincerity.

Jim tugged on the reins of the horses, stopping them. "Hello, Meg," he said, his smile fading somewhat. Though he hid it well, he was confused by the conglomeration of emotions that hit him every time he saw her.

Megan peered up at him, feeling uncharacteristically uncomfortable and unsure of herself. Squinting, she shielded her eyes from the sun. "Mornin', Jim, Clarissa."

Clarissa clasped her hands together in excitement. "We're on our way out to the river bluffs for a picnic. Come with us."

Megan forced a smile, feeling excluded even though Clarissa had extended the invitation. "Thanks, but not today. I have business to attend to."

"Ohhh, please do come," Clarissa begged. She turned to Jim and placed her hand over his where it rested on the seat. "Tell her to come, Jim."

Jim stared down into Clarissa's eyes, then shifted his gaze to Megan. Despite his confusion at seeing her, he couldn't help but notice how pretty she looked today, dressed in a blue skirt and white shirtwaist. Her hair was loose around her shoulders in the unfashionably simple style he'd always preferred. Seeing her thus, the years swept away, and without knowing he did so, he offered her that familiar lazy smile that made her remember simpler times, other picnics—another river. "Come with us," he said, hoping she would.

"The river bluffs are truly beautiful," Clarissa said. "You must see them."

Megan's gaze flicked away from the picture of their clasped hands. Jealousy rose within her. She knew that no matter how much she accepted their courtship, she was not ready to tag along on their picnic. At least not this time. "Another time maybe," she told Clarissa. "But not this mornin'."

"Are you sure?" Clarissa asked, disappointed. She seemed to deflate back down into the seat beside Jim.

"Yes." Megan fought the desire to change her mind. "I'll see you soon, though."

But Clarissa wasn't ready to let her go yet. "I saw the Reverend Dunmire this morning. He said you two have already met."

"Yes, we have." Megan felt Jim's eyes on her. "He's very nice."

"Handsome, too," Clarissa added.

"Yes," Megan agreed, lifting her chin a notch. "Yep. He sure is."

Clarissa laughed.

Jim frowned.

"He's not married." Clarissa nudged Jim in the ribs, hoping he'd aid her in her matchmaking effort. Jim, however, offered nothing more than a bad-tempered grunt, which Clarissa ignored. "We'll come by and get you for church Sunday morning about nine o'clock. Will that be all right?"

Megan nodded. "That'll be fine." She allowed her eyes to link with Jim's for the space of several meaningful moments. "I'm looking forward to hearing the reverend preach."

Jim lifted his brows, telling her he recognized her attempt to make him jealous. It irritated him that her effort had worked.

She widened her eyes innocently and batted her lashes twice for emphasis.

They warred a wordless battle for a couple of seconds until he quietly huffed, looked away, and urged his horse forward.

"We'll see you then," Clarissa called out, waving.

"Fine." Megan smiled, finding little comfort in her small victory. She urged her feet forward, refusing to look back, and headed for the post office. She spent a few minutes talking to timid Mr. Tidwell, who, despite his initial surprise at her gender, turned out to be a kindly old gentleman with a wonderful sense of humor. After she had mailed her letter, she made her way over to the livery as she'd planned.

When she reached the building, she stood in the warm morning sunshine and admired Zach's brightly painted sign before entering the shadowed interior. Once inside, she breathed deeply. Scents of leather, animals, and smoke assaulted her. They were scents she loved, scents that made her comfortable, that made her feel at home. It felt good to stand there letting them seep into her.

A soft whinny called to her from one of the stalls at the far end of the barn. She wandered toward the sound, stopping before the horse. "Nice home you got here, fella." The horse was black and glossy, a beautiful specimen. His ears perked forward at the sound of her voice, and he blinked his heavy lashes in silent communication. She reached out and stroked his nose, falling in love with him immediately.

Yes, sir, she acknowledged silently, it was time to get back to work.

"Hello, Doctor."

Megan turned and looked up into the face of the man who had championed her the night of her arrival. "Howdy."

He smiled. "I wondered how long it would take you to find your way over here. I figured you'd be needing a horse and rig soon enough."

She grinned. "You were right. I would have come sooner, but I was worn out after the journey and my visit to your jail."

Noting the mischievous twinkle in her eyes, Zach laughed. "By the looks of the deputy, he'll need more than a day or two to recover."

"Well, he got what he deserved."

"He said you'd give him grief."

Megan winked. "He doesn't know the half of it yet."

They both laughed, finding they were quite comfortable with each other.

"I'm Zachary Davis," the Negro said and extended his big hand.

Megan took his hand without hesitation and squeezed hard. "Dr. Megan Hawkins."

"You're staying on, I take it."

"I'm gonna give it a try."

Zach smiled. "Jim said that once you'd set your mind to something you were like a possum after an egg."

"I guess I can be pretty stubborn at times. 'Specially if I think I'm right."

"Which is often, I suspect."

Megan grinned. "'Course."

A couple of barn swallows entered the livery, swooped low, then rose upward to find resting places on a beam above.

Megan grew silent for a moment, then looked Zach directly in the eyes. "I want to thank you for takin' up for me the other night."

He took a rag that was draped over his shoulder and mopped at the sweat on his brow. "No need to thank me. It was my pleasure. There are some folks in this town who need to be put in their places every now and then." He shrugged. "I suppose it's that way everywhere."

"I s'pose it is." She hesitated a moment. "But I still appreciate it."

He nodded.

She thought about the careful pronunciation of his words and voiced her thoughts. "You talk awful good. Almost perfect. You must have had quite a bit of schoolin'."

Zach smiled, and his expression mellowed with remembrance. "I was just a boy when Mr. Wells took me on as his apprentice here. My pa and ma had died the year before, and since I had no kin, the townsfolk over in Arrow Rock didn't know what to do with me. They sent me out to work on old Mr. Nelson's farm. One day when Mr. Wells came out to shoe Mr. Nelson's horses, he saw me hiding behind the corncrib, watching him work. Mr. Nelson caught me and wanted to whip me good for wasting time gawking around instead of working. But Mr. Wells wouldn't let him. He shod Mr. Nelson's horses for free that day and took me home to be his apprentice. He taught me the trade and all about horses. And he made sure I learned how to read and write, too. He and Mrs. Wells didn't believe it was right for any human being not to have that opportunity. In fact, Mr. Wells said if I wouldn't learn my letters, wouldn't apprentice me." He grinned. "So I learned."

"Well," Megan said, "Mr. Wells did a fine job of teachin' you. You talk better'n I do. Not that I can't talk just fine when I've a mind to." She gave him a look, just to make sure there was no misunderstanding. "But it's a hell of a lot more comfortable to slip into patterns of the past."

"That it is." He chuckled, then said, "So, what can I do for you, Dr. Hawkins?"

"Well, you're right, I need a rig and a horse."

"How about him?" Zach asked, gesturing to the horse she'd been petting. "He's one of my best."

Megan turned, opened the gate, and entered the stall. "What's his name?"

"Jesse."

"Jesse?" Megan cocked her head.

"James," Zach finished with a sheepish grin.

"A fittin' name," she said with approval. "I've always wanted to ride with a James."

"So I've heard."

"Is that a fact?"

"Jim told me a lot about you."

Megan's eyes went soft. She dropped her gaze and muttered, "Yeah, well, he talks too much. Probably told you a pack of lies to boot."

Zach grinned. "Without a doubt."

"How old is he?" Megan asked, forcing her attention back to the horse and away from thoughts of Jim Lawson.

"Five this past May."

"Well, that's fine. Just fine." She reached out to stroke his nose again. "Jesse, looks like you and me are gonna be a team." She ran a hand down his flank and over his back, then carefully examined his teeth. When she was satisfied he was in prime condition, she nodded her approval and said, "He'll do." She slid Zach a speculative glance. "Can I afford him?"

"He costs, but you won't find a better horse in Boonville."

She thought of the money Pa had lent her and decided a good horse would be worth the price. Pa always said you got what you paid for. Somehow she knew Zach Davis would be a fair man. "I'll take him."

"Good. Come on out back, and I'll show you the rigs."

The next day, Megan found her way to the office of Mr. Thomas Barton, the local land agent, to ask about purchasing a piece of property of her own. She didn't have much money, she explained to him, but she felt she needed a place of her own if she wanted to set up her practice. She couldn't imagine dragging a pregnant sow through Habel's foyer.

Mr. Barton looked Megan up and down twice, and although she was dressed in britches, shirt, and hat, he decided she didn't look nearly as tetched as Mrs. Pribble claimed she was. Actually she looked just fine and seemed like a real smart little gal. So, rather than chase her off as he'd been instructed, he set his whiskered chin stubbornly and told her there was indeed a certain piece of property available for sale, a couple of miles east of town on Rocheport Road. Although it wasn't much, it had a small house and a few outbuildings. He invited her to ride out and take a look at the place. He was instantly rewarded by a bright smile that made him forget all about the coming wrath of Mrs. Pribble, and the fact that the Pribbles lived on Rocheport Road, too, just a hop and skip down the way from the house he was sending Megan out to see.

Before Megan headed toward Rocheport Road, she ventured on down to the riverfront. She rode along in her buggy and thought about how it had been for Adam when he'd come to Poplar Bluff nine years ago. It had been hard for him, coming from an eastern city, to set up his practice in a small town in southern Missouri where he knew no one but his Uncle Ned and Aunt Chloe—where he was considered an outsider.

Now she was the outsider.

Just because she was born a Missourian didn't mean Boonville would adopt her as one of their own. She realized it would be as hard for them to accept her—a woman veterinarian—as it had been for Poplar Bluff to accept an easterner like Adam. There was no doubt in her mind that she had her work cut out for her.

She passed several establishments as she ventured down Water Street. One in particular caught her attention. It was a large yellow, two-story house that boasted the sign *Merilee's House of Entertainment.* She grinned, wondering if she could sneak in some evening and find out just what kind of entertainment Merilee offered folks. 'Course, none of the fine gentleman of this town would frequent such an establishment, she was sure.

She turned off Water Street and onto Main, then, as Mr. Barton had instructed, took Locust out to Rocheport Road. She decided that Boonville's locale was ideal. Besides being the county seat of Cooper County, it bordered the Missouri River, making it a hub for commerce and a gateway to the West. Yet somehow, for all its prime location, the town had remained small, retaining a unique charm all its own.

The surrounding land was beautiful. The hills were gentler than they were back home. Black willows, sycamores, red cedars, and poplars bordered the road, parting every so often to allow her a peek at the sun-dazzled ribbon of the Missouri River in the far distance. Goldenrods, sweet williams, shooting stars, and blue lobelias splayed their colorful wares throughout the lush terrain.

It struck Megan that she could be happy in this place if she could find a way to fit in and do what she loved best, which was caring for animals.

Well, Pa, she thought, *I can't say much for the townsfolk, but it shore as hell is pretty here.*

She took her hat from her head and allowed the sun to warm her hair and shoulders, while she relaxed and allowed Jesse to take his lead down the winding road. She passed a huge, vine-covered, two-story, red-brick house that sat in the middle of a meticulously manicured lawn.

It wasn't long after passing that house that she found the one Mr. Barton had told her about.

Gently she tugged the horse to a halt. Mr. Barton was right. The place wasn't much. The house was hardly more than a faded gray shack set on a small island of shabby, undeveloped land. Megan climbed down from her rig and let her gaze rove over the outbuildings. They weren't much, either. Sighing, she looked down and kicked at a clump of loose dirt. She bent down, scooped it up, and crumpled it in her hand. It was dark and rich and moist. She lifted her gaze. There was enough of it for her to pasture some animals of her own if she wanted to and put in a pretty sizable garden. She imagined the house and outbuildings sporting a fresh coat of whitewash and decided she could do a lot worse. If someday they needed a bigger house, they could always add on.

They? She made a face. Humph! Who were they? It was then she realized that she had entertained the thought, albeit subconsciously, of a husband and children, despite what she'd told Johnnie. Still, the face of her husband was as fuzzy as the faces of her imaginary children. She decided then and there that she would buy the piece of land from Mr. Barton. With or without a family, it was time to put down roots of her own.

She left the little farm and decided to ride on down the road to see more of the countryside. In time she turned the rig down a barely passable road and headed toward the river. It wasn't long before she came upon the river bluffs. She tugged Jesse to a halt. The bluffs were every bit as beautiful as Clarissa had said. She hopped down from her

seat and led Jesse under the shade of a large tree. Once
she'd secured him, she wandered over to stand on the edge
of the bluff and gaze out at the river.

The water was dark, but the noontime sun caused an
iridescent shimmer to radiate along its surface. She slid
her hands into her rear pockets as a soft breeze lifted her
hair away from her face. Way out on the river a steamboat passed and blew its whistle. She waved, though she
doubted anyone saw her. A few minutes later a long, low
barge cut through the water, creating a series of rolling
ripples that eventually reached the bank below her. Megan
supposed both vessels were headed for the Boonville docks.
From a field beyond, a whippoorwill called out a song,
while above Megan's head a bright goldfinch and his mate
darted and swooped.

A flash of movement, followed by a splash near the
water's edge, interrupted her serenity. She ducked under
an oak branch and made her way down the hill to inves-
tigate.

On silent feet she approached the young culprit, who was
squatted down on his haunches, unaware of her presence.
"Hey, there," she said to the little redheaded boy.

Startled, he dropped to his knees and spun. He stared up
at her, his eyes reflecting fear. The freckles on his face
stood out sharply.

"Well, just take it easy now," Megan said, approaching
him slowly. "I don't bite hard."

Young Daniel Kincaid relaxed, letting his breath out in
an audible whoosh. His mouth worked wordlessly for a
moment until finally he got out, "Jeez . . . I thought you
were Professor Lewis!"

"Me?" Megan widened her eyes and flattened a palm
against her chest. "Criminy sake, no!" She remembered
some of her professors at the veterinary college back east
and wrinkled her nose in distaste. "Who's Professor Lewis,

anyway?" She sat down on a log and stretched her legs out before her.

"My teacher over at Kemper." His heart beating furiously, Daniel tentatively took a seat on the log beside Megan. He stared at her, thinking his heart might thump right out of his chest.

"Kemper?"

"Kemper Military Academy."

"Hmmm," Megan said. She squinted up into the early afternoon sun. Without looking at him, she asked, "I don't s'pose you should be in Professor Lewis's classroom right now?" She turned a deliberate, very astute gaze upon the boy.

Holding his tongue, Daniel betrayed his guilt by blushing clear up to the roots of his carrot-colored hair.

"Ahhh . . . I see." Megan reached out and ruffled the boy's thick thatch of hair. "Well, I don't s'pose you'll go to hell for missin' a day every now and then, although my guess is your ma and pa would be a mite displeased about the fact."

Daniel snorted his agreement. "Father will probably take the strap to me."

Megan nodded. "I've had more than a few good whuppings in my time." She leaned in close. "You gotta learn how to pad up."

"Huh?" Daniel said, giving her a confused look.

"There's ways to take the edge off a whupping. Remind me sometime, and I'll tell you 'bout 'em. Right now, I'd like for us to get acquainted. My name is Megan Hawkins. What's yours?"

"Daniel." He blushed again.

"Daniel what?"

"Daniel Kincaid."

"I see. Daniel is a fine name. The Daniel from the Old Testament was a brave man, you know?"

"Yeah?"

"Why, sure. He stood up for what he believed in even when that ol' king threw him in the lion's den. Imagine that."

Daniel did and felt pride billow within him at having such a valiant namesake.

"Do you like to be called Daniel or Danny."

He observed her from big green eyes and answered, "Everybody just calls me Daniel."

"Well, I'm gonna call you Danny. If that's all right with you?"

He shrugged, his expression solemn. "I guess."

She elbowed him and grinned. "Don't you ever smile, Danny?"

Bemused, he stared at her, his eyes reflecting his growing infatuation. A hint of a grin teased the corners of his mouth.

She pointed to the pole he'd abandoned on the edge of the muddy riverbank. "That your fishin' pole?"

"Uh-huh."

"Well, then." Megan got up and retrieved it. "It's a sin and shame to let a good fishin' pole sit idle. Let's do some fishin'."

CHAPTER
6

On the first Sunday of July, Megan entered the sedate Boonville Presbyterian Church. She was dressed in her best Sunday silk and matching bonnet and, once again, looked the image of a refined, genteel lady. Her dress, a lovely shade of green, was fitted neatly through the bodice and waist. The sleeves were large and puffy, the skirt narrow and slightly flared at the bottom in the latest of eastern fashion. The dress caught the attention of many of the local women, earning their grudging respect. But Megan didn't seem to notice their stares of appreciation.

The church, larger than Preacher Mosely's modest parish back home, was not excessively affluent, but it boasted polished, hand-crafted pews and beautiful stained-glass windows of which she'd never seen the like.

She followed Habel down the aisle and passed Danny Kincaid seated stiff and silent between his handsome parents in a pew. She caught his eye, winked, and was rewarded with a twitch of a smile. He was dressed like a miniature replica of his large, imposing father. Her instincts told her there was much the father expected from his young son. Her heart contracted with empathy for the boy. How well she remembered the frustration of trying to fulfill someone else's dreams and expectations. It was a fruitless, impossible task. At one time Johnnie had hoped to mold her into a well-read, soft-spoken, refined young lady. But loving her as she did, Johnnie finally realized that her little sister might become well-read, but soft-spoken and refined was something she would never be. It simply wasn't in her nature to be anything but what she was. Megan suspected the same was true for Danny. The afternoon they'd spent together had revealed that he had the heart of a dreamer, a discoverer. The strict confines of military school stifled him. She wondered if his parents would ever realize the truth and set him free.

She continued down the aisle. George and Edith Pribble were in attendance, seated in what Megan surmised were their regular places. Beside them sat Sheriff Johnson and his wife, Gladys, who, though some twenty years younger, was the spitting image of her mother.

Unable to resist the temptation, Megan flashed a bright smile on the group. Edith Pribble and her daughter huffed their disparagement, but Megan was almost sure she noted a twinkle in Mr. Pribble's eye and a grin teasing one corner of Sheriff Johnson's mouth.

She recognized several others: Maxwell Fletcher, Silas Goldman, Mr. Tidwell, and Mr. Barton. She flashed them all the same devil-may-care grin and obediently followed Habel into her pew, taking a seat on Habel's right, with Clarissa on her left. Beside Clarissa, a silent, sulking Deputy Jim Lawson brought up the rear.

For the most part, Megan had ignored him all morning.

She knew she should be civil to him for Clarissa's sake. But after thinking about it, stubborn as she was, she decided she'd be hog-tied and fried in spit before she'd give Jim Lawson the time of day ever again!

When the Reverend Steven Dunmire noticed the small group, he left his seat on the bench beside his pulpit and headed straight for their pew.

"Dr. Hawkins," he said, his smile for Megan alone. He held out his hand. "I'm glad you decided to join us."

Megan placed her hand in his and returned his smile, pretending not to notice that he held onto her hand much longer than was necessary. "I can't say as I had a lot of choice in the matter," she admitted bluntly. "Habel here"— she glanced at her staid companion—"seems to think my soul could do with some preachin', and Clarissa"—she nudged her friend—"is worried I'll dry up and die if she doesn't find me a beau soon."

Clarissa blushed.

Habel coughed.

Jim scowled and slunk down farther into his seat.

The reverend's smile grew. "I doubt Clarissa is going to have much trouble with that task."

Megan shrugged and made a face. "Well, we'll see. I can be pretty picky."

"Humph!" Jim couldn't help but snort, remembering her constant rejection of him when they were children. Inwardly he smoked. It wasn't taking her long to warm up to the reverend. Her blatant flirtation with him irritated him so much he wanted to throttle her into unconsciousness.

But Steven Dunmire had no such inclinations where Megan was concerned. What he was considering had nothing at all to do with throttling her. Thoroughly charmed, he laughed at her animated expression and decided that if he had anything to do with it, she would pick him as a suitor—and soon. "I imagine you left a long string of suitors behind," he half-questioned, half-stated.

Megan's smile softened somewhat. She went silent for a moment, then finally said, "No, to tell you the truth, I can't recall a single one."

Caught off guard by her statement, Jim felt an unexpected twinge of disappointment. Truth be told, he'd once fancied himself her beau. Her only beau. He thought he detected an odd note in her voice, but when he glanced her way, her smile was bright as ever, her eyes sparking orneriness.

He got mad.

"Well . . ." Steven reluctantly released her hand. "We'll have to do something about that. At the end of the month, on the last Sunday after services, we're having a pie and box supper over at the schoolhouse. If you'd be interested in attending and participating, I'd be willing to bid generously on your donation. That is, if you'll give me a hint as to which one it is."

Jim's eyebrows dropped. His expression darkened.

Everyone waited.

Megan thought about her answer. It was an interesting invitation. Pie and box suppers were common events all over the Midwest, but they were especially popular in Missouri. They meant a day full of fun, feasting, and courting. Back home, they were held whenever the community wanted to raise money for some worthy cause. The unmarried women and girls of the community baked pies or prepared box lunches, decorated the boxes in fancy materials, ruffles, and ribbons, and everyone gathered at the local schoolhouse or church grounds, where the pies and boxes were auctioned off to unattached men and boys present. Purchase of a pie or box brought with it the companionship, for the day and perhaps the evening, of the girl who had prepared the item. Usually the owners remained anonymous until the highest bidder came forth to claim his due. A clever young lady had ways of sending a preferred suitor clues as to which was her item, however, often intensifying the excitement of the event.

Megan decided she had nothing to lose. "Why, Rever-

end, I'd be delighted. But I have to warn you. I'm not
much of a cook."

He smiled, his face ruddy with the pleasure of her acceptance. "I'll take the risk. And please call me Steven." He left
them then and returned to his pulpit. A moment later he
asked his congregation to rise, and he led them in prayer,
while Jim Lawson continued to sulk.

The Reverend Dunmire's Presbyterian preaching was
somewhat of a revelation to Megan. Unlike Preacher
Mosely, the young reverend never once turned red,
never once pounded his pulpit. In fact, comparing the
young preacher to Preacher Mosely was like comparing
strawberries to rhubarb. They might blend together if they
were stirred real good, but they were nothing at all alike.

Instead of attacking sin with fire and fear, as Preacher
Mosely would have done, the Reverend Dunmire engaged
a variant strategy. He wielded a sword of a different nature
by bringing his flock a message of love and compassion,
forgiveness and acceptance.

To Megan's surprise, his sermon was most effective. At
least with most folks. She glanced over her shoulder and
noted the sour expressions of many of the townspeople.
Megan decided there were just some folks who needed the
sky to drop on their heads before they were ready to open
their hearts.

Yet, despite the indifference of those hard-hearted few,
when the Reverend Dunmire finished his sermon, there
were plenty of repentant hearts who made their way to
the altar for prayer.

Had she been in different company, Megan might have
been moved to repentance herself. After all, triflin' with
the young reverend's affections just to get Jim Lawson all
riled was not only unkind, but also downright dishonest,
and she knew better. Pa would have whupped her good for
such deceitful antics. But, she comforted herself, raising her

eyes to sneak another peek at the reverend, she did like him fine. And in time, well, who knows, she just might grow to like him even better.

While the Reverend Dunmire asked for all heads to remain bowed for prayer, Megan kept her head respectfully downcast. But instead of closing her eyes again, she gave in to the temptation to steal a glance to her left. Being taller than Clarissa, she easily saw over her head.

Jim's head was bowed also, but before Megan looked away, she saw him slide a glance in her direction.

He raised an eyebrow in that knowing, perceptive way that made her heart slam sideways. It riled her. Before she could stop herself, she stuck out her tongue.

A grin appeared, and his mustache twitched.

She steamed and snorted her disgust.

Habel's and Clarissa's eyelids popped open. Jim's and Megan's eyelids slammed shut.

The Reverend Dunmire ended his Sunday sermon.

Megan bought the small homestead from Mr. Barton, even when she found out that her nearest neighbor—the owner of that impressive red-brick house down the road—was none other than Mrs. Edith Pribble herself.

Megan drove a hard bargain, one Mr. Barton would never forget, and got the place for bottom dollar. The money her pa had lent her had been put to good use in purchasing her rig, Jesse, and her home, but she knew what little money she had left would have to be conserved. It would take some time for the locals to accept her and allow her to treat their livestock, and even when they did, money would still be tight.

In the next two weeks she set about making her new home livable. It was no easy task. The house had been empty for years, and she had no furnishings of her own, except the old clock she placed in the parlor. It had been her mother's. Johnnie had sent it along with her so she'd have a bit of home to put in her new place. She was thankful the previous owners had left an old black cookstove and a scarred but serviceable table and chairs.

She slept on a bedroll of her own making and accepted the fact that her front room would remain empty of furniture for the time being. Still, she wasn't discouraged. In her mind, she saw the house and farm as it would be . . . someday.

A week later, on his way out to Megan's place, Jim told himself he was only doing his duty by looking in on her. After all, Habel had asked him to go. He told himself he wouldn't stay long; he would make sure she was all right, then he'd beat it on out of there quicker than a chicken-stealing dog.

He owed her family that much—to check on her every now and then. He knew if anything happened to her, her brothers would not take it lightly, being as she was in his jurisdiction—and therefore his responsibility. And since he valued his hide . . .

Right about then a frightening thought struck him. Surely he wasn't making excuses to see her! He shook his head, unwilling to accept the thought and told himself, *Whoa there, Lawson! You don't need the grief she'd give ya! How many black eyes do ya need before you figure out that she's a danger to your person?*

Reminding himself of that fact, he convinced himself that his purpose for visiting her was nothing more than common consideration, and the rest of his journey was a pleasant one. The July morning was fair and warm, the sky gloriously blue. The county crops needed rain, but Jim was glad the rain held off. At least for today.

When he reached Megan's property line, he guided his horse into the yard and into the dappled shade of a large maple. Then he dismounted and went in search of the lady. He found her absorbed in her work, scrubbing the inside of a huge old tub out on the back porch. She didn't see him at first, and he thought that was fine, since it gave him the opportunity to study her in private for a few seconds.

She'd always been tall and willowy. She still was—more so now than ever—but there was a softness about her now, a winsome womanliness, that belied the tomboy image she created in her faded britches and worn shirt. Her sunny hair was pulled back into a loose coil at her neck. Several tendrils had escaped and clung, dewy and damp, to her face and forehead. Bent over at the waist, she scrubbed the tub so vigorously that the coil of hair came loose and fell across her shoulder and down into her face. She flipped it back out of the way and softly cursed.

"Say damn, dammit," Jim urged quietly, unable to resist the temptation to repeat the order she had so often given him in the past.

She snapped to and whirled to face him. Her eyes and mouth rounded at once. Recovering, she became embarrassed, then mad. Her eyes narrowed, and she nearly spit venom when she hollered, "Goddammit, Jim! You nearly scared me outta my wits!"

He fought the urge to laugh. "I didn't mean to scare you. I only came by to see how you were gettin' on."

"As you can see, I'm gettin' on just fine!" She returned to her task, scrubbing the tub so hard her small breasts jiggled within the loose confines of her shirt. She didn't notice, but he did.

He took a step toward her. "I wondered, that's all."

"Well, wonder about someone else!"

Provoked by her waspish attitude, he asked, "What are you so goddamned mad about?"

She raised her eyes to him and slowly lifted one eyebrow. "I ain't mad," she forced herself to say quietly.

"The hell you aren't!"

"The hell I am!"

"Humph!" he said.

"Humph!" she said.

Glowering, they both became silent, and Megan returned to scrubbing the tub as though sin and hell were contained in the bottom and she were possessed by the spirit of Preacher Mosely.

Jim shifted his weight from one foot to the other, feeling fourteen and terribly awkward once again. Finally he spoke. "Why are you scrubbin' the bark off that old tub?"

"It's for my patients. So I can give 'em a bath if I need to. It has to be sterile."

"There won't be nothin' left of it, the way you're goin' at it."

She ignored him, wondering why he'd really come to see her.

"I heard you're staying out here at night now."

"Yep." She didn't look up at him.

"Habel's worried about you."

"I know. But she needn't be."

He waited a second, then said, "I'm not sure it's such a good idea for you to be out here all alone."

Her eyes snapped up to his. Still, she kept right on scrubbing that damned tub. "I think you know me well enough to know I can take care of myself."

He thought about that a minute. "I s'pose." He shrugged. His eyes dropped to her chest. She felt his gaze on her so keenly it was as though he'd touched her there in a very tender, soft way. Flustered, she looked away, while he looked on. The first three buttons of her shirt were open, and a thin layer of perspiration glistened over her chest and down into a place he couldn't see. Thinking about that place got him rattled. "Well . . ." He hesitated a moment, knowing there was no good reason to prolong his visit, knowing it would be wise if he left. "I guess I'll be goin', then."

"Ouch!" She straightened and shook her hand three times hard.

Quickly he closed the few steps between them. "What's wrong?"

She held her hand close, squinting hard while she examined her finger. "Oh, I got a damned splinter, that's all."

He snorted as if to say he thought she deserved it.

She gave him a look that told him he was courting danger.

He shot her one back that said he wasn't scared. "Here." He grabbed her hand and pulled it close. "Let's see."

She huffed, but allowed him to give her finger a look. "It's right there," he said, and before she could protest, he deftly plucked it out.

She snatched her hand back and studied the tiny dot of blood where the splinter had been. "Thank you," she said grudgingly, not looking at him.

"You're welcome."

She glanced up at him and found his gaze on her again. Awareness hummed through them like a swarm of locusts, and for the first time since they'd seen each other as adults, they both looked their fill.

She studied the fine, straight line of his nose, the mellow depth of his sleepy, dark eyes, his handsome mustached mouth, and wondered how many others that mouth had kissed since the day he'd kissed her so many years ago, when she'd been twelve and he fourteen. She acknowledged his height, the attractive width of his shoulders. . . .

She had no idea what a lovely sight she made. Her small nose was beaded with perspiration; her hair was loose around her shoulders. Her eyes, sky blue, wide, and wondering, stared up at him, unblinking. Her breasts pressed up against the soft cotton of her shirt, accentuating her tiny, willowy waist, nipped tight by a belt that held up britches far too large for her. He had the desire to pull her close, touch her, smell her. . . . "Meg," he said quietly, not able to keep from voicing his thoughts, "you're still the prettiest girl in Missouri."

A slow flush stained her cheeks, and she shrugged one shoulder as if to say she didn't believe him.

"Oh, there you are!" a voice called. Startled, they both jumped.

Megan recovered first. "Clarissa, hello."

"What are you doing out here so early in the morning?" she asked Jim, joining them, her expression happy.

Feeling caught and guilty, Jim tipped his hat forward so the brim fell just above his eyebrows. "I figured I should ride out and see if Megan was set up all right. Habel was worried about her."

Clarissa seemed naively unaware of the tension that still fizzled between the two. "If you asked me, I could have told you she was fine. I come out all the time. In fact," she stated proudly, "I helped her clear some of her flower beds." Nimble of mind, she often changed the subject without waiting for a comment, and she did so now. It was one of the few things about her nature that irritated Jim. "I brought some of my mother's blueberry muffins for Megan and me to share over tea. You can join us."

"Uh, well . . ." Jim fidgeted, searching his mind for an escape route.

Feeling as convicted as he, Megan empathized and saved him. "Didn't you say you were meeting Zach about something this morning?"

Jim exhaled. "Yes. And if I don't get goin', I'm gonna be late."

"Oh." Clarissa sighed, disappointed. "I'll see you later, then?"

Jim forced a smile. "Sure."

"After supper?"

"Fine." Relieved to make his escape, he left them with a brief wave, and Megan and Clarissa went in to have their tea and visit over Mrs. Westfield's wonderful blueberry muffins.

A month had passed since Megan had left Poplar Bluff for Boonville. It was late July, and the days had grown long and hot. Harvest was still far off, and the lazy summer evenings drew on. On one such evening, Megan's oldest brother, Matthew, sat within the cozy walls of the Hawkins home, reading his little sister's letter out loud to his pa and his youngest brother, Luke.

It took him a while to work through it, since he'd never been the best of readers. But then, his married brother Mark was only a little better, and Luke—well, Luke might be strong as a bull and have a heart as soft as cotton, but he wasn't known for the power of his mind.

Their sister Johnnie had taught them and herself book learning, and had done a right fine job of the task. But she'd been determined Meg would have the formal schooling that she and the boys lacked. Yes, sir. Meg was the schooled one of the bunch, and they were right proud of her.

But she was still their baby.

When he was done reading her letter, Matthew looked up with worried blue eyes and asked his pa, "We ever been up to Boonville?"

Calm and steady as always, Clarence Hawkins continued to concentrate on packing the bowl of his pipe. "No. Can't say as we ever have."

Perplexed, Luke glanced over at Matt. "Why?"

"Well," Matthew said, his handsome face troubled, "I could be wrong, but by the sound of this letter, I'd say Meg is homesick."

Luke shook his head vehemently. "Aw, Meg's too tough to be homesick!"

"She ain't cither!" Matt argued, giving his brother a look of disgust. "I swear you got cornmeal for brains, Luke!" He smacked Luke over the head with Megan's letter, and read on:

" 'I'm not sure I should have come here after all. I'm fine, so don't worry. But the folks here are different from those back home. I always thought Missourians would be the same all over, but I guess I was wrong. People are sort of stiff around here. Guess they need a good dose of our blue ruin to put some life back in them. You make sure you tell Adam I'm going to skin him alive when I come home to visit. Did you know he never told these folks I was a female veterinarian? You should have seen their faces, Pa. They were like to hang me. I miss and love you all. Tell Johnnie to kiss them boys for me. Tell Matt and Luke not to take on so and drive you crazy with their fighting. And don't forget to write and tell me when Mark and Ellie have their baby. . . .' "

Matthew looked up, his expression still reflecting his concern.

"Yep," Clarence agreed, "our baby's lonely all right."

Luke thought about that and said, "Jim's up there. I'm shore he's lookin' out for her."

"And who's lookin' out for him?" Matt asked. "You know them two always did git in a peck of trouble whenever they were together."

Recalling the past, Luke couldn't argue with that statement.

Matt folded the letter carefully and rose from his chair, stretching up to his full height of six feet six inches. "Well," he said, making a decision, "Mark's gotta stay here with Ellie, jist in case she decides to have that baby early.

So I s'pose me and Luke should take us a visit on up to Boonville."

Luke stood and stretched also, hoping, for all that he figured he was probably done growing at thirty years of age, that he'd somehow stretch that last half inch and match his thirty-five-year-old brother's height.

Clarence nodded his approval and eyed his sons with pride. Matthew was the oldest; Mark, who was married to Ellie, was the middle boy; and Luke was the youngest. From the time Luke had been old enough to talk, there had been an ongoing rivalry between him and his oldest brother.

At times they almost drove Clarence crazy with their bickering, but he could find little fault with them otherwise. They were good boys, and he knew they loved each other and would always stand by each other in the end. That was how he'd raised them. And they'd never once defied him. He supposed it would be good for Meg to see her brothers, though he knew she'd be just fine if she didn't. Meg was tougher than any of her softhearted brothers. His guess was they probably missed her more than she missed them. He bit the mouthpiece of his pipe and squinted through a thin veil of smoke. "I s'pose you better leave at first light, then."

"Shhh," Jim said, nudging the man at his side. "You're gonna get us hung!"

"I can't help it if I have to sneeze," Zach whispered, affronted. "Can't a man sneeze if the urge grabs him?"

"Not if the urge can cost him his neck!" Jim said under his breath. He peered through the shadows, trying to make out Zach's expression. "Your face is so goddamned black, you're safe. They can't see you. But they'd sure as hell see me!"

"I can't help it if you got that sickly white face!" Zach paused a moment, then said, "I don't know why we're out here tonight anyway."

"Because I saw him kick his horse yesterday."

Disgusted, Zach shook his head. "I thought we were only trying to get back the animals he was stealing from others, not take the ones that rightfully belong to him—like his dog," he couldn't resist adding.

"He shouldn't have kicked him either. Besides, look how happy that pup is now, an' he'll be that much happier when I get him a new home."

"Why the hell do you always got to be lurking around to see him get mean with his animals?"

"Hell, I don't know. I guess 'cause I'm the deputy. I get paid to lurk around."

"But you don't get paid for stealing animals."

"Then Fletcher shouldn't t've stolen them from other people in the first place. And," he added defensively, "he shouldn't be mistreatin' his own animals."

Zach sighed wearily. "You can't make the whole world right, Jim," he said, even though he admired his friend for his desire to do so. But he also knew that Maxwell Fletcher had been stealing and swindling the people of Boonville and the surrounding communities for years. And they let him, because he hid his dishonesty behind his family name, his wife's money, and the false illusion that he was a fine, upstanding citizen of the community.

That riled Jim Lawson to no end. "One of these days he'll make a mistake, and I, or someone else, will be there to catch him and make sure he never cheats another soul."

"The folks of this town don't care, Jim."

"I care. You care. Anna cares. How else are we gonna get her father's cattle back for him if we don't take them back? You know he can't afford to replace them." He thought a minute, then added, "Did you ever think that her father just might take a likin' to you, if you helped him out?"

Zach snorted. "That man would as soon shoot me as look at me. And Anna will never marry me once she finds out I'm a thief."

Jim snorted. "We ain't really thieves."

"The hell we aren't. We could get hanged for this. This is about as close to being an outlaw as you can get, friend!"

"It ain't either," Jim argued. "We don't shoot people or nothing like that. We just take back what belongs to others and return it to them."

"They'd still call it rustling."

"They can call it anything they goddamn want. I call it justice."

"You call taking Fletcher's horse justice?"

"Hell, no," Jim said, grinning through the darkness at his friend. "I call that fun. Come on." He took off, keeping low to the ground. He slid from tree to tree, edging his way closer to the barn where Maxwell Fletcher's horse waited patiently.

CHAPTER
7

The days flew by, and July wore to an end. Although she'd yet to treat a patient, Megan made the acquaintance of many of the townsfolk and most of the local farmers. She talked to them all, unaffected by social station or gender, determined that sooner or later they'd need her services in some way, and when they did, she'd be ready. From some she felt blatant antagonism, but from others she sensed an ambivalent sort of acceptance.

She was not disheartened, however. She was far too busy creating a home for herself and a place to treat the patients she believed she would someday have.

Often she had company. Besides Clarissa, Habel was a constant visitor at her house. Twice, Steven had ridden out to check on her, though he'd stayed only the sparest of prudent minutes.

As for Jim, other than his one and only visit, he'd been conspicuously absent. What had passed between them that day still mystified her. For a moment she'd almost hoped he'd kiss her. For a moment she'd forgotten Clarissa and realized that for all her denials, she'd always thought of Jim as hers alone.

Since that day, she'd seen him several times on her way through town, and every Sunday at church. But they'd exchanged only the shortest of greetings, carefully avoiding any need for deeper conversation. There was an awkwardness between them now, and they both respected the need for distance.

She learned much about herself as the days passed. She found that her solitude gave her time to think, time to reflect on the past, time to hope for the future.

Her new friends were a source of enlightenment, also. The one who surprised her most was Habel.

Megan suspected that in the past Habel would never have thought of leaving her home and boarders alone for an entire day. But she left them now and came out to Megan's place daily to lend a hand wherever it was needed.

Habel enjoyed every minute of it. She'd made it her mission to look after Megan, having promised Deputy Lawson she would, and just because Megan no longer resided under her roof, that did not mean she could shirk her duty where the younger woman was concerned.

Besides, the more time she spent in Megan's company, the more unshackled she felt. It seemed as though she'd spent her lifetime bound by chains created by others. And now, by some miracle, those chains were falling away, setting her free, and she saw things differently through eyes that belonged to herself instead of others.

One day Habel sat in Megan's kitchen, watching her as she stood on a stool, stretching to reach into a small hole in the wall beside a cupboard.

"Do you really think it's wise to put your hand up in there?" Habel asked, worried.

"Hand me that rag, will you?" Megan realized the folly of not protecting herself. Any varmint, wild or otherwise, could be rabid.

"There might be something living in there," Habel said,

hesitant to comply with Megan's request.

"I'm sure there is. That's why I need the rag."

Reluctantly Habel handed up the piece of cloth. Megan took it and wrapped it around her hand several times. "There." Satisfied, she sent a knowing grin Habel's way. "Most critters are mean when cornered." She turned her attention to the hole.

Habel palmed her cheeks in worry. "Oh, Megan, sometimes you worry me."

But Megan ignored her and stretched upward again, shoving her arm into the hole clear up to the elbow. "Gotcha!" she exclaimed a moment later and withdrew her arm to reveal a baby squirrel. "I bet you got brothers and sisters in there, don't you?" She got down from the stool. "Well, you're all big enough to find a home of your own now. This one's taken." She took the animal to the door and set him free, then repeated the process two more times, while Habel looked on in amazement.

"You're not afraid of anything," Habel said, respect evident in her eyes.

Megan grinned. "Well, sure I am. I'm afraid of lots of things. I'm afraid this town might never accept me, and if the day ever comes when they do, I'm afraid I'll do something wrong and disappoint them." Her eyes grew sad, and her expression mellowed. "Sometimes I'm afraid of being alone. I don't admit that very often, but it's true. I've been thinkin' about it a lot lately. I'm afraid of never having a man to love. Of never having my own young 'uns."

Habel nodded, understanding. "Yes, I know," she said softly.

Realizing what she'd said and how it must have made Habel feel, Megan felt awful. "Oh, Habel, I'm sorry."

Habel waved off her apology. "It's all right. At my age one doesn't dream about such things anymore. Not that I ever really did."

"Thirty isn't so old, Habel."

Habel smiled indulgently. "Old enough."

Megan decided to change the subject. "I'm not afraid of critters, though. You just gotta know how to handle 'em. The same goes for most folks, too."

Her elbow resting on the table, Habel leaned her jaw into her palm. "I wish I were more like you."

Megan took a seat on one of her wobbly chairs. She flattened her palm against her chest and pressed forward. "Like me! What for? You're respectable and polite and nice."

Habel screwed her tiny face up into a wrinkled frown. "I'm tired of being respectable, polite, and nice. Most people in this town don't even know I'm alive. God himself wouldn't know if I didn't pray every night. But you," she said, admiration in her voice, "why . . . you're not afraid to do anything, say anything, be anything but who you are."

Megan thought about that. "I s'pose that's 'cause my family loved me. Really loved me no matter what."

Habel's lovely gray eyes grew soft and velvety. "That must have been wonderful."

"It was."

They sat in companionable silence for a little while. Then Megan got an idea. "What would you like to do more than anything right now? Today?"

Habel thought a minute, then a reckless giggle bubbled forth. Gathering her courage, she blurted, "I suppose if I could choose, I'd like to learn how to swear."

Megan's eyebrows shot upward. "Why, Habel! I'm surprised at you!"

Chagrined, Habel blushed. "Imagine what my boarders would think."

"Perish the thought." Megan rose from the table and affected a stance of authority. "All right. If that's what you really want, I'll teach you." Megan's brows tightened. "You ever cuss at all before?"

Habel blinked twice. "No. I can't say that I ever have."

"Holy shit!" Megan muttered, realizing the enormity of her task. She sighed and decided to start small. "All right. Say darn!"

Habel straightened her back in the chair. "Darn," she repeated so softly Megan had to lean forward, not sure she'd heard anything at all.

Disgusted, Megan plunked her hands on her hips. "Oh, for heaven's sake, you can do better than that, Habel! Now say it so I can hear it."

"Darn."

"Louder!"

"Darn!"

"Say it like you mean it!"

"Darn! Darn!" Habel rose from her chair, her expression determined. "Darn!"

Megan nodded her approval. "Now you're cookin'. Now say heck!"

"Heck!"

"Thatta girl!" Excited, Megan began to pace the kitchen. "Now say damn!"

Silence.

Megan waited expectantly. Finally, tired of waiting, she stopped pacing, snorted, and plopped herself down onto the shaky kitchen chair. "Well, what's wrong now?"

Habel shrugged and crossed her arms over her chest. "It just seems so . . . vulgar."

"It is," Megan agreed. "It's s'posed to be. It's cussin'. But it's fun. So try it."

Habel moaned.

"Do you want to be invisible all your life, Habel?"

"No."

"Well, then . . ."

"Oh, all right." Habel finally relented. She turned her profile to the window so that she wouldn't have to look at Megan. "Damn." It was barely more than a whisper.

Megan shook her head in disgust and rolled her eyes to the ceiling. "Criminy!"

Affronted by her friend's attitude, Habel experienced something very odd, very wonderful within herself. She got mad. Facing her friend, her back went ramrod straight, and she let loose a loud "Damn!"

"Atta way, Habel!" Megan jumped up from the chair. "Now look real mean and say a whole sentence like— Dammit! Get the hell outta my way, you goddamned pecker-head!"

Totally appalled, Habel looked about to collapse. Her face blazed.

Noting her shocked expression, Megan explained, "You gotta know how to do it right if you ever need to do it."

"I suppose you're right." But Habel didn't look so sure.

"I am."

Habel took a deep breath, made the most awful face she could muster, closed her eyes tight, and bellowed, "Get the hell outta my way, you goddamned pecker-head!"

Megan jumped up and down, applauding. "Hot damn! Now you got it, Habel!"

Habel punched both fists into the air. "I do! I do! Good heavens, but this feels wonderful!"

They practiced for the next hour, until Habel thought God would strike her dead or, worse yet, her tongue would rot from all the profanities that rolled off it. But her tongue held fast, and God didn't strike her dead. The sense of freedom she'd begun to experience of late grew even sharper, even sweeter. When they were done, she was totally exhausted and surprisingly content.

"Now, listen, Habel." Megan felt she ought to warn her. "Just 'cause you know how to say all those words now don't mean you gotta do it. It's knowin' you can if you need to that counts. Understand?"

Habel nodded. "Indeed I do. Oh," she said, her adventurous spirit taking hold, "there's something else I've always wanted to do."

"What's that?" Megan asked, curious.

"Well, I've always wanted to pay a visit to Merilee's House of Entertainment and find out exactly what goes on in that place."

Megan grinned. "Imagine that. I've been thinkin' I'd like to do that myself sometime."

After several days of spotty rain and unbearable warm temperatures, the day of the pie and box supper dawned bright and clear and pleasantly cool.

Jim Lawson stood before his washstand, shaving. He thought about shaving off his mustache. Clarissa had complained that it itched her when he kissed her. But he decided to leave it where it was for the time being.

He scowled into the mirror. He was not in the best of moods, but then he hadn't been for quite some time now. And he knew the reason why.

Megan Hawkins!

Although he couldn't quite figure out what she'd done to agitate him, she'd done it and done it good. He thought he had conquered his infatuation with her when he left Poplar Bluff. Now he wasn't so sure.

She'd hexed him, he decided. She was more of a witch than Granny Grady ever was. At least Granny was honest and open about her dabbling. Megan, however, worked her hexes in a different, far more subtle manner.

Yep! She'd hexed him good, dammit!

Despite his affection for Clarissa, he'd barely thought of her since the day he'd gone out to Megan's place. Even when he kissed her, it was Megan he thought of.

A ridiculous thought struck him: He wondered if Megan would mind his mustache. Irritated with himself for even entertaining the thought, he discarded it, jamming his Stetson onto his head.

He was going to take care of the problem today, by God! He would have him a good time even if it killed him. And if she'd let him, he was going to kiss Clarissa, mustache and all, till his lips hurt.

And Megan Hawkins be damned!

Jim was not the only man in town who'd been preoccupied with the subject of kissing. Steven Dunmire had been doing his own share of thinking on that matter. Today, as he turned his rig into Megan's narrow drive, the thought of kissing her was first and foremost on his mind.

He'd been taken with Megan Hawkins from the first day he'd met her; there was no denying that fact. She was spontaneous and fun, unpretentious and unaffected.

She was different.

He knew there were several members of his congregation who would not approve of an alliance between their reverend and such an unconventional young woman. But he was not deterred by that thought. Times were changing, and fast. They lived in a time of great progress. Contraptions such as telephones and telegraphs were sweeping across the country, opening communication lines and aiding advancement like nothing before. If such wonderful things could happen to this country, why couldn't a minister like him fall in love with a woman like Megan Hawkins?

He slowed his horse to a halt, then hopped down from the buggy. He crossed the recently weeded and trimmed yard and climbed the steps of the porch. He was about to knock on the door when it swung open.

"Hello," Megan said in greeting, looking lovely and trim in her blue-and-white-checked skirt and crisp white shirtwaist.

He stared at her, awed and speechless for several seconds, then finally managed to return the greeting. "Hello.

My . . . you look wonderful."

Megan cocked her head and smiled. "Thank you. So do you."

He did, dressed in creased dark trousers and a white shirt that he'd left casually open at the neck. He was so young, so appealingly handsome, he hardly fit her picture of a preacher. But then, that was all right.

Dipping to retrieve a large basket from the floor, she stepped out onto the porch and pulled the door shut behind her.

"I've been looking forward to today." His light blue eyes echoed the truth of his words.

"I have, too."

He stole a peek at her basket, hoping to get a look at her offering inside. But she had a towel tucked over and around the supper box, almost completely hiding it from curious eyes. He caught a glimpse of a crisp white ruffle, however, sticking out from beneath the towel.

She caught him peeking and arched an eyebrow at him.

He grinned sheepishly, then laughed, and she did, too. He led her to his buggy and gallantly helped her up, all the while wondering how he could manipulate the opportunity to claim a kiss today, and if she would mind if he did so.

The preparations for the pie and box supper were well under way by the time Megan and Steven arrived. Mrs. Pribble and her ladies were in charge of the arrangements, and they marched about, like captains of the cavalry, ordering their men and children to this task and that, tolerating no laziness or lack of cooperation.

The auctioneer, Mr. Barton—the land agent himself— wore a bright red vest over his fanciest duds and stood on a small stage outdoors that had been constructed for the sole purpose of the event. On the stage was a table, laid out in grand fashion, waiting to be decorated with the young ladies' fancy offerings.

Mr. Barton reveled in his role of auctioneer. He liked to think he drove the hardest bargain of any man in town, but he silently conceded, since meeting Megan Hawkins, that there were some who could best him. Still, he did have a way with words. And although the bidding had not yet begun, he kept busy amusing the audience with witty remarks and jibes, preparing them for the time when he'd relieve them of their money.

After Steven helped her down from the buggy, Megan snatched her basket from behind the seat before he could get another look and took off for the schoolhouse, where her donation would be given a number.

"You'll give me a hint?" he called out after her, his face bright with hope.

Megan laughed. "You already got one. I saw you peekin'."

"But I didn't see anything but a ruffle!"

"That's plenty!" she hollered over her shoulder.

The air was heady with celebration and excitement. Tempting aromas wafted about from the many tables of food that littered the schoolyard, ready to be served to those who did not participate in the bidding, along with the unfortunate swains who lost to a higher bidder.

Megan strolled through the throng, past a thriving lemonade stand, around a group of farmers discussing their crops, in front of an assemblage of women gossiping and trading recipes, behind a gang of laughing children playing a game of base ball.

Caught up in the festivities around her, she didn't notice the boy at her side until she felt a tug on her sleeve. Halting, she looked down into Danny Kincaid's freckled face. "Well, hey, Danny!"

"Hello, Dr. Hawkins."

Megan gave him a gentle look of reproof. "I thought we agreed my name was Megan to you."

Abashed, he pinkened. "I forgot."

"Well . . . that's all right." She leaned down and kissed his cheek. He silently vowed he would never wash it again, no matter what his mother threatened.

Megan straightened. A little girl with dark brown pigtails, tied at the ends with bright pink ribbons, turned her tiny upswept nose into the air and sashayed by, making sure they both saw her. She carried in her arms a box supper wrapped in white material, pleated with ruffles, that she didn't bother to hide. It was decorated with pink roses and big, misshapen pink cloth hearts she'd obviously cut out and sewn on herself. "Hi, Daniel!" she called out, batting her eyelashes.

Daniel pretended not to notice.

Megan smiled and couldn't resist asking, "So do you plan on biddin' on one of those suppers yourself?"

His blush deepened, and he frowned. "No."

"Well, why not?" Megan bent over, the better to get eye to eye with him. She rested one palm on her knee. "That little girl is makin' cow eyes at you."

"Oh, that's just Amy Applegate." He rolled his eyes upward.

"My . . ." Megan shook her head, clicking her tongue. "She sure is a pretty little thing."

"She's a pest!"

"A pretty one, though."

"Humph!" Danny wrinkled his nose in distaste.

The past rose up to greet her, and Megan remembered a time when she'd felt much the same about Jim. She ruffled Danny's bright head and gently told him, "Be careful, young sir. There may come a time when you'll be lookin' at that girl differently, and she'll be lookin' at someone else the way she used to look at you."

"I won't never!"

Megan's eyes went soft. "Never is a very long time, Danny. People change." She shook off the nostalgia by changing the subject. "We gonna do some more fishin' soon?" His eyes lit with excitement. But before he could respond, she added, "You try to make sure it's not on a school day, though, all right? I'd hate to have your ma and pa after me for teachin' you bad doin's."

He nodded, happy that she wanted to spend time with him.

Mr. Barton began his bidding, and Megan realized she was late. "Well, I s'pose I better get this on over to the schoolhouse, or I'll be eating this lunch all by myself."

She left him to find Habel and Clarissa, who were inside the schoolhouse, waiting for her.

Habel, who'd never in her life even considered the fool notion of participating in the event, did so now after days of pestering from Megan. She reluctantly placed her colorful box among the others and nervously waited for Mrs. Barton to assign both her and her supper a number, knowing she'd probably end up spending the day and evening with Sam Sweeney.

Seeing Megan, Clarissa rushed her. "Oh, Meg, let's switch boxes!"

"Why?"

" 'Cause it's more fun that way."

"We won't know who we'll end up with."

"We won't know that anyway, unless you gave the Reverend Dunmire a hint."

Pretending to be offended, Megan looked disgusted. "That wouldn't be fair. Of course I didn't!"

Clarissa slid her a knowing glance and smiled. "Megan Hawkins, from what I've come to know about you, playing fair is only a state of mind where you're concerned."

Megan's expression changed, and she chuckled, her eyes bright with amusement. "I can't argue that."

"Well, then?"

"Oh, all right."

*   *   *

Coming from the south end of town, Mark and Luke made their way up Main Street, heading due north toward the schoolhouse. The letter Megan had sent them had given Habel's address as her place of residence. So they'd stopped at a house on the outskirts of town and asked directions, only to be told that Miss Habershaw and her boarders would most likely be found at the schoolhouse grounds, attending the pie and box supper.

Since both Matthew and Luke were hungrier than homeless hogs, they wasted no time in finding their way to the festivities.

Twittering and excited, the women waited in clusters outside the schoolhouse door, anxiously clutching their numbers in their hands. When their suppers were won, they walked onto the stage, took their boxes from Mr. Barton, then waited to be claimed by their companion for the day.

Jim stood beside Steven, his arms crossed over his chest, watching while the box suppers were taken from the table and auctioned off. He'd bid on one, thinking it might be Clarissa's; but not sure, he'd let someone else top him and win the supper. Now he was greatly relieved. The last supper had belonged to Widow Higgins. And no young man this side of the Missouri River wanted to win Widow Higgins's attentions for the day. She had a face plainer than a lump of wood and a mouth that was never silent. And she was hunting a new husband. Her three previous ones were dead—they'd been talked to death, Jim was sure.

Still recovering from relief, Jim was the first to notice the arrival of the Hawkins brothers. Surprised, he left Steven and ran to greet them, his face beaming his joy at seeing them. "Matt! Luke!"

The two men reined in their horses and swung down to the ground. Jim was on them in a flash. They hugged and banged each other on the back and shoulders so hard they coughed.

"Hey, Jim!" Matt shouted.

"Whewee!" Luke hooted and hugged Jim around the waist, lifting him high into the air.

"Sheeeeyit!" Jim exclaimed. "It's good to see you boys!"

"It's good to see you, too," Matt returned.

"What the hell are you doin' here?"

Matt grinned. "We come to make sure Meg was doin' all right."

Luke nodded. "She wrote us a while back and seemed a bit homesick."

Jim sobered a minute. The thought of Meg being homesick had never occurred to him. She'd always seemed so strong, so self-sufficient.

"Pa thought we should take a ride up and visit for a spell," Matt said while he scanned the crowd for his little sister's head.

Jim gestured to the group of women hovering around the schoolhouse. "She's over there, waiting for her box supper to go up for bidding."

Matthew and Luke found her.

Luke's eyes settled on the pretty young woman at his sister's side. "Gawd dang, but I'm hungrier than a motherless pup!"

Matt nodded, his stomach grumbling. "Me, too."

Standing between the two, Jim draped an arm around their huge shoulders. "Come on, then. You two might as well get in on the biddin'. Now that Widow Higgins is taken, it's a pretty safe bet you'll end up with someone worth spendin' the day with."

Matt grinned. "I sure as hell hope so!"

CHAPTER
8

The words poured off Mr. Barton's tongue in a waterfall of sentences. Laughter and hoots filled the air, as suitors lost to higher bidders, and those who won the boxes won a girl other than the one they had originally intended to win.

Megan calmly waited her turn. On each side of her, however, Clarissa and Habel wrung their hands—Clarissa in excitement, Habel in nervous apprehension.

Habel watched as her box supper was set before Mr. Barton. "Now . . ." He paused a long minute to build tension. "Who is gonna start the bidding on this fine offering?" He bent down and sniffed noisily. "Something sure smells good."

A bidder called out a figure.

Affronted, Mr. Barton glared. "You can do better than that, Samuel Sweeney!"

Habel squeezed her eyes shut tight.

"Going once!" Mr. Barton called out. "Twice!" His voice echoed finality, while his gavel began its heartless descent.

"Two dollars!" someone hollered boldly.

The gavel halted in midair.

Megan searched the crowd for the owner of the deep, dear, familiar voice. "Matt," she whispered, her heart swelling at the sight of his handsome face. "Well, criminy! It's Matt and Luke."

Habel gasped, oblivious to Megan's words. Stunned, she was completely overcome by the offer, which was generous by anyone's standards.

"Do I hear two-fifty?" Mr. Barton waited about two whole seconds. "Two dollars once, two dollars twice." He paused one more moment. "Sold!" he announced and brought his gavel down hard. "For two dollars to the big gentleman over yonder!"

"Oh, my! Oh, my!" Habel twittered, overwhelmed.

"It's all right, Habel," Megan comforted, nudging her gently. "That's my brother, Matt. You'll like him fine. Go on." She aimed her toward the steps of the stage and gave her another nudge.

On wobbly legs, Habel descended the steps of the schoolhouse, climbed the steps of the stage, and crossed it to stand beside a grinning Mr. Barton. She clutched her number tightly in her tiny hand and self-consciously waited for the man who had won her and her lunch, praying he would not be overly disappointed in his prize.

Matt took the steps three at a time, then quickly conquered the last few to stand before Habel.

Habel's mouth went lax. He was a giant of a man with a big happy grin, wheat-blond hair, and bright blue eyes that twinkled down on her in greeting, revealing not so much as a hint of disappointment. He whipped his floppy hat from his head and bowed before her gallantly. "Howdy. I'm Matthew Hawkins."

"Matthew Hawkins!" Mr. Barton held out the pretty box supper for the big man to claim. "This is Habel Habershaw, your companion for the day!"

"Thank you kindly." Matt took the box and crooked his elbow, offering his arm to the little woman with the soft gray eyes. She was a tiny thing and real pretty in her own way, he thought. He'd seen the panic etched on her face when that slimy old drunk had called out the first bid, and gentleman that he was, Matthew Hawkins couldn't allow the lady to go to such an evil-smellin' varmint.

Feeling young and extremely conspicuous, Habel silently accepted Matthew's arm and followed him across the platform and down the steps.

Mr. Barton picked up the next supper and opened the bidding.

Steven called out a bid, noting the white ruffle that circled the rim of the box. He realized he was taking a risk, for many of the boxes sported a similar decoration. Still, the intrigue of not knowing who owned the lunches heightened the excitement of the event. Another man called out a bid, but Steven bested him by raising his own. A moment later, when he learned the identity of the girl he'd won for the day, he laughed good-naturedly, while certain older ladies around him audibly gasped their abhorrence.

Libby Logan was one of Merilee's newest girls. She was young and pretty, with large, dark eyes and long, wavy dark hair. She had a remarkably innocent demeanor and smiled constantly. When she realized who had won her, she, too, laughed at the irony and went up to stand beside Mr. Barton to wait for the young reverend to claim her.

For the most part, Merilee and her girls shunned social events, but every now and then they came out to participate, mostly to spite Edith Pribble and her ladies, who tried their best to discourage their company. But Merilee and her girls were a stalwart bunch and were not so easily cowed. Besides, many of the ladies who belonged to Mrs. Pribble's circle had husbands who were well known at Merilee's establishment. One of whom was the seemingly respectable Maxwell Fletcher.

Since the wives of those gentlemen hoped to keep that information hushed, well, they knew they could not forbid the participation of the women from Merilee's, no matter how undesirable their company might be.

To the horror of most of his congregation, Steven claimed Libby without hesitation. But he hadn't forgotten Megan. Passing her, he waved and offered a sheepish grin, telling her he hoped to make up for lost time later.

Clarissa grasped Megan's hand. "Well, it won't be long now. There are only a few lunches left to bid on."

"I s'pose," Megan answered, her eyes sweeping the crowd for her brother Luke. It wasn't hard to find him. Other than Matthew, he was the tallest man present. He stood beside Jim, who was only slightly short-er. Although she was disappointed in losing Steven's company, she'd missed her brothers and hoped, since Matt was busy with Habel, that Luke would bid for her.

Although Luke was eleven years older than Megan, the age difference seemed irrelevant. Even when she was just a little girl, Luke hadn't seemed much older than her. He was sweet-tempered and kind and seemed to view life through the uncomplicated eyes of an overgrown child. It was this quality and his unconditional acceptance of people, not to mention his good looks, that had got him tangled up with that no-good wicked Sadie Thomas.

Thank God Matthew and Mark were looking out for him, Megan thought, remembering when Sadie had her claws all set to hook into her brother. Luke's escape had cost him a hexing, but a hexing was a small price to pay for escaping a lifetime with Sadie Thomas. Johnnie's old beau Robert was paying that price now, and Megan couldn't think of a more deserving party.

"Now, fellas. Here's an extra special one!" Mr. Barton announced, stealing Megan's thoughts away from her brother. Mr. Barton lifted the lid and peeked inside Clarissa's fancy box. He smacked his lips in comical exaggeration at the contents, while Megan clutched the matching number in her hand. "What do I hear for this one?" he asked.

The crowd of young eligibles noted the dwindling supply of unattached ladies, and the bidding became a bit more frisky. An offer rang out, followed by another and another. Luke called out a bid, but Jim bested him. He'd had a good look at Clarissa's and was certain the lunch he'd bid on was hers. On and on the bidding went until finally the crowd hushed.

Jim stood as the last bidder, topping Luke's two-dollar bid by fifty cents.

Groaning out loud, Megan stood on tiptoes and rounded her eyes, attempting to catch Luke's gaze, so she could send him a message to top Jim's bid. Beside her, Clarissa giggled good-naturedly.

"Criminy!" Megan whispered with feeling. "See what you've gone and done. Now I'll be stuck with that husk-brain all day." She jumped up into the air and waved at Luke.

Seeing her, he smiled and waved back.

She wanted to bean him.

"It'll serve the two of you right to have to spend the day together," Clarissa told her. "Maybe then you'll quit acting like you hate each other."

"Ohhhh, I owe you for this one," Megan threatened under her breath.

Not in the least worried, Clarissa laughed and rolled her eyes in mock terror.

Smug and confident, Jim crossed his arms over his chest and waited.

"Sold!" Mr. Barton hollered. "To Deputy Lawson!"

"Hoooey, Jim!" Luke called out and slapped his companion on the shoulder so hard it knocked him sideways. He watched Megan leave Clarissa's side. Luke assumed Jim had intended all along to bid on his little sister's box supper. "Git on up there and claim what's yers!"

Her expression pained, Megan found her way to Mr. Barton's side.

The smug look fell from Jim's face, and in its place came a look of surprise, followed by one of obvious displeasure. A hearty chuckle and another slap from Luke propelled him toward the stage. Within seconds he was claiming his due: Megan Hawkins!

He scowled down at her.

She smiled up primly, knowing it would agitate him all the more.

He yanked the box from Mr. Barton's hand, wishing he could ram a cucumber down his throat, then gestured with his head for Megan to follow him. She did so obediently, promising herself she'd fix him good for his arrogance and his lack of good manners.

They made their way toward a grassy spot on the lawn where they could set up a pretense of enjoying the contents of the supper. Not halting his steps, Jim angled her a suspicious glance and said, "I know this is Clarissa's box!"

Megan made big eyes at him and quipped, "Oh, you do, do you?"

"Yes." The word was clipped.

"You must have cheated and peeked."

"I did!"

"Humph!" Megan said, as though she wouldn't think of committing such an infraction of the rules.

He glared at her and pointed a finger. "Don't you 'humph' me!"

She skewered him with a glare of her own and dared him to test her patience further, crowd or no crowd looking on.

"What are you doin' with her supper?" he demanded to know.

"We switched!"

"Humph!" he said.

"Don't you 'humph' me!" She paused a moment, then admitted, "It wasn't my idea, it was hers!"

"Well, isn't this just dandy?" Jim snapped sarcastically. "We get to torture each other for the entire rest of the day and evening."

"I can hardly wait to get started!"

"Neither can I!" he yelled and lengthened his stride, purposely trying to leave her behind. His attempt was unsuccessful. Megan had very long legs. "And I planned to have a damn good time today," he snarled under his breath.

"So did I!" Megan hollered up at him, wounded by his attitude, though she hid it very well.

Glowering furiously, they found a spot beneath the leafy arms of a large oak, within safe calling distance of Matt and Habel—just in case their assistance was needed. But Matt and Habel were too preoccupied with their own situation to worry about Jim and Megan. Overwhelmed by the big man's presence, Habel's eyes were glued to her hands, while Matt's eyes were glued to her.

Without waiting to spread a blanket, Jim dropped the box to the ground and collapsed on the grass beside it, his brow furrowed by his bad temper. He reclined onto his side and crooked a knee, contemplating his bad luck. Yep, he was hexed all right. His foul mood deepened when Luke strolled by with Clarissa a moment later.

Megan ignored Jim by busying herself with laying out their lunch. Still standing, she shook out the tablecloth, snapping it in the air several times for good measure, taking pleasure in barely missing Jim's nose. She took her time spreading the cloth out in a neat, perfect square. When she'd milked that task to the limit, she knelt down on the tablecloth and withdrew the items from the box. She set out two plates, silverware, a small jar of strawberry preserves, fresh bread, some fried chicken, a few hard-boiled eggs, some cheese and pickles, and finally two slices of apple pie. Noting Jim's scowl, she didn't bother to offer him anything, but made an exaggerated performance of filling a plate for herself, all the while humming softly.

She commenced eating.

She'd made out just fine trading baskets with Clarissa. Although Clarissa wasn't much of a cook either, Mrs. Westfield certainly was. And it was her vittles Megan now enjoyed. Fortunately for Clarissa, Luke wasn't picky about fixin's, since it would be his sister's he'd have to eat. Luke was a gentle giant, a simple, uncomplicated soul. As long as the fare was edible and available, he'd devour it without complaint and be thankful it was there.

"Mmmm," Megan said, smacking her lips.

Jim growled under his breath and refused to look at her.

"Well," she finally said, disgusted with his bad temper. She deliberately shook a chicken leg under his nose, knowing it smelled mighty tasty. "The least we can do is be civil to each other." When he didn't answer, she went on, "The last time I saw you, you were more than civil."

That got his attention. His eyebrows arched and his head snapped around to face her. "What the hell do you mean by that?"

"That day you stopped by my place." She bit into the chicken leg and chewed slowly, then swallowed.

"So I stopped." He acted confused.

Her brows rose. "You were sparkin' me, and don't try to deny it."

Feigning ignorance, he gave her a disbelieving glare. "The hell I was!"

"The hell you weren't!"

"I wasn't!"

"You was!"

He snorted.

She did, too.

"You wanted to kiss me," she added, watching out of the corner of her eye for his reaction.

"The hell I did!"

"The hell you didn't!"

He grabbed one of the empty plates she'd set out and began to slop food onto it. Then, as though to spite her, he fell upon the food, stuffing his mouth so full he could barely chew.

"You're gonna choke to death," Megan scolded calmly, not caring if he did or not.

"Don' tell me 'ow t'eat my food," he mumbled between chews. He grunted something else, but she couldn't make it out. His eyes, however, told her it would be her fault if he did choke to death.

They ate in sulky silence, neither one willing to give an inch, until finally they were joined by Zach and the girl whose lunch he had won, despite the ardent disapproval of her father.

"Megan," Zach said, "this is Anna."

Megan dabbed at her mouth and stood, smiling. "Howdy, Anna."

"Hello," Anna said and curtsied. She had a honey-baked voice and large, dark eyes, like those of an anxious doe. Her skin was the color of coffee with a dash of cream, and her hair was softly curled and clipped to a short cap on her head.

She was, without doubt, beautiful. Megan thought Anna and Zach did each other proud.

She poked Jim with the sharp toe of her shoe, eliciting a bad-natured grunt. "We'd love it if you'd join us," she said, meaning it. Jim's company was about as lively as a dead tick on a dog.

Jim sat there a few moments longer, like a worthless piece of driftwood, until finally he realized Megan wanted him to back her on the offer. He cleared his throat and nodded, gesturing to the blanket Megan had spread. The one he himself had spitefully ignored.

Zach and Anna seated themselves, and the afternoon drew on. The four ate together, sharing the contents of both lunches, and in time Jim's mood lifted. After a while Matthew and Habel wandered over and joined them, too. Before long, Luke and Clarissa followed. They sat together as a group—laughing, talking, telling tales, some true, some contrived.

All too often, Jim found himself watching Megan. He noticed the way she drew Anna into the conversation, the way she put Zach at ease, the way she smiled, teased Habel, and how every now and then she touched the hands of her brothers, as though to assure herself they really were present with her.

Once, when reaching across Jim, her hand brushed his. He supposed it was an accident, but their gazes caught and held, and silently they called a truce and smiled at each other.

He noticed the tiny, appealing little creases that hovered above each side of her mouth, attesting to the fact that smiling was something she did often. He wondered why he hadn't remembered that about her.

He knew then what it was about her that had held him in thrall as a child. Most children, as he had, needed time to grow into who and what they would be. Megan, however, had always been exactly who she was meant to be. Even then. The only difference being that her body had finally caught up to her mind. And he couldn't help but notice that that particular development became her most exceedingly.

By the time the afternoon sun slipped into the horizon, he'd forgotten all about his promise of kissing Clarissa till his lips hurt, and once again he found himself toying with the dangerous notion of whether Megan would mind the feel of his mustache upon her mouth.

As for Clarissa, she wasn't thinking about Jim any more than he was thinking about her. She found Luke a most pleasant companion. He was attentive and kind, unassuming and considerate. She enjoyed her time with him so much, in fact, she had to fight down a pang of guilt whenever she glanced Jim's way. She was terribly found of Jim, but she'd never met anyone quite like Luke. . . .

Habel was feeling much the same as Clarissa. With Matthew Hawkins at her side, her brain could barely function. His totally male presence overwhelmed her, and his gallantry made her feel breathless and feminine. When Samuel Sweeney approached her later that afternoon—daring to think she might save him a dance—Matthew wasted no time in sending him on his way. For the first time in her lonely life, Habel felt as though she had indeed been won.

The evening hours brought more merriment.

Everyone wandered over to the courthouse, which was located on the corner of Main and High streets. It was a large, imposing square building, used for a variety of town functions. Once inside, the young men pushed the tables up against the walls and stacked the chairs out of the way. Then, those who were inclined found their ladies and swayed and dipped to the lilting waltzes of the local musicians.

Steven found Megan, and they joined in with the other dancers. After a lengthy series of sedate songs, Megan grew bored. Finally she could stand it no longer.

She halted her steps and left Steven staring after her, a puzzled expression on his face. Braving a barrage of astonished looks, she climbed the steps of the stage and went over to talk to Mr. Tidwell, who besides being postman of

Boonville was also an exceptional violinist.

But Megan wondered what besides waltzes he could play with that instrument.

She leaned in close and whispered into his ear. He drew back a moment, his expression surprised. Then he nodded, grinned, and turned to say something to his companions.

When he began to play once again, his foot started tapping, and the music from his violin became brisk and spirited. As the tempo grew livelier, the dancing grew freer, and the younger dancers formed circles. They clapped their hands and shifted and switched partners, hooking arms with one another as they passed by.

"Now, this is dancin'!" Megan yelled and kicked up her heels. "Hooee!" she called out, passing her brother Matt.

"Atta way, Meg!" Matt called approvingly, catching Habel by the hand and pulling her out onto the dance floor despite her soft protests.

Luke swung by, his brow knitted in confusion, trying his best to pretend he knew what he was doing. He didn't, though. He never could dance a jig, but he always gave it his best. Clarissa, who was not much better at such free-style dancing, realized his problem and stuck close, taking genuine pleasure in attempting to guide him.

Megan threw back her head and laughed, swept up in the joy of the moment. On his way by, Jim caught her, swung her, grabbed both of her hands, and spun her like a small tornado. Then he lifted her high into the air and whirled her once again.

Winded, she laughed, enjoying herself immensely. She forgot all her animosity toward him and remembered that he was the best square-dancing partner she'd ever had. They made a handsome couple, dancing together as one, having learned to do so many years ago.

Later that evening, when the festivities had ended, and the ladies had all returned to their respective partners, Megan reflected on that thought. She and Jim had learned to dance together as children. Never once had they attended a shindig where they hadn't paired off.

She thought about that some more on the way home, while Steven drove the buggy down to the waterfront to view the river through the thready light offered by a three-quarter moon. The crickets and bullfrogs sang out into the night. Megan stole a glance at her escort through the shadows, and despite a twinge of guilt, she found herself wishing he were another man.

She shook off the thought, and the guilt along with it, and turned her attention to the silvery river and the boat chugging downstream in the distance.

Eventually Steven broke the silence. "Did you have good time today?"

"Oh, yes."

"I did, too." He waited a moment, then said, "I like your brothers."

Megan gave a little laugh. "I like them, too. They're pretty special, though they can be real pains in the hind section every now and then."

"They're staying a while, I imagine?"

"I imagine they will. Pa said they could."

"The deputy seems real fond of them, too." Steven watched her reaction carefully.

Megan shrugged and nodded. "I s'pose. They sort of watched him grow up."

"You grew up with the deputy, I understand."

She paused a moment. "You could say that."

"You were close?"

"Sorta, I s'pose. We spent a lot of time together as kids."

"And now?" Steven felt he had nothing to lose in asking.

Megan grinned, and though she tried hard to hide it, the grin became nostalgic. "We aren't kids anymore."

Steven's eyes darkened. "I can see that."

"And he's Clarissa's beau," Megan said without pre-amble. "Besides, just bein' near him irritates the hell outta me."

Although he was not entirely convinced, Steven chuckled at her words. "Megan." He shook his head. "I'm never quite sure what's going to come out of your mouth."

"Oh, well," she said, "neither am I."

He flicked the reins and set the carriage in motion. They rode back through town and out onto Rocheport Road, remaining companionably silent for most of the way. When they reached Megan's drive, Steven tugged the horse to a stop and laughed out loud. "Did you see the look on Mrs. Pribble's and Flora Fletcher's faces when I went up to claim Libby?"

Remembering the shocked expressions of all Mrs. Pribble's ladies, Megan laughed, too. "The ladies will have plenty to chew on for the next few days." She gave him a devilish grin and said, "Libby looked to be a real nice girl, though."

"She is," Steven said without hesitation, meaning it. "Very nice." He slid across the seat and rested an arm behind her shoulders. "So are you."

"Edith Pribble doesn't think so."

"I'm not Edith Pribble." His arm slipped down to touch her shoulder, gently pulling her close.

She'd known it was coming. She had sensed his desire to kiss her from the time he picked her up that morning. So when his head descended, and his lips lightly brushed hers for the very first time, her eyes slid shut in silent anticipation.

His mouth was warm, his lips soft, his chest hard as he pressed against her. Curious, she lifted her arms to his neck and tipped her chin up, the better to accommodate the fit of their bodies.

It was a nice kiss. Easy, soft, and pleasant. Nice. But when he drew away, she was neither pleased nor disappointed.

The sound of hooves reached them.

"Your brothers are coming," Steven said with a grin, pulling back, the better to ease the tension that threatened propriety. He got down from the buggy and held his hand out to her. His palm was smooth and soft, the hand of a man who labored with his mind and not his body. She took his hand and hopped down at his side.

"I'm not so sure they'd take kindly to me kissing their sister in the dark without a chaperone anywhere within calling distance."

"I can't say whether they would or not," Megan answered with a smile. "I s'pose it might rile them a mite. They can be a bit overprotective at times."

"Thank you, Miss Hawkins," Steven said sincerely, leading her to her door, "for the pleasure of your company."

She smiled up at him, a playful twinkle in her eye. "Why, Reverend . . . it was my pleasure entirely."

CHAPTER
9

Matt and Luke did stay on.

With the crops in at home and harvest still a ways off, Clarence had told them not to hurry back. He, Mark, Adam, and Chester would handle the chores until they returned. Besides, Clarence figured Meg would need the boys more than he did if she'd bought herself a place like she'd planned.

Megan was glad to have her brothers with her. With them constantly underfoot, there was little time for loneliness. She realized now that she had been a bit lonely.

Surprisingly enough, Jim came by almost daily now, despite his previous absence.

She figured his visits were due to the fact that he enjoyed seeing the boys and wanted to spend time with them while he could.

She knew it couldn't have been her cooking that drew him. Unlike Johnnie, Megan could barely stir up a pan of mush, let alone cook well enough to please a whole peck of men. More often than not, Habel and Clarissa appeared at her door carrying something they'd brought for dinner. Since they seemed to enjoy making the gesture, Megan saw no reason not to accept their donations. Besides, she had no desire to send her brothers home skinny. Pa wouldn't take kindly to that.

The boys were hard workers and earned their keep many times over. They knew exactly what needed to be done to set her up so she could practice her profession and farm her land. They even pounded together a couple of bed frames and ordered her a couple of mattresses from Mr. Pribble's mercantile. They said it wasn't proper, her sleepin' on a bedroll.

Their kind gestures brought back memories. Years ago, when Adam had bought the old Miller place, which was a much larger farm than Megan's, they'd done the same for him. Unlike Adam, however, Megan didn't have a milk house to reconstruct into a laboratory, so instead they sectioned off a piece of her barn, making a small room for a laboratory, complete with a makeshift table for doctoring. Then they partitioned off a room for an office, with benches for folks to sit on while they waited.

Megan anxiously awaited the day she would have use for those benches.

The days passed quickly, and summer steamed on in Cooper County.

Jim, too, was plenty busy, though not particularly with deputy duties.

With time on his hands on a warm Wednesday morning during the third week of August, he brought the dog out to Megan. He wasn't sure why he'd decided to do it, but he figured the dog needed a home, and Megan needed a protector. Her brothers couldn't stay on forever.

He knew Maxwell Fletcher would never miss the pup. He had half a dozen others that had come from the same litter and looked almost exactly the same. This one was the one Zach had scolded him about. The one Fletcher happened to take his boot to the day Jim had ridden over to his place to check out the complaint of a missing horse.

So later that night, Jim had ridden back out and searched for the pup with the broken leg. He found him and took him to a safer place, a place where he could mend, until he could find him a home.

That was about seven weeks ago, and now he'd found him a home.

On this particular day, Matt and Luke were out in the barn working. Megan was on the porch, on her knees, slapping a fresh coat of whitewash onto the worn, faded boards.

Leaning back on her haunches, she watched Jim's approach, surprised to see him on the seat of a buckboard, instead of in the saddle of his horse. She stood and stretched, trying to relieve the kink that had taken hold in her back. She wiped her palms on her thighs and went down the steps to wait for him.

He eased the horse to a stop before her and agilely leapt to the ground. "Howdy!" He grinned sheepishly and slipped his hands into the rear pockets of his britches, as though he wasn't quite sure what to do with them.

"Howdy," she returned, squinting up at him. She wiped a drop of perspiration from her nose with her forearm and left behind a white streak of paint.

His grin grew, but he held his tongue. His gaze swept the perimeter of her property. "Looks like things are shapin' up around this place."

She nodded. "I've had plenty of help." Almost as an afterthought she added, "I appreciate all you've done, too."

He shrugged. "It was kinda like old times. I didn't realize how much I missed the folks back home till your brothers showed up."

"Yeah, well, I felt the same way when they came up to visit me one summer while I was in school. Just seein' them brought back a whole flood of memories. I missed them somethin' fierce after they went back home."

He gazed down at her, thinking, *I missed you, too, Meg, all those years. More than you'll ever know.*

But he couldn't tell her that.

A soft whimper came from the bed of the wagon, pulling their attention away from each other.

"Oh," Jim said, as though he'd just remembered his reason for making the visit. "I brought you somethin'."

"For me?" Megan asked, her eyes wide. Surprised and curious, she approached the wagon bed.

"Come on out of there, boy!" Jim said and whistled.

A furry yellow head appeared above the slats of the bed.

Megan's breath caught in her throat at the sight of the pup. "Oh, my," she said softly, approaching the wagon. "My, my, my." She leaned into the wagon and hugged the dog's head to her breast. He lapped at her face, whimpering with excitement. "Oh, he's pretty, isn't he?" She turned a happy smile on Jim, unaware that by doing so, she caused his heart to do about five good flip-flops.

"I figured you'd like him."

"Where'd you get him?" She took the dog's head in both hands and pressed her paint-tipped nose to his sloppy wet one.

Jim took off his hat and scratched his head, then sat his hat back on his head, tipping the brim upward. "I guess you could say I sorta adopted him."

Her curiosity aroused, Megan raised an eyebrow. "Sorta?"

He nodded and hoped she wouldn't press him for details. "Yeah, sorta."

She reached over the side of the wagon and lifted the pup out. "He isn't even full-grown yet. But he's an armful already."

"I figure he's about six months or so."

"He doesn't belong to anyone? Really?" Her eyes were wide with hope.

"Not anymore. He belongs to you now," Jim said quietly. "That is, if you want him."

"Are you kiddin'?" She looked at him as though he had beans for brains. " 'Course I do! I've been wantin' a dog ever since I came here. Willy's been lonely for a friend! Haven't you, Willy?" she asked the cat who sat curled and content on a chair Megan had set out in a sunny spot in the yard. She set the pup on his feet and watched while he sprang about, yipping and running circles around her. She hooked her hands on her hips and laughed. "I'd say you're 'bout right. He's six months old or so. He's too frisky to be very old." She knitted her brow, studying the dog, then dropped down on one knee. "He's got a limp, don't he?" She called the dog, and when he came, she ran her hand over his leg.

"He had an accident a while back."

"It feels like it was broken, but it seems to be mendin' all right." She turned him loose to run once again. "He sure looks a lot like granny's Sigmund, don't you think?"

"Yeah." Jim dropped to his haunches beside her. "From the minute I laid eyes on him, I said, 'Boy, you look like an old friend of mine, an' I have the perfect home and the perfect mistress for you.' "

Megan slid him a dubious glance. "And what did he say 'bout that?"

"He asked me if she was purty." Jim made a serious face. "I told him she was uglier than last year's cow droppings! A real old hag!"

Megan's eyes crinkled with amusement, and she slugged him hard in the arm.

"Owww!" he hollered, laughing. He paused a minute, then his voice grew soft and earnest. "Do you really want to know what I told him?"

Megan shrugged, pretending indifference.

"I told him she was the prettiest girl in Missouri."

Their eyes caught and held for a moment, then, becoming flustered, Megan snorted and eyed him with suspicion. "You sparkin' me again, Jim Lawson?"

"Me?" Jim sounded affronted, his eyes mischievous. He drew back slightly. "Hell, no!"

Despite herself, Megan grinned and looked away, forcing herself to study an annoying gnat that buzzed around the pup's ear. "Does he have a name?"

Jim shrugged. "Not that I know of."

"Then I think I'll call him Samson. That's a brave, strong, noble name. I'd call him Sigmund, but there really was only one Sigmund, and out of respect for his memory, I think it'd be proper to leave it that way."

Willy watched the pup from his place on the pillow. His eyes narrowed in utter annoyance. He growled low in his throat, and his tail bushed out indignantly. The hair rose up on his back.

Curious about the furry critter, Samson bounded toward him. But Willy was in no mood to be friendly with the young whelp. He let loose with a frightful hiss, and when the pup came close enough, he whacked him good across the nose with an open paw, drawing two bright stripes of blood immediately.

Samson yelped and jumped back, then turned tail and hid behind Megan. Willy looked smugly satisfied at the dog's reaction and got comfortable on his chair once again.

Jim chuckled.

Megan snorted her disgust. "Willy, you're a bully!" She pulled the pup close to her side and scratched behind his ears. "Well, Samson, you got a pretty impressive name. Do you think the real Samson woulda run from that ol' cat? Hell, no, he wouldn't. Although," she said conspiratorially, "if he'd had a lick of the good sense God gave him, he'da run for cover at first sight of Delilah. But he didn't. He was big and dumb." She angled Jim a glance that said she thought much the same of most of the male species. "So," she went on, returning her attention to her dog, "if you're gonna live up to that name, you're gonna have to learn to stand up for yourself—"

"Give him time," Jim interrupted. "He just needs to grow up some and gain some confidence."

Megan thought about that a minute. She thought about how Jim had grown up some, then lifted quiet blue eyes to his. "Thank you."

"For what?"

"For bringin' me the dog."

"You're welcome."

"I know why you did it."

"Why?" He pretended ignorance.

" 'Cause you're worried 'bout me out here all alone."

He made a face and snorted. "I'm more worried 'bout the fool who might find you out here all alone than I am about you!"

"Is that so?" she asked, knowing he lied.

"Hell, yes!"

They fell silent, gazing at each other, both caught up in a web of confusion, held prisoner by an awareness that had been growing between them since the day she'd come to Boonville. They both began to speak at once—safe words, careful words:

"How's Clarissa?"

"How's Steven?"

"Fine," they both said, and their eyes shot away from each other.

The uncomfortable silence took hold once again, until finally Megan could stand it no longer. She stared down at the ground and scratched a picture in the dirt with her finger. "I had a good time at the pie and box supper."

Jim's gaze found her face. He stared at her, not sure of how to respond. He thought about it a minute, then quietly said, "I did, too."

Her eyes lifted to his. "I guess we're not fightin' anymore, are we?"

"I guess not."

"I don't know if that's good or bad," she told him honestly, her confusion mirrored in her eyes. She dropped her gaze once more.

"I s'pose it could be both." He, too, was honest.

"Well . . ." She shrugged.

"Well . . ." He mimicked her automatically, as he'd done so often in the past. He waited a moment, decided, then leaned in toward her.

Startled, she looked up to find his mouth just inches away from hers. She swallowed, her stomach doing the same kind of crazy flip-flops his stomach had been doing earlier. "You plannin' on kissin' me?" she asked bluntly, her throat suddenly dry.

"That depends."

"On what?"

"On whether I'm gonna sport a black eye for the attempt."

Megan stared at his mouth for several seconds, forced thoughts of Clarissa from her mind, then lifted her eyes to his. "I s'pose you'll have to take a chance on it."

"I s'pose I will."

They studied each other some more, both still on their knees, while the hot Missouri sun beat down on them. An annoying horsefly buzzed around their heads, but neither noticed. She still wore a stripe of paint down her nose; he still wore his hat, the brim tipped up toward the blue, blue sky. Ever so lightly, his hand touched her back, then slowly slid upward to rest beneath her hair. Gently he squeezed her neck.

They both felt anxious, afraid, a little bit guilty.

As she waited, her eyes slid shut, and she held her breath. She'd been wanting this for a very long time.

He forgot about black eyes, about a girl named Clarissa, about anything at all except the girl whose lips he sought.

They kissed then. Old memories faded, and new ones were born. This kiss was smooth and rich and wonderful. It began slow and easy, then grew adult and heady, ripe and fervent. It was all that a kiss should be—all that a kiss had never been with any other for either of them.

Her hand came up to touch his neck.

His hands sought her face and cradled her cheeks in a gentle, tender way that made her breath trip and her heart shudder. His palms were rough against her skin, calloused from the hours of work he'd done here on her farm, helping her brothers. From out of the past came the memory of herself as a child, trying to comfort Johnnie over the loss of her shiftless fiancé, Robert.

"I never did like Robert anyhow," she'd said to her sister.

"Ya didn't?" Johnnie had questioned. "How come?"

" 'Cause his hands are soft. Pa's aren't. And neither are Matthew's, Mark's, or Luke's. Don't seem fittin' for a man to have soft hands. The man I marry is gonna have hands like Pa's and the boys'."

She silently acknowledged the existence of the memory, while the kiss went on and on and on, until finally, still aching with the desire for more, they slowly separated.

"Criminy," Megan whispered, breathless.

"Yeah, criminy," Jim mimicked, yearning to continue.

"I don't s'pose we ought to be doing this," Megan said, not meaning it, her mouth barely an inch away from his.

"No, I don't s'pose so," he agreed, but didn't move away.

While the sun burned hot and the flies still pestered, while Willy slept and Samson looked on, two heads pressed close once again. They leaned into each other, and tongues came searching. This time the kiss was deeper, wetter, a lusty promise of something finer to come.

When at last they broke apart, they were shaken, confused by the heat that had risen so quickly between them.

After a couple of seconds Jim grinned. "That sure as hell is different than when I was fourteen."

Megan stared at him. She swallowed, remembering how he'd kissed her those many years ago, so inexpertly, all sloppy and wet, and wondered where he'd learned to do it the way he'd done it today. "Yes," she said at last, her gaze still voicing her surprise. "It sure as hell is."

She stood and led him out to the barn where Matt and Luke worked.

As it turned out, Samson was an egg-stealing, chicken-chasing, ditch-digging nuisance most of the time.

But Megan loved him.

He had a lot to learn about being a protector. In fact, he had everything to learn. But Megan believed there was hope for him in that area.

Willy put him in his place from the start, letting Samson know that Willy was the monarch of the household and intended to keep it that way. Samson accepted Willy's supremacy without challenge and only pestered the cat every now and then when his playful exuberance overcame him, earning him a few more bloody swipes across his big, spongy nose.

But that was the least of Megan's problems. Besides being an egg-stealing, chicken-chasing, ditch-digging nuisance, Samson was also a wanderer.

It was a good thing he looked like any other big yellow mixed-breed mongrel pup, because Jim soon learned that hiding him from Maxwell Fletcher would have been an impossible task.

It only took Samson about a week to wander off Megan's land and find Henry Holloway's cornfield. When he showed up on the jail steps early one morning carrying an entire cornstalk, roots and all, ears of corn still intact, ol' Henry in hot pursuit, Jim got a little nervous. But he knew he had real trouble when Samson discovered Edith Pribble's prized flower beds.

Yessiree, Edith Pribble did so love her flower beds.

She was mighty proud of that fancy yard of hers, too. But she was even prouder of her flower beds. So when she called on Jasper and Jim one day, wielding her broom and shrieking to high heaven about some vicious yellow dog that was eating the tops of her dahlias and stripping the roses clean off her bushes, Jim figured he knew who the varmint was.

He caught him in the act one morning and hauled him back to Megan, who seemed completely unconcerned with the state of Mrs. Pribble's dahlias and roses. Still, loving Samson as she did, she tied him to the porch for his own protection.

Jim wouldn't have been overly concerned about Edith's flowers either if he wasn't concerned with her blatant dislike of Megan. He knew Edith Pribble was a force to be reckoned with, and if Megan ever hoped to fit into the community, she needed to avoid antagonizing one of its driving forces.

Especially after what had recently passed between him and Megan, Jim found that he did want to see her happy. He wanted that very much, and since she had decided this was where she wanted to plant herself . . .

So he made apologies for Megan, covered as best he could for the pup, and wondered what the hell he'd gotten himself into by stealing that dog and kissing Megan Hawkins that August day in the hot noontime sun.

*   *   *

The townsfolk called a meeting right after evening services the second Sunday in September. The parishioners filed out of the Reverend Dunmire's church and herded on over to the courthouse, where business could be conducted properly.

Everyone was present: Maxwell and Flora Fletcher, George and Edith Pribble, Mr. Tidwell, Silas Goldman, Mr. Barton, Zach Davis, Sheriff Johnson and his wife, Deputy Jim, Colonel and Lucy Kincaid and Daniel—whom they sat in a chair near the wall with stern orders to sit and listen, not run wild with the children—Big John and his wife, Beulah; Matthew and Luke, who took seats near the rear; and Libby Logan, seated with Merilee, who was a pretty middle-aged woman who smiled a lot.

Megan entered the building with Steven at her side. On her way past Daniel, she stopped and ruffled his hair. "Hey, Danny."

"Hello, Megan," he returned, his somber expression lighting. "Reverend," he said, acknowledging Steven's presence, though reluctantly. It wasn't that he didn't like the reverend; it was more that he loved Megan with all his heart and soul and held tight to the fantasy that he'd someday grow up and marry her. The reverend's courtship of her just didn't fit into his plans.

"Catchin' any fish lately?" Megan asked.

"Nope."

"How come?"

He shrugged. "Demerits. I gotta stay in school till I lose some, or I'll be expelled."

Amused, Steven smiled.

"You don't say?" Megan said, impressed. For all the shenanigans she and Jim had pulled when they were children, they'd never come close to being expelled. The fact that Danny could manage such a dire disciplinary action sparked her respect. "I wondered why I hadn't seen hide nor hair of you lately."

"That's why. I've been behavin'." His expression told her he was about ready to bust with "behavin'."

"Well, come out and visit me sometime. I got a pup now. His name is Samson, and I have a feelin' you and he would get along just fine."

His eyes lit. "A dog! Wow!"

She smiled. "Come by after school so you don't get yourself in any trouble, and I'll introduce you proper."

Just then Amy Applegate came down the aisle. She was dressed like a princess with a four-inch yellow bow adorning the top of her head, and at least three layers of lace etched onto her dress. She wedged her way past Megan and sat her tiny bottom on the chair beside Daniel. Instantly he colored, then he gave her a glare that said he'd like to bop her a good one. She was imperious to his distress, though. Her eyes bright with adoration, she smiled at him, revealing a gaping hole where her two front teeth had once been.

Daniel looked sick.

Amy looked smitten.

Megan laughed, and she and Steven moved on. She nodded greetings to some of the locals she'd come to know and some she'd yet to meet. When she passed Jim and Clarissa, her footsteps never halted, though her heart did. She felt a sharp, unreasonable stab of jealousy at the sight of them together, but she smiled, expertly hiding the commotion in her heart.

Since the day Jim had brought her Samson, she'd wondered many times if he ever thought about that kiss.

She sure had.

At times she was sort of mad at him about it. At other times she wasn't. How could she be mad about something she had participated in? How could she be mad about something she had enjoyed?

She supposed she felt he had no right kissing her when he was Clarissa's beau. And of course she felt she had no right kissing him when she was Clarissa's friend.

And then there was Steven, who courted her and kissed her—whom she genuinely liked.

When she reached a table where Merilee and Libby sat, she paused and put thoughts of Jim from her mind.

Not caring what anyone thought, she took a seat beside Merilee, leaving Steven no choice but to take the seat next to her. "Howdy," Megan said to Merilee.

"Hello." Merilee smiled, her eyes sizing up the pretty young woman who dared to sit beside her—her a woman not highly respected by those whose opinions mattered in Boonville.

Megan offered her hand. "I'm Megan Hawkins."

Merilee shook Megan's hand. "I know."

"Pleased to meet you."

"Same here."

"What's all this fuss about?" Megan peered around the shoulder of the man seated in front of her in an effort to see the front of the room. "Back home, whenever a town meeting was called on a Sunday night, it meant serious business."

"This is. It's about cattle rustling and such," Merilee answered.

Megan's brows jumped. "You don't say?" Her eyes lit with excitement.

"So they say," Libby said, entering the conversation and turning a bright smile upon the reverend.

"Well, hell's bells!" Megan exclaimed. "An' I thought ol' Edith was makin' all that up!"

Surprised at her verbiage, the two women's heads snapped sideways to get a better look at their new acquaintance. Their eyes spoke their astonishment.

Habel had entered the courthouse after Megan. Seeing

Megan, Habel headed her way. She stood, awkward and uncertain before the group. Watching her fidget, Megan grinned and gestured to the chairs on her left. "Have a seat, Habel, for heaven's sake."

She hesitated a moment, thinking of the gossip such an action would generate. Then, thinking of just that, she accepted the offered seat.

The twittering of conversation died down as Jasper Johnson rose and made his way to the front of the room. He waited until all was silent, then in a serious, slightly ominous voice, he said, "As you all should know by now, we have outlaws among us."

A collective gasp went up around the room.

"Dangerous outlaws . . ."

Another gasp.

"Outlaws of the worst kind." He paused a moment, allowing his words to take effect. "Folks . . . we have among us the lowest form of humanity. We have horse thieves and cattle rustlers. . . ."

CHAPTER
❈ *10* ❈

The following Tuesday night Clarissa gave a reading at Thespian Hall.

Most of Boonville attended, though there were some who had no interest in such cultured activities and refrained.

Surprisingly enough, Matthew and Luke accompanied Habel and Megan. Both men were somewhat reluctant, mostly because they weren't used to such events, but Clarissa had asked them to come, and neither man had the heart to refuse her request.

Boonville's residents were proud of their theater. It was the cultural essence of their town, an impressive two-story Greek Revival structure, graced in front with four unfluted Doric columns constructed of wedge-shaped bricks. A balcony and cast-iron ornamentation added to the hall's distinction.

When Matthew and Mark entered the building, they stood, awkward and uncertain, feeling much like two big bears invading a dainty dressmaker's shop. The inside of the hall was as impressive as the outside. Red velvet curtains draped the walls and stage, and all the woodwork surrounding them was ornate and artistically designed. Above, an inner balcony sported box seats for the more influential of Boonville's residents.

Their wheat-blond hair, slicked back and still damp, gave evidence of their recent baths. The dress clothes that Megan had made them wear bound them, adding to their discomfort.

Extremely self-conscious, Matthew gave the place a good look and mumbled, "I never thought I'd see the day a Hawkins man would come to one of these places to hear somebody read some prissy dead man's writin's."

Luke was every bit as uncomfortable as his brother, but he gave him a scornful look. "Clarissa ain't jist somebody, and Mr. Shakespeare ain't jist any prissy ol' dead man."

"Oh, yeah?" Matthew said, cocking a brow. "An' jist how do you know so goddamn much about this Mr. Shakespeare?"

Luke colored. He held silent a moment, then leveled his gaze on his brother and said, "Clarissa told me about 'im."

"Is that right?"

"That's right."

Glaring at each other, they went nose to nose.

"Boys," Megan warned calmly, sensing a battle brewing. She knew it had been a long time since either of the men had wallowed in a good brawl, and they were itching to go to it, even if it was with each other.

Habel, however, was not used to such open antagonism. Alarmed, she wedged her tiny body between the two. "Please," she whispered, gazing up into Matthew's eyes. "This is not the time or the place for a confrontation. Please, Matthew."

It was Matthew's turn to blush. Properly chastened, he dropped his gaze, but not before he angled his brother a look that told him he planned to take the matter up later. "Beg yer pardon, Miss Habershaw," he said politely. "I didn't mean to git ya all shook up."

She nodded, accepting his apology, then shyly took his elbow to lead him down the aisle.

The four made their way to the front of the auditorium, stopping when they drew abreast of the row of seats where Jim sat. Seeing them, he stood and moved down the row, making room for them.

Matthew and Luke stepped aside and waited for Megan to move into the row, but she hesitated, not wanting to take the seat nearest Jim. When she didn't budge, Matthew gave her a gentle nudge and urged, "Go on, Meg. You ain't bein' polite leaving us standin' out in front of everybody like this. Folks gonna think we ain't civilized or somethin'."

So she moved down the row of chairs and bad-naturedly plunked herself into the one next to Jim. It was obvious she did so only to pacify her brother.

Jim nodded a greeting to the two men and Habel, but when he tried to catch Megan's eye, she baldly ignored him.

Confused and burned by her treatment of him, he got mad. He folded his arms across his chest, snapped his head forward, and glared at the stage.

She pretended not to notice, even while she felt awareness sizzle between them.

Finally Jim leaned in toward her. "Least you can do is say hello."

"Hello."

Silence. He waited for five good seconds, then asked, "What the hell are you mad about now?"

"I'm not mad," she said quietly and lifted her eyebrows in mock surprise.

"The hell you aren't!" His voice was embarrassingly loud.

Her head whipped around to face him. "Shhhh!"

"You are," he accused. "I can tell. I could always tell."

"The hell I am."

"Humph!" he said and snapped his gaze toward the stage again.

"Humph!" she mimicked and did the same.

They sat there, simmering inwardly, confused at their antagonism toward each other.

He didn't want to be angry at her, but he was.

She didn't want to be angry with him, but she couldn't help herself. Their anger kept them both safe.

His feelings stung, he sulked. Lately he'd thought of nothing but her. Even when he was with Clarissa, his mind was on Megan. If he were being honest, he'd have to admit he'd thought of little else since she'd come to Boonville. Even his occasional nights out with Zach had lost their attraction, though he still wanted to continue with his plan. He'd gone too far to turn back now.

Look at you, Lawson, he silently berated himself. *You're simpering all over yourself for that mule-headed girl again.*

He was disgusted.

And what about Clarissa? He'd been courting her and thinking of another. Why, it was downright contemptible of him.

But, oddly enough, Clarissa had been distant herself lately. He blamed himself. Deep down, he figured Clarissa must sense something was different with him. He felt bad about that, but not terribly guilty. Although they had been headed in a serious direction a few months back, no words of love had ever been spoken between them; no promises had been given.

His thoughts were interrupted when the long velvet curtains parted and Clarissa walked onto the stage. She looked like an angel in her gown of ivory satin. The gown was embroidered in ivory silk braid and pink roses, and edged with ruffles of chiffon. Champagne-colored festoons trailed gracefully down the back from a large bow tied to the ribbon that encircled her tiny waist.

She stood in the center of the stage and patiently waited till all was hushed and still. The low hum of conversation that had filled the large room faded throughout the auditorium. Then she began her reading. She recited her favorite verses of *Romeo and Juliet* from memory. Her voice, though loud enough to hear, was soft and smooth as butter, her bearing as regal and refined as any queen's. She held her audience captive with the musical intonation of her words and the beatific expression on her face.

Megan felt pride in her friend. She understood, though it hurt her, why Jim would choose to court her.

Though Matthew and Luke didn't understand some of the words Clarissa spoke, her voice, eloquent enough in itself, told them all they needed to know. When at last she uttered these final words:

> " 'The sun, for sorrow, will not show his head:
> Go hence, to have more talk of these sad things;
> Some shall be pardon'd, and some punished;
> For never was there a story of more woe,
> Than this of Juliet and her Romeo,' "

there rose from the audience a host of sentimental sighs and more than a few noisy sniffles, of which both Hawkins men were guilty.

Surprised, they glanced at each other, blinked, then quickly averted their gazes. Embarrassed, Matt nudged his brother roughly. "Quit yer wallerin', you bugger-brain!"

Luke's eyes got big. He wasn't sure what a bugger-brain was, but he knew he didn't want to be one. "Shhh, yourself, shithead!" He thought a shithead had to be worse than a bugger-brain.

Matthew looked affronted.

Luke looked satisfied.

The applause of the crowd diverted their attention from each other. Both Matthew and Luke joined in the clapping with hearty enthusiasm, forgetting their antagonism for at least this moment.

Yes . . . that evening Clarissa Westfield touched many a heart as she delivered her finest reading, with all the eloquence and verbal grace of the world's most accomplished readers.

That night Matthew Hawkins learned respect for Mr. William Shakespeare.

And that night Luke Hawkins fell hopelessly in love with Miss Clarissa Westfield.

Still smarting, Jim was determined to put thoughts of Megan from his mind.

After she and her brothers had left the hall to see Habel to her door, Jim walked Clarissa home through the town at dusk.

The night was lovely and peaceful—a proper compliment to Clarissa's hauntingly beautiful reading. Jim took her hand while they walked, but they remained uncharacteristically silent with each other.

When at last Jim spoke, his voice seemed strained to his own ears. "You gave a fine reading tonight, Clarissa."

She turned and favored him with a grateful smile. "Thank you. I'm glad you enjoyed it."

"I did. So did Megan and Habel."

She gave a little laugh and dropped her gaze. "I suppose Matt and Luke thought it was pretty silly."

"I don't think they did at all," Jim told her honestly.

She halted her footsteps and turned to face him. "Really?"

"Really."

He gazed down at her, hoping to feel the rush of excitement, the heady flow of desire he felt when he was with

Megan. He didn't. It wasn't that Clarissa wasn't beautiful enough. She was indeed. She was also kind and sweet-tempered. To the right man, she would be everything.

Looking up into his eyes, she waited, realizing he meant to kiss her. She wished she could feel the anticipation she'd once felt.

But she didn't.

She could tell he didn't feel it either. Something had happened between them, and neither one knew what it was or how to explain it.

He kissed her anyway. But when he did, there was no passion in his touch. The kiss was kind, benign, chaste. It made him wish for the lips of another. It made her wish for someone with wheat-blond hair who had no mustache to prick her.

When they parted, there was no need for words. They felt no sadness, but silently acknowledged the truth.

They locked hands once again, smiled understanding at each other, and continued the walk to Clarissa's house.

"I'm shore gonna miss ya, Meg," Matt told his little sister a week later.

Luke nodded his agreement but couldn't speak the words. His throat got tight. He'd always hated good-byes. They were hell on his feelings. So, instead of saying anything, he gathered her up into a big bear hug, nearly crushing the air from her body.

"Holy hell, Luke," Megan complained, her eyes damp. "You're squashin' my bones!"

When Luke released her, Matt gave her more of the same treatment. "Pretty soon pa'll be sendin' Adam and Mark to fetch us if we don't git home. Won't be long till frost hits, and the crops'll need to come in."

Megan nodded and blinked the wetness from her eyes. She hooked her hands on her hips and looked embarrassed. "It seems like you boys just got here. Time goes too damn fast."

They stood on the porch, in the cool of the early autumn air, gazing out at the surrounding land and buildings. The trees had yet to heed the season's call and still stood green and resplendent. The two brothers had accomplished much in the seven weeks they'd stayed. Megan had a home she could be proud of. Though not elegant and filled with affluent finery, it was neat and tidy and comfortable, just as she'd hoped it would be.

She was sorry to see her brothers go. Their presence had lightened her heart, filled her days with laughter. "I'm gonna miss you boys somethin' terrible." The tears welled up in her eyes. She'd always been one hell of a crier—as a child it had been her most viable weapon.

"Aw, now, Meggie," Luke said, confused and alarmed as he'd always been whenever she cried, "we'll be back. Come Christmas, maybe even 'fore that. Maybe Thanksgivin'. You'll see."

She drew herself up and impatiently swiped the moisture from her eyes. "You tell Pa and Johnnie I'm just fine, you here? I don't want them worryin' 'bout me."

"We will, Meg," the two men said in unison, nodding their heads as one. From the day she'd been born, she'd known how to handle her brothers. They were like clay in her hands.

Her eyebrows dropped. "An' I don't want Pa writin' me and tellin' me you two showed up with black eyes and split lips. You get on together. No fightin'!"

"Yes, Meg." Again they nodded, their expressions innocently solemn.

She looked up at them, felt the lump return to her throat, and held silent a moment. Then very quietly she said, "I love you boys."

Matthew sniffled and got embarrassed. "Oh, hey, Meg,"

he said and gave her another fierce hug. "We love yew, too."

"Thanks for everything you did for me."

Luke jerked his handkerchief out of his back pocket and blew his nose, honking loudly.

"Oh, get on with you, then," she said gruffly and pushed them both toward the steps. "It'll be lunch soon, an' I'll have to feed you all over again."

So they tied their bundles to their horses and swung up with a grace that belied their great size.

"You look after Habel," Matthew said, turning his horse to the dusty road. "She's a little thing an' she needs protectin'."

"I will," Megan promised. "Don't worry."

Luke nudged his horse gently, following his brother. On his way down Meg's drive, he turned in his saddle and yelled, "Tell Clarissa I like Mr. Shakespeare jist fine!"

"I'll do that," Megan said and waved.

"Git over on yer own side the road, goddammit!" Matt yelled at Luke.

"I'm on my side of the road, you hog!" Luke glared and kicked his horse into a canter, taking the lead.

"The hell you are . . ."

"The hell I ain't . . ."

As Megan went into the house, their voices faded off into the distance, and she thought the silence didn't sound quite so bad after all.

Megan doctored her first patients two days later.

She awoke one morning to the sound of someone knocking on her door. Watchdog that he wasn't, Samson slept soundly on the rug beside her bed, but Willy, his sleep disturbed, issued an irritated meow.

Megan sat up, shoved her arms into a robe, tied it around her middle, then made her way to the kitchen door.

She opened it to find Danny on her doorstep. She stepped out onto the porch. Beside Danny was a boy who looked to be a few years older, probably about twelve. Danny was dressed in his impeccable military school uniform; the other boy was dressed in mustard-colored work trousers and a thin cotton shirt, dented by a pair of well-worn suspenders.

The two boys stared up at her wordlessly.

She waited patiently for a minute. When still they held silent, she smiled and quietly said, "Well, mornin', boys."

The older boy shifted his weight from one foot to the other, then angled a suspicious gaze up at her. "You Dr. Hawkins?"

"I am."

"She is," Danny put in.

"Pa said you was a girl." It was almost an accusation.

"I'm that, too," she said easily. "What can I do for you?"

"This is Theo Skeets," Danny said. "We're friends."

"Hello, Theo." Megan extended her hand. After shaking the boy's hand, she asked, "Aren't you boys s'posed to be on your way to school?"

"Theo doesn't go to school at Kemper. He goes to the community schoolhouse in town."

"I see." But that still didn't explain why neither boy was in school.

"Theo's pa sent him," Danny finally explained. "Their pigs are sick."

"I see," Megan said again, understanding this time.

Theo blushed hotly. "Pa said to ask ya to come. He said to tell ya we ain't got much money to pay ya, but I could come over and do chores after school." He shuffled his feet again, then hurried to say, "We don't take charity. But our pigs . . . well, we can't afford to lose any more of 'em." The proud lift of his head tried to belie the embarrassment his words caused him.

"Chores'll be fine," Megan said without preamble, hiding the swell of compassion she felt for the boy. She knew he would not tolerate her pity. "My brothers just left for home a couple of days back, so I'll be needin' some help every now and then." She turned to the door. "You boys have a seat out here on the porch while I get dressed and get my bag." She opened the door, and Samson shot out to greet the boys. He lapped at their faces and wagged his tail so fast his behind was nothing more than a blur.

"Oh, look, Theo!" Danny yelled, bringing a smile to Megan's face. "A dog! A dog! Isn't he the best thing you ever saw?"

While Megan dressed, she thought that every boy should have a dog, especially a little boy like Danny Kincaid.

The boys rode in the rig beside her. They headed back into town, then continued west, out onto Old Georgetown Road, until they were well out in the countryside. The boys were impressed with Jesse, who shamelessly preened for them all the way to the Skeetses' farm.

Megan had reluctantly left Samson in the house with Willy, knowing the two would probably tear the place apart, but she felt that that was the lesser of two evils. She didn't relish chasing the pup all over Cooper County when she came home.

The Skeetses' farm was about three miles out of town, off Old Georgetown Road, on a barely passable road that headed down toward the river.

The farm was a simple place, unadorned by detail. Some would have called the house "mean." But Megan was not one of those. Her home in Poplar Bluff hadn't been much more elaborate, but at least it had been bursting with love and happiness. It wasn't how much folks decorated a house that made it a home, she knew. The people who lived inside the house made all the difference.

When Megan swung the rig into the Skeetses' barnyard, Mr. Skeets came out of the house to meet them. Alice Skeets, obviously pregnant and looking ready to deliver at any moment, came to the door, holding a baby who straddled her hip and looked to be about a year old. Two other children, not much older than the one she held, clutched Alice's skirts and stared at the new arrivals curiously.

The man looked tired—old, too, though Megan guessed he wasn't much past forty. A life of struggling often took its toll by aging a body.

The smell of pigs hung heavy in the air. It was a stench few could tolerate, and in some communities, owners of a pig farm were often scorned. A scrawny chicken stalked by, pecking every now and then at a few straggly grains of corn. A trio of hawks rode the sky above them, waiting, watching, sensing the sickness that plagued the farm.

Megan tugged Jesse to a halt and hopped down from the rig, not waiting for anyone to offer aid. The two boys jumped down behind her. She wore a pair of faded britches and a plain white cotton shirt, the sleeves rolled up to her elbows. A wide-brimmed hat kept the sun from her eyes. Her bright hair was tied back from her face by a thin strip of leather. She tipped her hat back and met the man's eyes squarely. "Mr. Skeets," she said, "Theo said you had some trouble here."

He eyed her silently for several seconds, sizing her up, taking note of her britches, her hat, her straightforward manner. She certainly was different—like no woman he'd ever met. He wasn't sure if he liked or disliked her, and he supposed it didn't matter much either way. If she could help him save his pigs, that would be enough. "I do."

"Well," she said, waiting for him to go on, "I'm here to help if I can."

"You shore ya know how to doctor animals?" His question was blunt, his gaze skeptical.

She shrugged and grinned. "I'd say I'm pretty good at it. I do my best. Just like any other doctor would." She waited a moment, then said, "Man or woman."

He believed her.

They all walked to the barn together, while Mrs. Skeets looked on. Once they were inside, the stench hit them in their faces like a fetid blast. Megan stopped before a pen that held three large pigs. One was lying on its side, barely breathing. The other two were standing, but they were lethargic, their eyes dull and lifeless. All five had blotchy red lesions on their skin.

Megan donned the rubber apron she'd pulled from her bag, then climbed into the pen. She dropped to her knees beside the pig that was on his side, and touched his ears. They were hot and scarlet. Not a good sign. She ran her hand over the pig's side, down to his belly, which was hot and swollen, too. "It could be cholera," she said more to herself than to Tom Skeets.

Tom nodded. "I feared as much."

She lifted a worried gaze to him. "There's always a chance it could be swine erysipelas. When did this start?"

"A couple of weeks back."

"You gotta separate the sick from the healthy."

"I know. It's jist I ain't got the space."

"Then you make the space or turn the healthy ones loose. Better to turn 'em loose than lose 'em all to fever," Megan said quietly, keeping the reprimand from her voice. She looked around the barn. Each pen held at least three pigs. "We'll sort them best we can. We'll see how many are still healthy and how many are sick. Then we can decide how to pen them." She glanced around the barn again. "If it's cholera, the sickness is held in the droppings. We need to get the pigs out of the barn." She glanced back up at the man. "How many pigs do you have?"

"I had thirty head. I'm down to twenty-two."

"You buy any new ones lately?"

"Two. Mr. Fletcher got a litter in from St. Louis a while back. I rode over and bought two."

"I'd like to get a look at them. Where are they?" Megan asked.

"Dead. They were the first to go."

Megan thought about that, but held her tongue, wanting to be certain of her suspicions. "Well . . ." She rose and wiped her palms on the sides of her thighs. "Let's get to work. If it's cholera, we'll know soon enough."

"And then?" His eyes spoke his dread.

"Then we have to shoot the whole herd and burn the carcasses." Her eyes were sympathetic. "You know that."

Mr. Skeets nodded and swallowed. "These pigs and this farm are all I got. I lose these pigs, I don't know how I'm gonna care for my family."

Megan placed a hand on the man's shoulder. "Don't you worry 'bout that right now. Let's just get to work. Theo and Danny," she called, gesturing to the two boys, "over here."

For the rest of the day and on into the evening, they worked. It wasn't until the sun began to set that Jim showed up looking for Danny. Danny's mother had heard from Professor Lewis that he hadn't shown up for school that morning. And when he didn't come home that afternoon, she got worried. Jim had also heard from Big John that Tom Skeets had trouble with his pigs. Liking the Skeets family as he did, he was concerned and decided to take a ride out to see if he could help.

When he entered the barn and realized what was happening, he asked no questions, but silently joined in, following Megan's orders along with the others.

Megan examined every one of Tom Skeets's pigs, young and old, sows and boars. If any appeared even slightly less than healthy, they were taken off and penned separately elsewhere. They sectioned the barnyard off into small pens, using boards and slats.

Megan washed her hands often, careful not to spread the infection to the healthy, and the day wore on. Although it was long, tedious work, no one complained.

Jim watched Megan work, his respect for her growing by the minute. She labored on, doggedly putting her heart and soul into saving this man's pigs, his livelihood.

When it was time for supper, Mrs. Skeets sent one of her younger boys out to get them all. Megan liked Alice Skeets immediately. She was a shy, quiet woman, and her face was pleasant and artlessly kind. She served them a hearty meal of ham, new potatoes and gravy, and green beans with fatback. Then she followed the meal with blackberries on biscuits for dessert, and strong coffee to wash it all down. Megan and Jim thought it was one of the best meals they'd had since they'd left home; Danny thought it was the best meal he'd ever had.

They returned to the task and didn't finish until long after dusk.

When at last they'd completed the examination and separation of all the pigs, night settled down around them, and Megan climbed up onto the seat of the rig. She extended her hand, helping Danny up beside her.

"I can take him home," Jim offered, noting the weariness in her face.

"I better do it." Megan smiled. "He's gonna catch all. Not only did he play hooky today, but he ruined his fancy outfit, too. It's my fault. I shoulda sent him on to school."

"Then I'll come with you." He swung up on his horse.

"Suit yourself," she told him, secretly glad he'd offered.

Mr. Skeets held his hand up to Megan. "I can't thank you enough, Doc."

At the sound of that title, Megan's heart billowed. She shook his hand and smiled down on him. "You just did, Mr. Skeets. I'll stop by in a few days to see how things are goin'. If you need me, you know where I live. Theo," she said and turned to the boy, "I'll expect you sometime next week, after things settle down around here."

"Yes, ma'am," he said respectfully. To Danny he said, "See ya, Danny."

"See ya, Theo."

"Git up there, Jesse." Megan gave Jesse's reins a snap.

With the harvest moon beaming down on them, Megan turned the rig toward Boonville.

CHAPTER
11

By the time Jim and Megan reached the Kincaid house, Danny was sound asleep. His young body was pressed close to her side; his head bobbed lightly against her shoulder. His nearness made her feel warm, maternal.

She stopped the rig in front of the ornate iron gate that guarded the beautiful house, and gazed at the structure a moment, pondering its occupants. Lights shone from several of the windows, testifying that those occupants were still awake and waiting.

Jim reined in his horse, then swung down to the ground. After he tied his horse to the gate, he went to help Megan with the boy. She eased Danny away from her shoulder and down into Jim's arms. Then she jumped down to the ground and walked beside him up the long brick walk.

"You all right?" Jim shifted Danny into a more comfortable position in his arms.

Megan nodded. "I'm fine."

"You look tired."

"You do, too."

He paused, searching his mind for the right words. "You

did good today, Meg." His voice held a note of surprise, as well as respect.

"You did pretty good yourself." She offered him a weary smile.

"I didn't know the first thing about what I was doin'. I was just followin' orders."

"Well, you did that all right, too, for a change."

They shared a chuckle at that.

"I guess I never much thought about you knowing how to do all that doctorin'. I always figured you could, though. Even before you went away to school, you knew so much about takin' care of animals. I should have expected you'd be good at it."

She glanced his way, grinning. "I surprised you a little, didn't I?"

"I guess you did." He returned her grin, thinking she looked mighty pretty, despite her frazzled appearance.

At the door they halted their steps and knocked.

Within seconds the large, heavy door swung open, and Colonel Kincaid's stern gaze met Jim's. Slowly the colonel lowered his gaze to Megan.

"Deputy," he said stiffly. His eyes rose to Jim's face once again.

"Colonel," Jim said respectfully, though he was unimpressed with the older man's tone of authority.

Lucy Kincaid stood at her husband's shoulder, her expression anxious. Seeing her son, she gave a soft cry of relief and reached for him. Daniel stirred and woke. Jim eased him down onto his feet, then gently prodded him toward his mother.

The colonel's gaze left Jim and locked with Megan's. "I certainly hope you have a good explanation."

"I do, Mr. Kincaid," Megan said respectfully.

"It's 'Colonel' to you, Miss Hawkins."

Megan chafed at the rebuke, and a fire lit in her eyes.

For Danny's sake, she forced herself to keep silent.

Jim, too, was irritated by the colonel's attitude, but he tried to smooth things over by saying, "The boy was out at the Skeetses' farm, Colonel. He was helping Dr. Hawkins treat Tom Skeets's pigs. When I got there and saw how much work had to be done, I stayed, too. That's why I didn't bring him home sooner. They've had a run of bad luck out there. It was mighty kind of Danny to help out like he done. The boy is one helluva worker. You can be proud of him. He—"

"Had no business out at the Skeetses' farm," Colonel Kincaid cut in. "They're not his kind. He belongs in school. At Kemper. With those of his own social stature." Having said that, he turned to his wife. "Take the boy to his room, Lucy."

"But, Father, I—" Danny lifted his gaze to his father, his eyes wide with entreaty.

"Now!" the colonel said in a voice that would brook no argument.

Lucy hesitated. "Stuart," she said softly and placed her hand on his arm. "Please."

"Now!" he repeated coldly.

She dropped her gaze in silent defeat and took her son's hand. "Come, Daniel." Obediently she guided the boy toward the commanding staircase. Danny glanced back at his two friends, his eyes speaking the apology his mouth was denied.

Jim felt fury rise within him. But prudent man that he was, he held his tongue, fearing that provoking the colonel would only make things worse on the boy and Megan.

Megan was not so prudent, however. Once Danny was safely up the stairs and out of earshot, she drew herself up and pushed back the sweat-stained hat she still wore. "Pardon me, Colonel. Exactly what do you mean by 'not his kind'?"

"You know exactly what I mean, young woman."

"That's 'Doctor' to you, Colonel," she told him firmly. "And let me set you straight on somethin' else, too, while I'm at it. Just in case you're too pompous and self-righteous to know it, that little boy"—she pointed toward the staircase—"is just that: a little boy." Her voice softened somewhat when she added, "He's a good boy. A fine young person. He worked real hard today to help out a friend. His friend. 'Cause he cared about him. It didn't matter to him whether those folks plowed fields for a living, raised pigs, or managed a bank. He did what he did 'cause he was there and he was needed. He's gonna be a fine man someday. But he's got a ways to go yet. He still needs to laugh and play and discover things. He needs to feel and do what other children feel and do. And you're tryin' to make him into what he can't be. Maybe he'll never be what you want him to be. Not 'cause he doesn't love you and want to please you. But because he just can't."

Colonel Kincaid's face turned an angry shade of red. His hands clenched at his sides. "That will be quite enough!"

"Yes, I s'pose it will," Megan said, her eyes sad, realizing he didn't understand—couldn't possibly understand: He was not her kind.

Jim reached down and clasped her hand, holding it tightly within his own much larger one. "Come on, Meg. It's late, honey."

She lifted weary eyes to him, grateful—oh, so very grateful—for his presence. She felt a warmth flood her. He understood. He had always understood about these things.

Lucy Kincaid stood at the bottom of the grand staircase, holding onto the glossy, polished banister. Tears filled her eyes. She blinked them back, knowing her husband hated such a display of feminine weakness.

Megan sighed and dropped her chin to her chest. She felt Jim squeeze her hand gently. "Please don't be too hard

on Danny," she begged softly. "It was more my fault than
his. I should have dropped him off at school 'fore I went
on out to Tom's place." Without waiting for the colonel to
deny her request, she turned and allowed Jim to lead her
out of the house and down the walk to her buggy.

In silence he rode his horse beside her rig, down the
moonlit road to the welcome familiarity of her home.

Bone tired, Jim saw her to her door and was about to
leave when she glanced up briefly and said, "Thanks for
being there today. For helpin' like you did."

He saw the tears in her eyes, and something about the
way she looked at him went straight to his heart. "Aw,
Meg," he whispered, aggrieved. In all the years he'd known
her, he'd never seen her cry. His chest got tight. Feeling
inept, he touched a hand to her cheek, angry at the colonel
for being such a coldhearted fool. "Don't feel bad about the
colonel," he told her. "He's not worth it, honey."

She blinked hard to erase the tears, but the weariness in
her overrode her stubborn heart. They came anyway. She
dropped her chin and sniffled loudly. "I don't feel bad
about him. I feel bad for Danny. He's just a little boy.
He should be allowed to be what he is, for a little while,
anyway."

"I know, Meg. I know." Instinct took over, and he gathered her up against his chest. She went into his arms will-
ingly, closing her arms around his waist. It felt good and
right and natural, like fitting two halves that had always
belonged together back into one perfect piece. He held her,
stroking her back comfortingly, murmuring soft, unimpor-
tant words of comfort. "Danny'll be all right. You'll see.
He's a pretty tough little boy." He took off her hat, pitched
it onto the rocking chair beside them on the porch, then
rested his chin on the crown of her sunny head, while
the night deepened around them and the bullfrogs croaked
out their nightly serenade. At length, she yawned, and he

reluctantly let her go. "You go on to bed, honey. I'll see to Jesse."

"Thanks . . ." To his surprise, she reached up on tiptoe and kissed his cheek. "Jim . . ." Her face was close to his, her gaze direct and unflinching.

"Yeah?"

"Are you gonna marry Clarissa?"

Surprised by her question, he hesitated only a moment, then very quietly answered, "No. I'm not."

"Does she know that?"

"Yes."

"Is she sad about it?"

"I don't think so."

"Good." She kissed his cheek again, then went into the house, closing the door softly behind her.

Bewildered, Jim stared at the door for a long minute. He tipped his hat back and scratched his scalp, while a nagging inner voice taunted, *Well, there you go. She got to you, didn't she? You're all moon-eyed for her all over again.*

"Humph!" Jim huffed.

He went about the motions of putting Jesse up for the night, then stood for another long moment staring at the dark windows of Megan's house and pondering the words of that damned inner voice. Finally common sense descended, and he swung up onto his horse and slowly headed back to town—to the bed that waited for him at the quiet, empty Cooper County Jailhouse.

As it turned out, Tom Skeets's pigs had swine erysipelas and not hog cholera as he had originally feared. The news of Megan saving his herd stampeded through Boonville. He lost five more pigs before the sickness claimed its final victim, but the rest of his herd survived. He would recoup his losses in time, thanks to Doc Hawkins.

When young Theo came by on Tuesday, a week and a

half later, he brought her two young piglets, one male, one female.

Clarissa was visiting that day, and out of respect for her readings, Megan named the piglets Romeo and Juliet. Clarissa was delighted and said Mr. Shakespeare would probably turn somersaults in his grave, but that was all right.

The most influential residents of Boonville still shunned Megan, unable to accept the fact that not only was she an intelligent, outspoken young woman who mingled with anyone she chose, despite their social station, education, or occupation, but also she was proving herself to be a damned good animal doctor.

Whether they liked it or not, however, talk of her selfless attitude and successful treatment of Tom Skeets's pigs spread from farm to farm, earning her the respect of many of the townsfolk and most of the farmers.

It didn't take them long to start showing up on her doorstep. She was, after all, the only veterinarian this side of Kansas City, and they decided it would profit them to take advantage of her learning regardless of her gender.

Besides, she was a likable sort, and surprisingly enough, some had begun to think of her as one of their own.

Megan was glad to be working with animals once again. Although she'd been busy settling into her home, she still felt she'd been idle far too long. And with Matthew and Luke gone, the days sometimes stretched on endlessly.

The following week brought her two more patients, and a visit from Henry Holloway, who stopped by to ask after Tom Skeets.

Since he was already there, he wondered if she would mind taking a look at his mare, Mildred, who'd been actin' a bit peaked lately. So Megan took a look and found there was nothing wrong with Mildred other than a few extra pounds and a crotchety temper. She told Henry that Mildred

had many good years left in her, and to quit allowing her to
be such an old tyrant.

Henry was so grateful to know Mildred was all right, he
sent a whole wagon load of vegetables from his garden
for Megan to set by for the winter, and promised her
a pup from his pregnant dog, Lillian. Megan rode out
to thank him for the vegetables and ended up treating
his cow, Agnes, who had torn a hole in her leg trying
to push through the fence. Agnes, Henry said, never did
respect a fence. And ever since Maynard Owens, who
owned the farm next door to Henry's, had bought that
new bull, Agnes had been pushing at that fence with a
vengeance.

The next week Megan made a trip out to check on Tom
Skeets, just to make sure all was well with his stock. To her
surprise, she found Alice Skeets in labor. Back home, she'd
helped many a mare foal, helped struggling cows deliver
their calves, and participated in the delivery of countless
litters of pigs.

But birthin' a baby—a real, honest-to-goodness little
human person—was an entirely new experience. She was
scared. She was exhilarated. She was awed.

But she did it.

When little red-faced Melody Skeets slid into the world,
tears of joy slid down Megan Hawkins's cheeks. And when
she cleaned the mess from the baby's perfect, tiny body, a
yearning lit within her breast that seemed to spread outward and encompass her entire being. *A baby*, she thought,
brushing the tears from her cheeks. *Well, Lordie. Isn't she
somethin'. How precious! How wonderful!* And she began
to wonder what it would be like to have a child of her
own. . . .

When Tom Skeets took his wife's hand and gazed down
into her eyes with the look of a smitten young swain, it was
obvious he still thought her the most beautiful woman in

the world. Megan thought Alice Skeets was, by far, one of the luckiest women she'd ever known.

Time passed, and her practice finally began to take hold. Her small laboratory was put to good use, as she spent countless evenings mending wounds or examining her neighbors' animals for one reason or another.

For the most part, Megan began to feel fairly content in her new home. Willy, Jesse James, Samson, and Romeo and Juliet kept her company.

If only those damned nights weren't quite so long . . .

September rolled into October, bringing pungent scents of fall and the first bright splashes of color. The air was crisper. The moon beamed brighter. Life seemed sweeter.

Steven visited Megan often, though he stayed only as long as prudence permitted. Megan enjoyed his company and looked forward to his visits. He was an excellent conversationalist, and they often passed the time of day arguing their views about the Almighty.

But it was Jim's visits Megan waited for, although she'd rather have been dragged buck naked through cow manure than admit it.

Despite the truce they'd drawn, despite the understanding they'd shared after that day on Tom Skeets's farm, there remained between them an awkwardness, a tension of sorts.

When he came, Zach or Jasper was often with him, and he stayed only long enough to ask after her and give Samson a few good pats, before heading on over to ask after one of the other farmers.

When he left, she always felt oddly disappointed and more than a little bit lonely, and sometimes just plain mad at him. She felt he was avoiding her, and by God, she was determined that he wasn't going to get away with it.

Not while she had breath left in her body!

Megan found the hollow on a particularly brilliant autumn morning.

October was blazing a path across the land, leaving behind a splendid trail of color.

She was able to observe it firsthand, for she was out in the midst of it, looking for Samson, who, for the fifth time that week, had chewed clean through the rope that bound him to the front porch.

She'd seen him take off down the road and shoot off across a field, so she wasted no time in chasing after him. Since Habel and Clarissa were visiting, they were elected to join the posse. The two other women followed in the buggy, while Megan rode Jesse.

Megan turned an exasperated glare on them. "That fool dog is gonna get his head blown off!" She left the road to search a long stretch of trees and brush nearby. She returned shortly. "Sooner or later he's gonna steal the wrong man's chickens, or Edith Pribble will see to it that he isn't able to bother her damn flowers anymore. She'll probably get her ladies together and strip the hide from his worthless bones. If that don't happen, he'll hang himself with that goddamned rope he's draggin' around!" She snorted her disgust and nudged Jesse on, then turned back toward the two women. "Wait here! I'm gonna have a look over that hill. While I'm at it, you two keep an eye out for him." With that said, she trotted off, yelling, "Sa-a-amson! Come on, boy! Sa-a-amson!"

Once over the rise, she rode on for a while longer, hoping to see some sign of the dog. To her surprise, she came around a small clump of trees and spotted him. He lay beneath the shadowed shade of a large tree, panting, seemingly waiting for her. "Samson! You stay right there, dadburnit!"

He didn't, of course. He shot off, disappearing over another small rise.

Madder than a provoked porcupine, Megan urged Jesse on, while she cussed the hair from the pup's hide. Halfway over the hill, she jerked the horse to an abrupt stop and stared, totally flabbergasted. "Well, I'll be . . ." she whispered softly, gazing at the large corral before her. It held at least fifty head of cattle and several horses.

Samson, that scoundrel, sat by the corral gate, looking for all the world as comfortable and at home as a bee on honeycomb.

Megan remembered Jasper's announcement at the town meeting and the discussion that had followed: Many of the local farmers' animals were being stolen right out from under their noses, head by head. Even, God forbid, Maxwell Fletcher's.

Instinct told her that the cattle in the corral were the missing stock. She prodded Jesse on and examined the area around her. The hollow was well hidden, a furrowed-out depression of sorts placed in the center of a thick grove of trees. It was the perfect place to hide stolen animals. She discovered the burned remains of a campfire and noted that the surrounding grass was flattened, like squashed collard greens, as though someone or several someones had made their beds on it.

She swung down off the horse and continued her investigation. She was so involved in her thoughts that she lost track of time.

"Mega-a-an!" she heard Clarissa call out. "Mega-a-an, where are you?"

"Over here," Megan yelled and turned to see Clarissa coming over the ridge on foot, with Habel huffing close behind.

Both women were winded. They were armed with short tree branches, which only added to the ridiculous sight they made. Clarissa's lovely hair had come loose from its neat nest and hung in disheveled wisps around her face. Her fashionable clothing, wet with perspiration, molded itself to her skin.

Habel's face was red and blotchy from the heat. She looked even worse for wear than her companion.

Clarissa looked worried. "You were gone so long we thought maybe Jesse had thrown you or something."

The "or something" was what had caused them to leave the safety of their buggy for the wilderness of the brush, searching out weapons from among fallen tree branches.

Seeing the bedraggled state they were in, Megan doubted either woman would have been able to wield her branch should the need have arisen.

"My word!" Clarissa said, noticing the corral. She stopped so suddenly that Habel ran into her back. Their mouths dropped open.

Habel steadied herself by clutching Clarissa's arm. "Oh, my, oh, my, oh, my," was all she could say, while she teetered back and forth.

Regaining some of their composure, they joined Megan and stood silent in their confusion.

"Well, ain't this somethin'?" Megan said quietly. She turned to her companions and continued, "I think we've found those missin' animals Jasper was tellin' us about. I could almost swear that's Henry Holloway's Agnes over yonder. I got a pretty good look at her that day I put a poultice on her leg."

"Good heavens," Clarissa whispered, aghast.

"Indeed," Habel said, alarmed.

Clarissa turned to Megan, her eyes wide. "We should tell Jim."

"Yes," Habel agreed, her eyes darting to the brush and trees beyond. She pressed closer to her friends. "We should tell him at once. Now! Immediately!" She was silent a second, then said, "The outlaws could return at any moment." Her complexion paled. "They could find us here." At the very thought, her voice grew panicked, and her head bobbed with fear. "Why, they could kidnap us, or, or, they could rob us, or," she stammered, and her eyes nearly popped from their sockets. "They could have their way with us. . . ."

"Good heavens!" Clarissa gasped and clutched her throat in horror.

Megan thought a minute, then said, "Oh, Habel, quit it. You're workin' yourself into a fit of vapors. There isn't nobody gonna have their way with us 'less we want them to. As far as kidnappin' us—well, I s'pose we could make them regret that soon enough. All we'd have to do is talk enough. And I doubt they'd bother to rob us. We don't have two whole dollars between the three of us." She scanned the area around them, her mind clicking with ideas. "No, whoever these outlaws are, they won't be doin' any of those things."

"How can you be so sure?" Clarissa asked.

"Call it a gut feelin'," Megan said simply. "Real outlaws wouldn't be pennin' the animals anywhere near the area they'd taken them from. They'd have enough sense to get them the hell outta Cooper County soon as they could. Besides," she said, walking toward the corral, "I have a feelin' there's a lot more going on here than just the theft of these here animals." She paused a minute. "I think we should wait for a while before we say anything to Jim or Jasper."

"Wait!" Habel croaked.

"For what?" Clarissa asked.

"Until I've had time to think about this some more."

Clarissa looked frazzled. "But this is a matter for the law, Megan."

"Yes, the law!" Habel reiterated.

Megan nailed them both with a disgusted glare. "Oh, hell! The law didn't find this hollow, did they? We did. With Samson's help, of course." At the sound of his name, he joined the women, wagging his tail furiously. The rope still trailed from his neck.

Megan forgot her earlier anger at him and patted his head. "You done good, boy." She studied him silently, cocking a brow. "You knew exactly where you were going today, didn't you?"

The weeks passed. The first frost covered the land, and mornings glistened in a new light. Halloween came. The town held wagon rides and parties for the children. The county held a pumpkin-growing contest, awarding the owner of the largest one a coveted melon-colored ribbon.

Harvest ended, and the fields were put to rest for another year, while autumn in its full-blown glory draped the county in various shades of gold and scarlet. Huge mounds of hay stood as sentries in the fields, while nature's smaller animals sought shelter to shield them from winter's cold breath.

The three women said nothing about their discovery.

Megan didn't want to.

Clarissa wanted to, but didn't.

Habel didn't dare.

Megan made them promise to keep the secret—at least for a little while. She threatened them with a hexin' if they so much as leaked a word, though she'd never hexed a soul in her life and had no intention of doing so. Although she toyed with the idea of hexin' Mrs. Pribble every once in a while, if she ever got the chance.

In the meantime, with Samson keeping her company, Megan visited the corral weekly. She was careful not to be seen and always went in the bright light of day. A makeshift shelter went up in anticipation of the coming cold weather. Feed and supplies filled one whole corner of the shelter. It was obvious that the "dangerous out-laws" planned to take good care of their booty and had no intention of moving the animals out of the county anytime soon.

It amused her to see recently reported stolen stock appearing in the corral, while others, like Henry's Agnes, were miraculously returned to their former owners.

Miraculously! *Humph!* she thought, but she said nothing to anyone and bided her time, while the good folks of Boonville shivered in their beds at night, confused and anxious, fearing the dangerous desperados who were stalking their land.

November turned cold. The nights were often dusted with stars, and the days ranged from a cloudless, chilly blue to an overcast dismal gray.

Megan spent the night before Thanksgiving trying to make an apple pie. It was an awesome, daunting task. Clarissa's mother, who turned out to be a sweet, open-minded woman, had shared her favorite apple pie recipe with Megan, and Megan was giving it her best effort. She ended up with a sloppy mess for the crust. But she'd promised Habel, who'd invited her for Thanksgiving dinner, an apple pie for dessert, so after beating the dough into some semblance of obedience, she plunked the lump of crust on top of the apples and hoped for the best. She supposed Habel's boarders might be a little put off by her presence tomorrow, but when she voiced that thought to Habel, Habel had softly replied, "I can invite whoever I please to my table, and I'm inviting you."

While the odd-looking creation was baking, Megan got comfortable in a chair and read from a veterinary journal she'd received through Mr. Tidwell's post office the day before. The hour grew late. The flames inside the stove flickered cheerfully against the glass doors, sending warmth to her body and spirit. Samson snuggled in a ball near her feet, while Willy snoozed contentedly in the chair beside her.

From outside the windows the night wind whistled through the treetops, promising a frosty day for feasting.

When she smelled the pie, she rose and took it out of the cookstove as Mrs. Westfield had instructed. She set it on the table to cool and went back to her book.

She had just begun to nod off when she heard the commotion outside her door. . . .

CHAPTER

12

"Git the hell outta my way!"

"Why do you always git to be the first one to the door?"

" 'Cause I'm older!"

"You're dumber, you mean."

"I ain't the dumb one, you are. You're dumber than a tree trunk."

There was a silence, then came a muffled thump, followed by a loud "Ouch! Goddammit!"

Megan whipped the door open. She planted her hands on her hips and forced her meanest frown. It was hard, though. She was so damned happy to see her brothers.

She glanced from one brother to the other, sizing up the situation. Matthew was holding his bloodied nose with one hand and winding up with the other to wield a blow to Luke's noggin. Luke was armed and ready for him, though. He held a huge turkey poised above his head, ready to bean his brother again if necessary.

"Enough!" Megan stepped between the two. She pressed a palm to each man's chest and pushed them apart. "What the hell's the matter with you two, standin' out here squabblin' like a couple of fools on the night before Thanksgivin'?

Why, it's almost sacrilegious. Pa would whup you both!"

Matt pointed an accusing finger. "He hit me with the goddamned turkey!"

Megan turned to Luke. "Why'd you hit him with the turkey?"

" 'Cause he said I was dumber than a tree trunk, and everybody knows a tree ain't got no brains! That's pretty goddamned dumb!"

Megan couldn't argue that. "All right, then." She turned back to Matthew. "Tell Luke you're sorry."

"Hell, no!"

Megan narrowed her eyes in a manner that told him she meant every word she was about to say. "You tell him you're sorry, or I'll write Pa and tell him you've been fightin' again."

Matthew's jaw bulged stubbornly.

"I mean it, Matt."

Matthew shot his brother a look of disgust and begrudgingly whispered, "I'm sorry."

"That's better," Megan said. She turned to Luke. "Now you tell Matt you're sorry for beanin' him with the turkey."

Luke made a face. "Do I gotta, Meg?" He angled Matt a look of pure animosity.

"What do you think?" Megan answered.

"Oh, hell." Luke fidgeted, shifting his weight from one huge foot to the other. "All right." He glared over at Matthew. "Sorry."

Megan nodded and smiled. "Well, now, that's fine. You're even. Now come on in outta this weather and get warm."

Glowering furiously, the two men elbowed past each other, both trying to fit through the door at once. They popped through it like two unplugged corks, then stumbled into the kitchen.

Hiding her smile, Megan got out the jug of "blue ruin" they'd left behind from their last visit. She poured them both a generous cup and held it out to them. "Here. Now, you two make up."

They did. Sort of. After a couple of good swigs, their moods mellowed, and they passed the next several hours chewing over the news from back home: Mark and Ellie had had their baby. Another little girl. Mark wanted to name her Emily, but Ellie insisted on Grace. Pa was fine. So was Uncle Chester. Harley and Hurley Baker said to say, "Hey!" Johnnie and Adam were fine. Their boys were getting big. Adam had had to whup them again last week. They'd let a jar of baby snakes loose in the classroom, and Mrs. Oglebee almost suffered a stroke. . . .

On and on the two men chattered, sometimes arguing over the tiniest details, but Megan didn't mind. She leaned back in her chair and sipped her own cup of "the devil's brew," and when at last the old clock in her parlor chimed midnight, she left them to argue and went on to bed, content and happy to have voices fill her house once more.

Habel was thrilled to have Matthew and Luke at her Thanksgiving table.

Her boarders, however, were not so enthusiastic.

If they'd found Megan's table manners lacking, they found her brothers' all but nonexistent.

But Habel paid her boarders no mind. She hadn't had so much animation at her table since Megan first came to town and stayed with her. She loved having the Hawkins men there. She fluttered and fussed shamelessly over the two, earning herself many a sharp glance and more than a few coughs of disapproval.

The boys had brought the turkey, and Megan had brought the pie, and the four ignored the covert glances cast their way from Mr. Higley and the rest of the stuffy group, so that, oddly enough, Thanksgiving dinner passed quite pleasantly.

Later that evening, when the table had been cleared and the few leftovers wrapped tight and put away, the four rode over to visit Clarissa. Luke had suggested the visit, and the other three agreed it was a wonderful idea.

When Clarissa opened the door to see the group on her porch, she let loose with a happy shriek of surprise and hugged both brothers as though they were her own.

She invited them in for another round of desserts, served by Mrs. Westfield. While chewing a mouthful of pumpkin pie, Matthew looked up from his plate and asked, "Where's Jim?"

"Yeah," Luke said, suddenly realizing his absence, "where's Jim?" He blinked his bewilderment.

Megan had been wondering the same thing. All day, in fact. She glanced over at Clarissa, who lifted her brows and shrugged as if to say she had no idea where he was.

"I asked him to join us," Habel said, "but he said he wasn't sure he could make it."

"Excuse me." Megan rose from her chair. She found her coat, shrugged into it, then left, heading straight for the jail. Once there, she knocked twice, and when no one answered, she let herself in. She found him sitting alone at his table, before a plate of cold beans and countless dirty dishes, looking for all the world as if he'd lost his best friend. Her heart contracted with tenderness. She felt a need to go to him and hug his neck and say, "Come, let me make it better."

Hearing her footsteps, he looked up.

"Hello," she said, stopping before the table.

"Hello." He looked surprised to see her.

"We wondered where you were today."

He shrugged. "It was my day to do duty here." It was the truth, though there was little duty to be done. He could have left anytime he wanted to.

He'd stayed, though. Partly out of confusion, partly out

of stubbornness. He'd been trying to work through his feelings for Megan for weeks now. He had come to terms with the fact that Clarissa and he were wrong for each other, but he hadn't quite figured out where he stood with Megan. He wasn't even sure where he wanted to stand with Megan. He knew Steven still visited her regularly, and he wanted to ask her about that, but pride had held him stubbornly silent.

"Ah." She nodded, keeping her expression serious. "I see. You have dangerous outlaws locked up back there, do you?"

"Sam Sweeney."

She thought of his fetid breath and bad manners and nodded. "That's dangerous enough, I s'pose. Did you get him fed?"

"Best I could."

Silence, then: "Habel said she asked you to join us."

"Yes, she did."

"You missed my pie. I baked one, you know. Apple."

He didn't bother to hide his grin. "Now, that had to be somethin'. Sorry I missed it."

Megan laughed out loud. "You shoulda seen ol' Mr. Higley trying to choke it past his big bushy mustache."

Jim chuckled at the picture her words elicited.

"So," she said when their laughter had faded into self-consciousness. "Did you have any turkey?"

He shook his head and dropped his gaze. "I don't care all that much for turkey an' fixin's anyway."

"Liar."

He cocked an eyebrow, and his gaze shot back up to hers.

"You always loved turkey, an' don't try to deny it."

"Yeah, well . . ."

She pulled a chair out and sat down across from him. "There's plenty of leftovers. And Matt and Luke are here. Came in last night. They must've brought us the biggest turkey in all of Butler County, although it was nothing short of a miracle they got it here in one piece. They almost beat each other to death with it on the way up."

"Yeah?" He tried to sound disinterested, but his eyes lit at the thought of some real food. God, he was hungry! The beans he'd been trying to force down all afternoon were about as exciting as Widow Higgins, and just about as deadly.

"You're welcome to what we got left." She held out her hand, palm up. He stared at it a second, then took her hand. His eyes lifted to hers, and they sat for a while, allowing a wonderful warmth to sluice through them.

At length he asked, "Is the reverend still courtin' you?"

She shrugged. "He visits."

"You plannin' on marryin' him?" He thought he had nothing to lose by asking.

She smiled a slow, mischievous smile. "What do you think?"

"I think you'd make one helluva preacher's wife."

"I think so, too. Scary thought, huh?"

Jim chuckled, then said, "Does he know your intentions aren't serious?"

"I think so. If he doesn't, he will soon."

"Good," Jim said. He leaned across the table and, without asking permission, pressed his lips to hers.

She reached up and hugged his neck, sighing inwardly, finding a satiety in his nearness, while he deepened the kiss with the pressure of his mouth and the touch of his tongue. Time seemed to stop, fluttered, then passed, while each acknowledged the reality of the spark that burned, alive and hot, between them. Neither knew where it would lead for certain, or what it would bring them. They only knew they shared a bond that had existed for as long as each could remember.

When finally they parted, he drew away reluctantly and sat back down, thinking about her, about him, about some very important things.

"So," he said, "you have some of that mangled turkey left, huh?"

"Yep." She smiled.

"How 'bout some of that apple pie?" His gaze was skeptical.

"Nope." Humor flashed in her eyes.

"Good. Then I think I just might take you up on that invitation."

Matthew burst in the door, not bothering to knock. "Hey, Jim!" The others followed behind.

There followed a long episode of shoulder-banging and whooping, and before he could change his mind, Jim abandoned his beans in favor of Megan's smile, the leftovers at Habel's boardinghouse, and the company of his friends.

Jim rode out to see Maxwell Fletcher during the second week of December.

He'd grown tired of the game.

The farmers needed their stock returned so they could care for the animals through the coming winter months. For the most part, Jim had outsmarted Maxwell's men and stolen the stock back, one by one, before the animals could be sold out of the county. Those he'd taken, he'd penned and cared for as best he could until he could figure a way to unobtrusively return them. Still, there was a constant list in the jail of new missing stock. It seemed to grow daily.

The game was becoming too difficult, too dangerous.

Up to this point there had been no real danger. He knew Maxwell could not make accusations against him without putting himself at risk. How could he accuse Jim and Zach of stealing what he had stolen from someone else? Maxwell would have to figure out a way to frame them, leaving himself in the clear. Jim didn't put it past him to try that strategy sooner or later.

In the meantime, Fletcher's thievery went on, making Jim and Zach work doubly hard to keep up with the game. Fletcher had more men to do his bidding than Jim had. And Jim was running out of room in the hollow. So, before anyone could get hurt, Jim decided to do what any good ol' boy would do and go directly to the source of trouble and speak his piece.

Besides, someone had discovered him. He'd found telltale tracks in the dirt to testify to a new presence.

He'd been putting off the confrontation with Fletcher, hoping to draw him out and expose his guilt to the townsfolk in another way. But Fletcher was a crafty old soul and eluded him at every turn. Still, Jim knew him for the varmint he was, and he planned to let him know he knew. Maybe then this foolishness could stop. It angered him no small amount that a man who had so much would steal from those who had so little. He just didn't understand the reasoning behind such practices.

When he reached the Fletcher farm, Flora answered the door. She was a tall, handsome woman, who would have been beautiful had she not been so pompously filled with her own self-importance. She was one of Mrs. Pribble's ladies—the only one who ever challenged Edith's position in the group.

She held the door open a fraction, barely wide enough to allow Jim to enter. "Deputy Lawson." She greeted him with forced civility. She was every bit as arrogant as her husband—maybe even a little more so, if that were possible. After all, she was the one with the family money. "Do come in. To what do we owe the honor of this visit?"

"I'd like a few words with Maxwell, if I could." Jim

removed his hat, held it between his hands, and stepped into the house. "Is he home?"

"I'm afraid not. He went to town."

"I see. You wouldn't know where he went, would you?" Jim asked the question for good measure, though he was almost certain he could find Fletcher.

"No, I don't," Mrs. Fletcher lied. She knew very well where he was, and it galled her no small amount that her husband preferred such coarse company to her own. One of these days she was going to get even with that man for all the humiliation he'd caused her. One of these days . . .

"Well, thank you anyway, ma'am." Jim placed his hat on his head.

"You're welcome, Deputy," she said and saw him out.

He stood on the sprawling porch that encircled three-quarters of the house. The house was a huge, dignified three-story structure that had been in Flora's family for generations. Jim's gaze swept the perimeter of the yard, outward to the fields in the distance, then back to the small separate corral near the barn. He felt Beauregard's eyes on him and wondered how any creature could be so damned cantankerous. The bull was Fletcher's pride and joy. Fletcher thought the sun rose and set on him. But the folks of Boonville did not share his sentiment. They thought the bull was a dangerous nuisance, though few had the guts to admit it. He'd run the fence many times, nailed several of the area farmer's cows, and gored Frank Bozemen's youngest boy, giving him a limp he'd carry for the rest of his life. Yep, Jim thought, making his way down the steps to his horse, that damned bull was gonna get his due someday. Just like Fletcher.

A cold wind swept down through the hills, chafing his cheeks and chilling him. The season's first stinging flecks of snow hit his face. He flipped the collar of his coat up around his neck, swung up onto the back of his horse, then headed due east, back toward the riverfront, to the big, yellow two-story house whose windows always glowed with life.

Merilee let him in.

The place was lively as usual. Lights glowed, and peals of laughter were heard. Cards snapped and dice thumped. The sound of voices, male and female, mingled with the clink of glasses and the din of someone banging out a melody on a piano. The overly sweet smell of cheap perfume warred with those of cigar smoke and incense.

Jim took off his hat respectfully, while a slow grin caught at his mouth. "Merilee," he said in greeting. "How's the entertainment business?"

"Slow," she answered and chuckled, eyeing his handsome form. "How's the outlaw business?"

"Slow."

She shook her head in mock disgust. "You always say that."

"So do you."

They both laughed, knowing exactly where they stood on the issue of the law. Merilee's place was no ordinary gathering spot for the local men. It was a clean establishment, and she intended to keep it that way. Her girls were not for sale, though the men could look to their fill. But no touchin' was allowed. That was Merilee's law! She allowed her girls to entertain the men by dancing and singing and performing skits, and she offered the men a variety of choices for their drinking pleasure and gambling entertainment, but she was firmly against the coarser practices that many riverfront establishments offered.

As for the deputy, well, they understood each other. He was not one of her customers, but he'd always treated her with the utmost respect and kindness. And he was one fine looker, too. Had she been a bit younger . . .

"I'm looking for Fletcher," Jim told her, his gaze sweeping the room.

Merilee cocked her head toward a set of open double doors on the left. "You'll find him in the main room, playing cards with some of the others."

"Thanks," Jim said, smiling. He left her to make his way through the gaping doors, then stopped for a moment and looked again around the room. On the stage before him three women paraded, sashaying and dipping, keeping time with the music. Their faces were painted and rouged; their hair was swept up high and sported feathers in a pretense of sophistication. They wore dresses, fitted snugly through the bodice and waist, with full short skirts, which were ruffled around the bottom. Stockings, topped by lacy garters, encased their legs, and on their feet were fancy high-heeled shoes.

Jim's gaze left the ladies and found Maxwell, who was seated across from a trio of other well-dressed gentlemen.

He drew Maxwell's attention immediately by stopping before his table. "Fletcher," he greeted.

"Deputy Lawson," Fletcher returned, though his gaze remained distracted.

Jim smiled, but his smile was guarded. "I think it's time we had a little talk, Fletcher."

"I'm engaged right now," Fletcher said with forced pleasantness, gesturing to his companions, who waited for him to make his move. He looked down at the cards he held in his hand and studied them intensely, while the fingers on his free hand tapped out a nervous rhythm on the polished tabletop. "Couldn't we do this another time?" he asked absently.

"No. I think tonight is gonna have to do." Jim crossed his arms over his chest and waited. It suddenly occurred to him that Maxwell's finances might not be as secure as he pretended—that maybe he'd dug himself into a hole with his gambling, that maybe he stole from his neighbors to cover his debts and hide the truth from his wife, who the whole town knew disapproved of the sinful practice, especially when it was done at Merilee's. Flora Fletcher could be a force to be reckoned with, every bit as formidable as Edith Pribble herself.

The assumption only fueled Jim's exasperation with the man. "We can talk about this in private, or we can do it right here," Jim said.

Maxwell glanced up at him sharply.

Jim's eyes were steady. "It's your call."

The veins in Maxwell's forehead looked about ready to pop through the top of his head.

Jim grinned.

Abruptly Maxwell rose and flung his cards onto the table. "All right, then, Deputy." His jaw was tight with suppressed anger. "We'll do it your way." He followed Jim across the room, to a corner where no others could overhear their conversation. Once there, he turned to Jim. "What is so important that you need to speak with me about it now?"

"Well," Jim said as he leaned his shoulder against the wall and studied the man before him. "I guess it has to do with about one hundred fifty head of missing cattle and at least two dozen stolen horses."

Maxwell's gaze never wavered, but he blinked. Once. "Exactly what does all that have to do with me?"

"Just about everythin', I'd say."

"I don't know what you're talking about."

"Oh, I think you do." Jim straightened and nailed the man with a look that said he was done playing games. "You've been stealin' off your friends and neighbors for years now. And though they suspect you, they're too afraid of your name and your wife's money to make an accusation. Well, I'm not. They may want to deny the truth, but you and I know what's goin' on here, don't we, Fletcher?"

When Fletcher didn't answer, Jim went on. "Someone is on to you and stealin' back those animals before you've had the chance to get them out of the county." He paused a moment, then said, "Isn't that right, Fletcher?"

"You!" Fletcher said, his eyes narrowing at the affirmation of his suspicions.

Jim grinned. "Back home we have a thing called justice. Funny thing justice is—it don't always happen the way folks expect it to. Nature has its own set of rules and regulations." He leaned in close to the older man. "Be careful, Fletcher. Life has a way of making right what folks make wrong." He nodded. "Maude, a real smart lady back home, always said that, and I've yet to find her wrong."

Fletcher's hands clenched at his side. "I'll get you for this, Lawson."

Jim grinned. "Not if I get you first."

"Well, he goddamned got you, goddammit!" Zach said, helping Jim down from his horse. The cold December wind caught at his scarf, blowing it up into his Jim's face. "I better take you out to the barn, till I make sure there's no one but the doctor home."

Jim batted the scarf out of his face and yelped at the sudden movement. He glared through the moonless darkness at his friend's almost invisible face and placed his hands on Zach's shoulders. "Take it easy, will you!" He eased his buttocks away from the saddle and attempted to slide down into Zach's waiting arms. His rear brushed against the back of the horse and elicited another muffled yelp.

"I told you this would happen." Zach caught him, holding him steady for a moment. "I told you—"

"You told me we'd get hung. I ain't hung, I'm shot!"

"Shot or hung, they both get you dead." Zach hugged Jim's waist, supporting him, while together they began to hobble toward the barn across a thin, crunchy crust of snow.

"I'm not gonna die."

Zach shook his head. "Probably not. But you might never sit up straight again." A sudden chuckle broke from his chest and rumbled out into a fit of laughter, which he fought hard to suppress.

Jim's eyes shot daggers at his friend. "Go ahead! Laugh! You think it's so goddamned funny, do you? Well . . . you just wait! Your turn's comin'!"

"We never should have gone out there tonight. If we hadn't, you wouldn't be shot. He set us up, stealin' those pigs from Tom Skeets. He did it on purpose, knowing we'd try to get them back before Christmas."

"Aw, shut up," Jim muttered churlishly, limping at Zach's side.

Zach gave him a look of disgust. "Anybody ever tell you you're a lousy outlaw?"

Stung, Jim snorted. "Well, you ain't no Frank James yourself."

Zach stopped before the barn doors. "Can you stand by yourself for a minute?"

"I got buckshot in my ass, not my legs."

Zach stifled another burst of chuckles, unlatched the barn doors, and swung them open. It was dark inside. He walked back to Jim and helped him through the doors. They groped their way against the wall until they came to a mound of hay.

"I sure as hell hope there ain't a pitchfork hid in here." Slowly Jim got down on his knees and patted the mounds with his hands.

Zach did the same, carefully feeling for anything hard or sharp and pointed. "I never thought he'd try to shoot us."

"I made him mad that night I talked to him at Merilee's."

"I guess you did."

"He wants us out of the way now that he knows it's us who's been ruining things for him."

"Lay down," Zach said, rising. "I didn't feel anything in the hay. You wait while I go get the doctor."

Jim grunted a response and slowly stretched out belly flat on the mound of hay to wait for his friend to return.

CHAPTER
13

Megan didn't get a chance to talk to Steven until Christmas Eve. It had snowed sporadically throughout the day, making the ground crystalline and white. The air was sharp and cold, abetted by the harsh norther that had hit Cooper County the day before. The naked tree limbs clacked together, creating a music both lonely and lovely, keeping harmony with the soulful keening of the wind.

The weather drove most folks indoors to seek the warmth of their stoves and fireplaces. Megan, too, had been house-bound and felt a need to get out and visit with her friends.

The house seemed especially quiet since the boys had left for home two weeks ago. They wanted to check on Pa, but they promised to return for Christmas, and since they'd never broken a promise to her yet, she expected them back tonight, or at the very latest, tomorrow.

With time on her hands, she'd hitched Jesse to the buggy, braving the weather to head into town to watch the children's Christmas program that was to be held at the Presbyterian church that night.

The snow made the journey slower than usual, though not overly difficult. With the trees bare, the river was easily seen from the road. It swirled, dark and alive, not yet frozen by winter's cold breath. A frosty rime lined the riverbank. A lone duck swam down-current, seemingly oblivious to the water's chill.

When Megan reached the church, she secured the rig and Jesse and went in to sit with Habel and Clarissa. She automatically searched the chapel for Jim. But she didn't see him, nor did she see Zach, for that matter. So she focused her attention on the children, who stood on a small stage at the front of the room, in a solemn cluster around a cradle, in which lay a baby—little Melody Skeets. The children were dressed in makeshift robes and headdresses reminiscent of those worn by the blessed few who were present at the event of that first holy night. After all the children had spoken their lines, they raised their youthful voices together in song. Some voices were so terribly out of tune they brought smiles to the faces of many. Some were so perfectly lovely they brought tears of wonder.

When the program was over, Megan sought out Danny. He was dressed in his oriental king's costume, complete with a crown. He stood alone near the door, obediently awaiting his parents, who were busy exchanging Christmas greetings with those townsfolk they thought counted.

"Hey, Danny," Megan said.

"Hey, Megan." Danny smiled, obviously glad to see her.

"How've you been?"

"Good."

She cocked her head. "You sure?"

"Yep."

"Doin' all right in school, are you?"

He rolled his eyes in disgust. "I guess. I been there."

"You look mighty fancy in your costume."

He shrugged and wrinkled his freckled nose in distaste. "I wanted to be a shepherd, but Mother and Father said I had to be one of the three kings of the Orient."

"Ah," Meg said. "Well, that's fine! You look handsome as a king." She laughed at his doleful expression. "I bet Amy thinks so, too."

Danny snorted and rolled his eyes again.

Megan reached into her reticule, pulled out a small tissue-wrapped package, and handed it to him. "I brought you a present."

His eyes lit with excitement. "Wow. For me? What is it?"

"You'll see," she said with a small, secret smile, thinking of the collar she'd bought over at Mr. Pribble's store. It would fit the neck of the pup Henry Holloway had promised her. The pup would be Danny's, even if she had to keep it at her place. "This is only part of your present. The best part won't be ready for about four more weeks. When you can do it without gettin' yourself in trouble, you come out and see me. All right?"

"Sure." His eyes glowed with adoration. "Thanks."

"You're welcome." She bent over and kissed his cheek. "Merry Christmas, darlin'."

"Merry Christmas, Megan," he returned happily. Then, seeing Amy headed his way, he shot off in the opposite direction, the smile still stretched clear across his face.

Megan sought out Clarissa and Habel next. She hugged them both and wished them the merriest of Christmases, then waited patiently for the others to leave so she could have a moment alone with Steven.

When Steven had seen all of his parishioners out, he closed the church doors and came to her. He took both of her hands in his. Smiling that boyishly pleasant smile of his, he gazed down into her eyes. "I'm so glad you stayed, Meg." His gaze swept her form appreciatively. "You look lovely."

"I need to talk to you," she said quietly. She felt sad-

dened to steal away his joy, and on this holy night, too,
by telling him what she must. But it was the right thing
to do, the fair thing. Although their courtship had never
progressed beyond lively conversation and the lightest of
caresses, she could tell he wished for more. Her instincts
told her it would not be long before he pressed his suit
further. Though she held a true affection for him, she knew
she did not return his devotion equally.

What she felt for him was not what she yearned to
feel toward a man—the man who would be her husband.
Steven's kisses, though pleasant enough, did not stir her;
his touch did not set her heart thrumming, almost pressing
out to greet him.

She'd only known those feelings with one man. Only
one. Even as she acknowledged that fact, it brought her
confusion. At one time she never would have believed it
possible. But she was different now, and so was he. There
was unfinished business between her and Jim Lawson. What
was between them needed to be settled and given its proper
due—one way or the other.

Sooner or later she planned to see that it was.

For now, she must think of Steven's feelings.

He led her to a bench near the back of the room and
waited while she seated herself. Still holding her hand, he
sat down beside her and asked, "Now, what is it you must
talk with me about that would make you look so sad?"

She laughed a short, quiet laugh that held little humor.
"Am I sad?" She raised deep blue eyes to his much light-
er ones.

"Yes." His easy smile also grew sad. "And I think I
know why."

She waited for him to go on, her gaze steady.

"You fear I care for you more than you do for me, and
you do not wish to hurt me. Am I right?"

She looked down and nodded, feeling a knot congeal in

the back of her throat. He was a very special, very kind man. "Oh, hell," she muttered softly, not realizing that her use of profanity widened the smile on his face, and lifted away some of the sadness.

"There's someone else you have feelings for. Am I right?"

She nodded again, her expression so morose he almost chuckled, despite the fact that he was truly reluctant to lose her. But he knew she had never been his. Not really. She'd always belonged to another, even if she didn't know it herself.

"Deputy Lawson is a fine man," Steven said.

Her gaze shot up to his. She frowned. "Just 'cause I have feelin's for him doesn't mean he's fine."

Steven laughed. "Well, he is. But if he doesn't do right by you, I'll get your brothers after him." Gently he touched a hand to her cheek. "Because I think you're wonderful."

Grateful for his understanding, Megan stared at him for several moments, then impulsively leaned toward him and took his face in her hands. She planted a whopper of a kiss dead center on his mouth. Then she rose, strode to the door, and, without looking back, walked out into the wintry night.

Megan had just finished filling her brothers' socks with fruit, nuts, and new red scarves and gloves when she heard the knock.

Fierce warrior that he was, Samson slept on at her feet, while Willy, in his chair, woke and growled low in his throat.

She rose from her place before the fire and went to unlatch the door, thinking it must be Matthew and Luke. Pulling her robe around her, she opened the door and was surprised to find Zach shivering on her porch. "Zach, what a pleasant surprise! I wondered where you were tonight. I expected to see you and Jim at the Christmas program."

"Yes, well . . . we had business to attend to."

Megan stepped sideways, gesturing him in. "Come on in and warm up by the stove."

"Actually, Doctor," he said with a smile, "I was hoping to bring you out with me. I would have brought him up to the house, but I wasn't sure if you had company or not. Jim said Matt and Luke were due back soon."

Megan got confused. "They are. But they aren't back yet." Her brow knitted with concern. "Is it your horse, Zach? You said 'him'?"

"No, it's not my horse." Without telling her more, he said, "You better bring your bag, though." He paused a moment. "And a lantern."

"I'll go get changed—"

"No need," he told her. "We aren't going far."

Baffled, she left the door open and went to get her coat and bag. Hearing Zach's voice, Samson had woken, stretched long, then happily wagged his way to the door to greet his friend.

Megan shrugged into her coat, then took the lantern down from a cupboard shelf and lit it. She grabbed her bag from where it sat on the floor by the door and joined Zach on the porch, all within minutes, allowing Samson to follow her out before pulling the door shut behind him. "Where are we going?"

Zach pointed to the barn. "Over there."

Completely puzzled, she raised her brows in question. The lantern pierced the darkness with a flickering glow of light. She turned to Zach for an answer, but all he did was take the lantern from her hand and offer his other arm. Together they crunched across the ground toward the barn, Megan's long nightgown sweeping a path in the snow behind her.

The wind burned their cheeks and stung their eyes,

though they reached the building within minutes. Quickly Zach swung the barn door open so they could slip inside and close out a strong blast of December chill.

Megan stood in the barn for a moment, letting the lantern illuminate the area around her. She looked around the floor, then froze when she saw the mound of hay in the far corner, which Samson had already found and was nudging incessantly, eliciting moans from the hapless victim.

"Criminy . . ." she whispered and moved toward the figure that was flung out over the hay mound. The rear of his trousers was speckled with about half a dozen dark holes, each surrounded by a small dark circle of blood. "Criminy," she said again.

Zach was right behind her. He held the lantern over the wounded one.

Hearing them, Jim rose up on his elbows and cocked his head their way. He frowned fiercely, trying hard to cover his embarrassment.

Megan's gaze went from Jim to Zach, then back to Jim again. "What in tarnation happened to you?" She dropped to her knees beside him, setting her bag down at her side, her nightgown and coat billowing out around her.

"I think that's pretty damned obvious," Jim snapped. "I got hit with a load of buckshot."

"In your . . . your—" She stifled a giggle and pointed to his hind section, trying to keep the grin from creeping onto her face.

"My ass," he shouted.

Zach turned his head away and tried to muffle his laughter with a cough.

"But how?"

It took Jim a few minutes to answer, not sure if he should tell the truth or a bald-faced lie that might salvage his dignity. He decided the truth would save a later explanation. "I was runnin'."

"From who?" Lightly she touched a hand to his rear. He jumped as though she'd scalded him with a kettle of hot water.

He jerked away from her and scowled, ignoring her question.

She'd not forgotten she'd asked it, though. She looked up at Zach, expecting an answer. "Who the hell was he running from?"

Zach looked sheepish. Megan could have sworn he was blushing beneath his dark skin. "Well . . . we were both running—sort of."

Growing impatient, Megan waited for him to continue. She lifted her brows in expectation and pursed her lips.

"Well," Zach said, shifting his weight, making the lantern jiggle and cast dancing shadows across the walls, "we were sort of running from Maxwell Fletcher."

"But why?"

Zach sighed. "We were stealin' a couple of pigs."

"Pigs?" Her eyes got big. Her pupils expanded as facts began to come together in her brain.

"Yeah," Jim said, glowering, "Tom Skeets's pigs."

"The ones that were just stolen from him?" Megan asked.

"Yep," Zach said. "Those are the ones."

"Where are they now?"

Zach gave her a sheepish smile. "We left them and got the hell out of there while we could."

"Aha!" she yelled, springing to her feet. She stabbed a finger toward Jim's inert form. "It's you two, isn't it?"

Caught, both men remained silent.

"I knew it all along." She paced a circle around them, excited by her discovery, delighted that she'd been right about her suspicions. "Hot damn, I knew there couldn't have been any real outlaws!" She scorched both men with a look of scorn. "You two are some scary desperados, all right! Huh! You're 'bout as slick as a couple of pieces of sandpaper, leaving evidence all over the place and keeping those animals down in the hollow for anyone to find! Besides," she said as she narrowed her eyes in gleeful satisfaction, "Samson went right to that place. Probably was his home at one time, too, huh?"

Annoyed by her attitude, Jim sullenly watched her pound around the dirt-packed barn floor. He thought about stifling her. For good.

"It's Fletcher who's been taking those animals, isn't it?" She didn't wait for either of the men to answer, but continued on in a long run of words. "Why, that low-down, no-good, thievin' son of a bitch! Then you two steal 'em back and hide 'em for a while, hoping you'll draw him out. But you haven't been able to yet, have you? So you return the animals 'cause you never really intended to keep them anyway, and 'cause no one is quite sure who's stealin' from who, and everybody's confused, but happy to have their stock back. . . ."

It was the craziest scheme, but where she came from, crazier things were done. She angled a disgusted look Jim's way, centering her gaze on his peppered buttocks. "I always said you'd make a sorry outlaw."

Zach chuckled at that, thoroughly enjoying the dressing down, now that it was directed at his friend alone.

Jim, however, was not enjoying the episode at all. He got mad. Really mad. His face turned red as a radish, while a vein took to throbbing in his temple. He'd had enough of her heckling, by God! She'd always got the best of him. Even when they were children. And it irked him no small amount. Well, he'd had a bellyful of her carping.

He rose up on his knees and glared holes through her head. "Zach. Get me outta here. I'm goin' home!"

Suddenly alarmed, Zach's expression got serious. "But you need doctoring."

Jim pointed a finger at Megan and roared, "Not from her, I don't! I'd just as soon bleed to death! And she isn't a human doctor anyway!"

Zach set his chin. "If I take you in to see Doc Andrews, he's going to ask questions."

"I don't give a damn!" Jim tried to get to his feet, using Samson's back for support. Samson, however, did not take kindly to being used as a prop and took off like a shot to the other side of the barn. Jim fell back onto his knees, his face reflecting his pain.

"Well, I do!" It was Zach's turn to get mad. "Anna's father is just beginning to like me a little. And I do mean a little," he added with emphasis, "and only because I found his cows for him. If I want to ask for her hand by spring like I'd planned, I got a lot of work to do to win him over."

"And whose idea was it to get his cows back for him?" Jim asked.

"Yours," Zach admitted honestly, "and it was a good one, too, but how do you think he'll see it once he finds out you and I had those cows penned up for a week before I gave them back?"

Jim scowled his answer.

"Well, I'm not taking the chance of losing Anna, and you're not going into town to see Doc Andrews! And besides," he added, "it's Christmas Eve, and I'm supposed to be spending it at her house!" That alone seemed like a good enough reason for abandoning his friend. He turned to Megan, handed her the lantern, winked, and marched to the door. "Merry Christmas, Doc!"

"Hey!" Jim yelled. "You can't leave me—"

But Zach ignored him and let himself out into the darkness, slamming the door behind him. "Merry Christmas, Jim!"

Still on his knees, Jim stared, dumbfounded, at the door,

while he listened to the sound of the wind buffeting the barn.

In time his gaze reluctantly found Megan's. She was grinning at him, her eyes dancing with mirthful satisfaction.

Incensed, he decided he would drown her. Yep! That would be a fittin' end to her harping. He would wait till the river waters rose high in spring, then he'd bind her feet and hands and cast her in. First he'd gag her, though.

He felt better immediately.

She dropped her gaze and pretended to study her fingernails. "Well, Mr. Jim Dandy Deputy," she drawled. "Do you want that buckshot outta your hind-section, or are you waitin' for it to become a permanent part of your anatomy?"

The thought of her coming demise allowed him to force a secret, almost demonic half-smile. His mustache twitched wickedly. "I suppose I don't have much choice in the matter."

"It would be easier to work on you up at the house if you think you can make it there." Suddenly her voice was free of sarcasm.

Despite the pain it caused him, he gritted his teeth and used a support beam to help him rise to his feet, hugging it all the way up.

"I made it here, didn't I?"

Megan picked up her bag from the floor. In her other hand she held the lantern. "You wanna hang on to me?" She felt a twinge of guilt at watching him suffer.

He set his jaw firmly and eyed her. "What do you think?"

"Fine!" she huffed and turned.

"Fine!" he returned and hobbled after her.

She sashayed off toward the barn door, leaving him to follow. He did, but his journey was agonizingly slow. At the door she slid him a derisive look. "It'll be summer 'fore we get to the house. We could freeze to corpses if you don't let me help you."

Bent over like a man four times his age, he almost snarled with annoyance. He fixed his hat on his head and turned the collar of his coat up around his neck.

Vexed, she rolled her eyes to the beams above her head and tapped out an impatient rhythm with her foot, while holding the door open so he could shuffle through. Samson bounded ahead, out into the night, barking at every shadow he saw. Megan dropped the barn door latch back into place and followed Jim's arduous trek through the snowy night.

When they reached the house, she felt frozen indeed. She shot around him and hurried up the porch steps to throw open the door and let Samson and herself in. She almost pinched Jim in half in her hurry to get the door closed behind him.

He scowled.

She smiled.

She shrugged off her coat and forced him to allow her to help him get out of his. Then she hung their coats side by side on matching pegs on the wall.

"I think we'd better do this on a bed," she said as she set the lantern down on the table.

Her words caught him off guard, and his gaze collided with hers. His eyes swept down her robed form, then rose back up to her face once again. His cheeks flushed beneath the dark shadow of his beard.

She shrugged and widened her eyes innocently. "I don't know how else we can do it. Come on." She headed down the narrow hall toward the back of the house. "We'll put you in the room Matt and Luke use when they visit." She left him no choice but to follow.

She reached the bedroom before him and lit two lamps, sending the darkness to flight. He entered the small, tidy room and stood in one place, uncomfortable and uncertain.

He'd known her most of his life, yet never once had he been in a bedroom with her. The furniture was plain, the floors bare, but as in the rest of her house, there was a hominess that was evident and welcoming. He watched her turn down the quilt and the rest of the bedclothes so he could lie down. The sight of her bent over, performing the simple chore, struck him as intensely intimate and caught him off guard again, producing a warmth that spread throughout his chest and down to his stomach.

"Get outta those britches and drawers," she instructed calmly, bringing him back to reality—to the real reason he stood within the room with her. "Lay down belly flat." She turned to him, her expression vague and unreadable.

He hesitated a moment, feeling totally emasculated.

She lifted an eyebrow. "Do you want infection to set in?"

Bristling, he grumbled an unintelligible response so vulgar it would have burned her ears had she heard it. But he obediently made his way to the bed.

"You go ahead and get ready," she said quietly. "I'll go back outside and get your horse bedded down for the night." Though she was loath to admit it, she sympathized with his discomfort and felt no need to provoke him further. Besides, it was late, she was tired, and he was in pain. And she never could stand to see a critter in pain, even if it was a human one like Jim Lawson.

After she left the room he stood with his back to the door and unbuckled his belt. He undid the buttons on his britches, then, very carefully, eased his trousers and drawers down and stepped out of both, leaving them in a dark puddle on the floor. In one last act of defiance, he kept his shirt on, though she hadn't told him he couldn't. He crawled on hands and knees across the bed and lowered himself onto his stomach. He eased a sheet up over his bare backside, desperate to preserve a measure of his dignity, hoping not to soil the sheet with dried blood. He decided it was worth the risk. He could always buy her a sheet.

Tired and sore, he laid his head down on his folded arm and waited for her return.

She didn't take long, but when she returned, she found him dozing, his buttocks and thighs covered by the sheet, his muscled, darkly furred calves exposed and bare. She walked to the bed and studied him in silence, while an odd, possessive tenderness caught at her heart. He was, indeed, a handsome man. His hat lay beside him, though it was still clutched in his hand. His thick, dark hair was mussed, falling onto his forehead in a careless, boyish manner that made her remember his younger days. She was bewitched by memories. She struggled with the desire to touch him. "Jim," she said softly, sitting down on the bed. She gave in to the temptation and touched his shoulder lightly.

"Huh—" He stirred and woke. He turned his head to get a better look at her. She looked serene and lovely. Her hair, bright and loose, fell around her shoulders in a soft tangle of waves. He felt an urge to touch her hair, to see if it felt as silky as it looked. Then she withdrew her hand from his shoulder, and he remembered the pellets in his backside.

She focused her attention on the bed, where she'd laid out several clean towels, a small metal pan to hold the buckshot once she'd extracted it, and a long pointed implement. On the nightstand she'd placed a kettle of hot water so she could cleanse his wounds before she began the operation. She smiled and handed him a jug she had lifted from the floor. "Here. Matt left this. Take a couple of good swigs. We'll give it time to take effect 'fore we get started." She'd anesthetized animals in the past with ether, but she'd never attempted such practices on a human. She didn't want to begin with Jim.

"If the shot didn't go deep, it shouldn't take too long to get out." She paused, her blue eyes soft and earnest. "It's gonna hurt some. You'll just have to trust me."

"I hate it when you say that," he said, remembering their earlier days. Trusting her had gotten him whupped more times than he cared to remember.

"This time you won't regret it. I promise."

"An' if I do?"

"Then I'll let you get even."

"Humph!" He looked away.

She leaned in close and captured his gaze. "I promise."

He studied her, remembering her steadfastness in caring for Tom's pigs, her compassion with Danny, her unwavering dedication to doing her best at everything she'd ever done. He knew, deep within himself, she would do her best with him. Besides, if he were to be truthful with himself, he'd have to admit he was glad it was her who would be digging into his hide instead of Doc Andrews. Doc Andrews's eyesight was failing, though he hotly denied any such thing. Were Jim at his mercy, it would have been a very long, very painful night.

Resigning himself to his predicament, Jim lifted himself onto one arm, crooked the jug in his elbow, and took a good long pull of the fiery liquid within.

CHAPTER

14

"Well . . . I guess we better get started," he said, surprising her.

"I guess we better." She took a deep breath, then closed her eyes a moment. When she opened them, her gaze fell on his britches where they lay on the floor. The realization that he was naked beneath the thin covering of the sheet hit her with force. She remembered the day she'd followed him through the jail, admiring his backside, and consoled herself with the thought that now she'd get to admire it firsthand.

Just the same, it was an unsettling thought.

She had yet to see a man without his drawers. The closest she'd come was seeing the boys washing up at the well or heading for the outhouse in their drawers.

She tried to remind herself that the man on the bed was just Gordie. Just plain ol' Gordie Lawson, the boy she'd grown up with—the boy she'd fought and played with for the biggest part of her life.

They'd even gone skinny-dipping together many times. But she'd been young, and so had he, and though he'd begun to cast covert glances her way, she'd thought him an addle-brained idiot, who was more of a pest than anything else.

Glancing up, she caught him staring at her and was reminded that many years had passed since then. She was no longer a child, and he was neither an addle-brained idiot nor a pest, regardless of what she'd told him over the past few months.

Bemused at her hesitation, Jim watched the emotions play over her face. Her obvious discomfiture surprised him. It should have brought him a measure of satisfaction, but it didn't. He wanted her steady and confident when she went to work on him. To bolster her spirits, he grinned and rolled over from his side onto his stomach. "Well, Doc," he said, indicating his readiness. Mellowed by the moonshine, he was beginning to feel tranquil and sleepy.

"Yes," she said, gathering her composure. "Of course. Let's get started." She pulled back the sheet, widened her eyes, and blinked several times. With his buttocks completely exposed to her, she felt her cheeks heat. She hesitated several moments, then reached out and touched him. He jerked slightly, then went still beneath her hand. "Looks like you got about seven shots in you," she said quietly.

He stared straight ahead, trying to pretend he didn't feel the warmth of her palm upon his buttock. "Seven less than I thought. That's good."

"They don't look too deep, either."

"That's good, too."

She withdrew her hand and dampened a clean towel with warm water from the kettle. Gently she cleaned the areas surrounding the wounds. "Well . . ." She paused. "Here goes."

He squeezed his eyes shut and waited for the pain to come. It never did. She was surprisingly gentle. He felt the prick of the implement each time it entered his skin, but her hand was cautious and steady, deftly withdrawing the buckshot, causing him very little discomfort. When she dropped the pellets into the pan, they made a twangy, musical *ping*. He counted each note as it sounded.

"You all right?" she asked once, pausing to give him a moment to recover.

"I'm fine." They both knew he would have told her he was fine even if he weren't.

Time passed, and Samson, wanting company, wandered into the bedroom to join them. Sighing greatly, he flopped down on the bare floor beside the bed. Within minutes, Willy came, too, though he tried to be inconspicuous and took the chair by the window, curling into a tight, snug ball.

"You missed a nice program tonight," Megan said, trying to make conversation.

"I had hoped to make it," Jim returned.

"But you had business to attend to." She couldn't keep the gentle note of reproof out of her voice. "Outlaw business."

"Yeah." He didn't bother to deny it.

"You shoulda known you was dealin' with a polecat."

He winced slightly when she extracted another pellet. She dropped it into the pan with another *ping*. "I guess I should have," he agreed amiably, his temper assuaged by the moonshine. "Fletcher was just tryin' to draw me out. He probably figured with most everyone in town attending the program, it would be as good a time as any to get even with me for threatenin' him like I done."

"You threatened him?" Megan stopped her prodding to stare at the back of his head, digesting his words.

"Yep. I chased him down one night over at Merilee's and told him I was on to his thievin'. I told him I'd get him eventually." He laughed a short, derisive laugh. "He got me first, though."

"Oh, hell," Megan huffed, going back to work, wondering about Merilee's, though she didn't voice her curiosity.

"He hardly got you at all. This isn't nothin' but a little ol' spray of buckshot. Now, if he'd shot you dead center in the gut, that's gettin' ya." Despite all she'd said earlier, she felt a need to buffet him, to comfort him, to lift some of the self-recrimination from his voice. He was, after all, only trying to do the right thing in returning Tom Skeets's pigs to him. It was hard to judge a man for attempting to right a wrong, even if he'd used bad judgment in the undertaking of that attempt. "It's just a shame this had to happen on Christmas Eve, for criminy's sake."

Jim laughed. "Don't it figure, though?"

They both went silent, as memories of other Christmas Eves assailed them. They thought of home, of family, of simpler times when they both knew their roles and exactly what they expected of each other. One memory in particular surfaced and burned bright for both of them.

"Bet you're thinking about that gun," Jim said, remembering his own gift of a gun and the huge community Christmas tree that had stood center stage in the Poplar Bluff courthouse, holding his gift within its bountiful limbs. Megan's gun had come from her sister. It had been purchased that magical Christmas Eve and passed on to her by the local Santa, who was none other than her lovable Uncle Chester.

She smiled, remembering. "Yeah, that gun and those britches."

"That was the best Christmas ever."

"It sure was."

"Your sister always was a real special lady."

Megan nodded. "Yes, and she still is." She chuckled, her heart warmed by the memory. "That was the year she finally gave up trying to make me into a lady. That gun and those britches were the best presents she ever could have given me." She paused a minute, thinking. "You know somethin'?" She cocked her head around to draw his gaze.

"We always used to spend Christmas Eve together. Isn't it funny that here we are again?"

He turned his head around to look at her, the memories and the moonshine allowing him temporarily to forget the bare state of his backside. He grinned. "Yeah. Here we are again." His words held a note of tenderness.

"Imagine that," she said softly and laughed. She returned to work, withdrawing the last of the pellets from his buttocks. "There," she said with satisfaction and dropped it into the pan—the final *ping*.

Jim let out a long whoosh of air.

She took the kettle of water and dampened another clean towel, then carefully washed his wounds once again. When she was finished, she dabbed the areas with an antiseptic to prevent infection. The sting of the antiseptic caused him to grit his teeth and inwardly cringe, but he held still for her, knowing his discomfort would soon pass. She covered his wounds with small bandages, hoping they'd stay put throughout the night. When she was finished, she drew the sheet up over him and rose from the bed. "I think you'll live, Jim Lawson."

He turned to her. Their eyes caught and held. "I imagine I will. Thanks, Meg." His voice was innocent of sarcasm, his sleepy eyes earnest and warm.

For a moment she felt confused once again. Her heart tugged toward him, and she thought about some very curious things that made her cheeks grow warm. To hide her emotions, she grinned. "It was my pleasure. Besides, you have a real handsome backside."

He scowled, pretending to be affronted by that statement. She laughed, thankful for the emotional reprieve.

She busied herself with gathering her materials. "I guess you might as well get some sleep. Come mornin' you should be able to ride into town. It's too late to give it a go tonight." She took a quilt from the bottom of the bed and laid it at his side. "This'll keep you warm enough, I s'pose. If you need another, let me know."

He wiggled his eyebrows and teased, "What if I get lonely in here all by myself?"

"Then ask Samson to come up and join you. He's got a real affection for beds."

Jim made an injured face. To get even with her, he asked, "What will the good ladies of Boonville think 'bout the lady veterinarian puttin' the local deputy up for the night?"

She turned and arched an eyebrow. "They'll think I'm a shameless wanton, I s'pose." She cast off the thought with a careless shrug. "I'll be back in a little while to see if you need anything." She left him to put away her supplies and instruments.

By the soft light of the lamp she stood by the stove, absorbing the warmth of the fire. She took off her robe and washed her face and hands. She decided to leave the robe off. It was spotted and soiled from her night's work, and she reasoned that her nightgown, buttoning clear up to her chin, was modest enough. She went to her room and ran a brush through her tangled hair, smoothing it out until it was once again soft and silky. Then she turned down the lamps throughout the house and made her way to the back bedroom to check on Jim before retiring herself.

She found him resting, his head lying limp in the crook of his arm, his face peaceful, his eyes closed. He'd taken off his shirt, and it lay by his side, wrinkled and empty, a lifeless lump of cotton without him in it. She gazed at his back, fascinated, finding it a glorious sight, so broad and bare and totally male.

A wondrous sweep of sensations hit her, making her hunger for something she'd yet to experience, that special something that could bloom and exist only between two people, two lovers. That special something that Johnnie had hinted at that day in her kitchen.

Megan sighed. There was a restlessness within her. It had been there for quite some time now, but lately it was a living thing, taunting, even haunting her.

She moved to the window and listened to the house settle itself into slumber. In another hour it would be Christmas, and she was glad to have someone with her, even if that someone was asleep. Christmas in Poplar Bluff had always been a happy time, a time of feasting and friendship, of love and family. She walked to the window and peered out into the night, watching the snow fall in a slow, lacy curtain that blanketed the pale countryside.

Behind her, Jim opened his eyes and studied her in silence. She looked like a Christmas angel, standing in the snow-washed light of the window, her sunny hair hanging free down her back. She was dressed in a long white night-gown that fell around her, sequestering her in an intimate cloud of material.

He swallowed and held his breath, while all remnants of his earlier irritation with her melted away to nonexistence. "Meg?" he said quietly.

Startled, she spun to face him. "I thought you'd fallen asleep."

"Almost. Not quite." Cautiously he rolled onto his side, pulling the sheet up around him to cover his nakedness. He eased himself into a sitting position and rested his back and shoulders against the walnut headboard.

She walked to the bed, her arms hugging her middle, unknowingly pulling her nightgown taut over her breasts. "You needin' somethin'?" Her face was soft with concern.

"Yeah." He gave her a slow, sleepy grin.

"You thirsty? Hungry?"

"Sorta." He reached for her hand and took it from around her waist, capturing it. "Come here."

He drew her down to sit on the bed, then leaned forward until his face was only inches away from hers.

She didn't move. Neither did he. The house creaked and groaned; the wind whispered a timeless song.

"Merry Christmas, Meggie," he said and brushed his lips across hers.

Surprised, she raised her hands to rest against his bare shoulders. She drew away slightly, her heart beating a frantic rhythm within her chest. She held silent, uncertain as to what to do or what to say. When at last she spoke, she said the only thing she could think of. "Merry Christmas to you, Jim."

The fact that they were alone, that no one could disturb or interrupt them, pressed in upon them both.

A small smile caught at her mouth, lifting away some of her uneasiness. "You back to courtin' me again, Deputy Lawson?"

His hand came up and gently touched her cheek. A grin teased his mouth. "I guess I am," he admitted. "I guess I always have been. Earlier tonight, I was thinkin' 'bout drownin' you come spring. Now that's the last thing on my mind."

Curious, she stared into his sleepy brown eyes. "So . . . what is it you're thinkin' 'bout doin' with me?"

Now it was his turn to be surprised. He was awed afresh by her directness. He decided to be equally direct. "I think you can guess."

"I s'pose I can." Her cheeks took on a pink glow, but her gaze remained steady, unflinching.

His eyes darkened with desire.

Silently they acknowledged that they'd been heading in this direction for a very long time. Long before Megan had come to Boonville. Long before she'd left Poplar Bluff.

The road they'd traveled since childhood had led to this night, and they both accepted that fact without question or false pretenses.

"Have you ever?" She was unable to keep the question to herself. She'd wondered about it so many times.

"Once," he admitted quietly. "Just once. A long time ago."

She turned her head away, hoping to hide the disappointment his words brought. "You always were a randy sort, tryin' to see up my skirt and all."

"Meg . . ." He fingered a lock of her hair, then brushed it away from her face. He caught her chin between his fingers, bringing her gaze back to his. "It wasn't anything like you think. And to tell you the truth, I was drunker than a bald knobber on a Saturday night. I can hardly remember it."

She snorted her disbelief, wanting to believe him.

He tried to make her smile again by saying, "I couldn't see anything under your skirts anyhow with you wearin' those darned britches all the time."

"Say damn, dammit," she reminded him softly, unable to help herself.

He chuckled, then obliged her. "All right, then, damn britches! The only thing I got to see on you were those two little mosquito bites you still had on your chest the last time we went skinny-dippin' together."

She grinned and looked down at her chest. "They aren't mosquito bites any longer."

He swallowed, his smile fading, his gaze focusing where hers was fixed. "No, they aren't."

She never stopped to think of right or wrong, about what Preacher Mosely would say, about what Edith Pribble and her ladies might think. She took his hand and, without saying a word, placed his palm over her breast. The fit was perfect, exquisitely perfect.

They went still as shadows, letting time and memories seep into them and remind them that there was much they did not know about each other. A surge of sweetness swept her, sending her stomach into a swift series of tumbles. Heat flooded him, making his groin tighten and his eyes sink shut.

When he opened his eyes, he lifted his gaze to hers and asked, "Have you ever, Meg?"

"No," she told him honestly, without hesitation, feeling a moment of uncertainty. "No, I never." She was an educated woman, a learned veterinarian, schooled in the ways of nature. She knew more about mating and breeding than most women twice her age, and yet she wondered if somewhere along the way she had missed something important about this mysterious act she was now contemplating.

His heart soared at her words. "I'm glad," he admitted, feeling a powerful surge of possessiveness. His hand left her breast, and with an almost impatient urgency, he pulled her into his embrace, clasping her close to his chest. The thought of her with another man tore at him. He wanted her for himself only. He'd always wanted her for himself. He rested his chin on top of her head. "This thing between us, Meg. It's been a long time comin'. We got things to settle." He waited, afraid she would move away, hoping she wouldn't.

She did move, but it was to press closer, instead of pull away. "Then I think it's time we settled 'em."

He absorbed her words, pondering on the wisdom of such a thing. "Are you sure?" His hand brushed her cheek. He lifted her away, so he could study her face.

"Yes," she said softly, her blue eyes steady. She leaned forward again and kissed him lightly, a mere brushing of her lips across his. The gesture surprised him. She smiled and playfully asked, "Your backside hurtin' too much?"

"What do you think?" he asked.

She reached eight fingertips out to explore the texture of the dark hair that spread across his chest, from shoulder to shoulder, down to where it disappeared beneath the sheet that covered his lap. Her hand ceased its journey when it came in contact with that sheet, reminding her that what lay beneath it was yet unknown to her. She lifted her eyes to his and told him, "You grew up to be real pretty, Jim Lawson."

"You think so, huh?"

Her eyes flashed with tender humor. "I do."

Moved, he drew her close once again and felt her breasts press into his chest. He returned her kiss with one of his own, one that was harder, much more urgent, his tongue delving deep, tasting of the whiskey he'd drunk earlier. He found her lips soft, her mouth warm and welcoming.

"Ahhh, Meg," he whispered against her mouth, turning onto his side and taking her down onto the bed with him. "I've been wonderin' about this for a long time."

"I have, too," she admitted. Her arms came up, and she hugged his neck, relaxing within his embrace, growing limpid and warm and supine. "More times than I care to admit."

He nuzzled her neck, her chin, her mouth, and realized that a woman could be sweet and submissive, eager and fervid all at once. She shivered within his embrace and realized that a mustache on a man was a wonderous thing.

"I like your mustache," she whispered.

His head came up.

She touched his mouth with her fingertip, trailing the curved shape of his mustache. "From the minute I saw you walkin' toward me the day I arrived. I liked it."

Pleased, he chuckled and dipped his head to capture her mouth once again. His tongue trailed her lips as her finger had his mustache. "I wondered if you would. Some women don't."

"This woman does."

Their kiss deepened and grew impatient and turbulent, heated and ardent—a reflection of all they'd waited for, all they'd sought, all they'd yet to learn.

He rolled her onto her back and allowed his hands to cup her breasts, reveling in the adult fullness, in the tautness of her nipples as they hardened beneath her gown.

The clock in the parlor sounded out the hour, ringing in the holy day, and he felt the urge to say once again, "Merry Christmas, Meg."

"Merry Christmas," she returned, her eyes soft with emotion.

He rose above her, and she forgot to breathe, as he tugged the sheet from between them, leaving him naked, exposing him to her gaze. Curious, she looked her fill and simply said, "Oh . . ."

He rolled to his side and propped himself on an elbow, then laid his palm on her stomach, spreading his fingers wide, hipbone to hipbone, over the gentle swell of her warm belly. Closing his fist, he gently grasped a handful of her nightgown and drew it up.

She helped him, lifting her arms, willfully releasing the last barrier between them.

Now it was his turn to say, "Oh. . . . " and silently marvel at the wondrous changes that nature had wrought on her willowy body. "Meg, you really are the prettiest girl in Missouri . . ." He left off, finding his words inadequate in their simplicity.

She reached up and drew him down to where his mouth barely hovered above hers. "You always did tell the tallest tales, Jim Lawson," she teased, hiding her self-consciousness behind a veil of humor.

They kissed then. Some of their kisses were slow and exploratory, others wild and heated—some placed on temples, some placed on shoulders, necks, arms, and breasts.

Hands came searching, learning age-old secrets that only other lovers had discovered.

He pressed down upon her, chest to chest, belly to belly, thigh to thigh, while he adapted a rhythm that rocked her. She clasped him to her, carefully avoiding his bandages, careful not to touch his wounds, gripping the bare skin of his firm backside beneath her hands. She marveled at how different his skin felt, heated and alive, so different from how it had felt just hours ago when she had worked on him.

His hands played over her sides, her breasts, her hips, her thighs, then searched deeper to find that secret place that yearned for him. She didn't move away, but went still beneath his touch, reveling that such amazing things could happen within a woman's body.

She touched him then, finding him hard and warm and smooth; she learned that not only did such blessed things happen within a woman's body, but they happened within a man's, too. He drew away from her and rolled her onto her back, then rose above her. He laced the fingers of both his hands with hers, holding them close to her temples, while he placed a gentle kiss upon her mouth. His dark eyes were open, gazing down into hers. "I don't want it to hurt for you, Meg. They say it can at first."

Touched by his concern, she felt a lump grow in her throat. "It won't," she assured him, offering him a smile. "I can't imagine all of this feelin' so good, to have it end in hurt."

"Aw, Meg," he said, and she knew at that moment that she loved him—that she'd loved him even before she'd come to Boonville, that she'd just needed time to figure it all out, to discover it. . . .

"Meggie," he whispered tenderly, calling her by the name he'd used so often as a boy. "You're somethin' else, you know that?" Unable to wait any longer, he lowered himself upon her, placing his body against her. Gently he pressed forward into her sweetness, joining them as one. She raised her hips in welcome, taking him deep, taking him home. Her breath caught in her throat, and he groaned and forced himself to hold still for a moment.

"Oh, my," she whispered, awed.

"You all right?" he asked, worried.

She nodded, while tears stung. "Oh, yes . . . yes . . ." Her tears were not of pain, but of wonder, of discovery, of completion. This thing they did could never have been learned any other way. It was a precious thing, glorious and beautiful all at once, and she was glad to take the journey with him, her first, her only love. . . .

He rocked upon her, slowly at first, then faster, harder. She clasped him close, feeling his breath beat upon her shoulder, his chest brush her breasts, his heart thud with hers. She gloried in his weight on her body and knew there was no right or wrong to this thing they did. It just was. It simply was.

She whispered his name; he spoke hers. He pressed deep; she arched to receive him. She sighed. He groaned. He thought her lovely; she thought him perfect.

Then came the last shudder, the ripples of feeling, the tarrying tenderness, the billowing of the love that existed between them.

In the following moments, they lay for a long time with his body still deep within hers. Megan sighed, listening to the sounds around her. From outside, the wind moaned. Within the house, the clock ticked in the parlor, and Willy purred while Samson snored. All seemed still, peaceful, hallowed . . . right. *This is what Johnnie meant*, Megan thought. These moments of rightness, of wholeness, this joy at being held and loved by the man whom you loved in return.

Soon Jim stirred and withdrew from her. He rolled onto his side, taking her with him, gathering her close. "I love you, Meggie," he whispered into her hair.

"Do you?" she asked softly, heartened, happy, gladdened by the words.

"I always have. Even when you had nothin' but mosquito bites on your chest."

"Imagine that." She snuggled closer.

"Yeah," he said, his voice sleepy. "Imagine that."

Before he drifted off to sleep, he could have sworn he heard her murmur, "Criminy . . ."

CHAPTER
—⚓⚓ *15* ⚓⚓—

A loud banging woke Megan on Christmas morning.

She lifted her head from Jim's shoulder and tried to place the noise. Rising up on an elbow, she looked down at the man by her side. Memories of the night before assailed her, flooding her heart with tenderness.

The knock sounded again, more insistent this time, bringing her thoughts back to the present.

Jim woke, also. His eyelids parted slowly. He focused his eyes on her and smiled, a sleepy, satisfied smile that made her grow warm and limpid once again. "Mornin'," he said, his voice husky. He pulled her down on top of him and kissed her, running his mustache and tongue gently over her mouth.

"Mornin'," she returned, brushing a lock of his hair back from his forehead.

Bang! Bang! Bang!

"We got company," she said softly, though she didn't get up.

"Maybe they'll go away." Jim's hands rode her hips, clasping her close.

Bang! Bang! Bang!

Jim groaned his frustration, and Megan rolled off him, scrambling to the edge of the bed. Her feet hit the cold floor, making her shiver. She grabbed her nightgown and whipped it over her head, enveloping herself in a sheath of white modesty, erasing Jim's view of her shapely backside. She glanced over her shoulder at him. "You'd better get your drawers on. Your britches, too."

He swung his legs over the bed. He winced at the soreness that reminded him of the reason he'd been in her home in the first place.

Bang! Bang! Bang!

"All right! I'm comin'!" She hurried from the room and down the hall to greet her visitors.

Samson followed her to the kitchen door and stood at her side, wagging his tail and whimpering with excitement.

She unlatched the door and threw it open to view a wintry background of frosted fields and snow-dusted tree limbs.

And her two brothers.

They stood before her, their brows locked into matching frowns of confusion. They looked like twin Santa Clauses, their red stocking caps pulled low over their ears, their bulky coat-shrouded shoulders powdered with snow.

Luke's arms were loaded with gifts, while Matthew held the trunk of a large fluffy evergreen.

"What the Sam Hill took ya so long?" Matthew asked, crowding his brother out of the way so he could force his way through the door first. He hauled the tree into the kitchen, bringing with him a thin trail of snow.

Megan threw her arms around his neck and hugged him till he coughed. She ignored his question. "I kinda thought you'd come last night."

Luke followed his brother into the house. "Aw, we wanted to, but we had to bring presents, and Johnnie and

Ellie wanted to send vittles. We had to wait till they had everything ready."

"Women!" Matthew snorted and made a disgusted face, as if the entire gender were solely responsible for muddling up everything on the earth.

"Yeah, women!" Luke agreed, mimicking his brother with a disgusted frown of his own.

A shuffle to their right drew their attention. Jim entered the kitchen, adopting a half grin of welcome. "Hey, Matt! Hey, Luke!" he called in greeting. He wore his britches, but his feet and chest were bare.

Matthew and Luke exchanged baffled looks. Matt drew the first conclusion. His eyebrows met in an arch in the middle of his forehead. Luke's eyes widened. Their gazes went from Jim to Megan, then back to Jim again.

Megan blushed. "Now, boys . . ."

"What the hell are ya doing here this goddamn early?" Matt asked Jim. Friend or no friend, Jim Lawson had no business in his little sister's house in the early mornin' hours struttin' around like a randy bull in only his britches. Nosiree, by God!

"Yeah!" Luke dropped the gifts on the floor, as understanding dawned. He puffed out his chest, ready to do battle for his sister's honor, though the bulky coat he wore would hamper his efforts greatly.

Jim lifted his palms in entreaty. "We didn't do anything we're ashamed of, Matt. You both know how I feel about Meg."

Matthew scowled. "Yeah, that's what's got me worried."

Luke lumbered toward Jim. "You're gonna do right by 'er, by God, friend or no friend, 'specially after you spent the night doin'—"

Matthew broke Luke's sentence off and stabbed a finger at his little sister. "You're gittin' hitched!"

"Yeah!" Luke poked a finger at Jim. "An' you are, too!"

Megan lifted her stubborn chin. "I'm not gettin' hitched!" she hollered, putting herself between Jim and the boys, irritated that they were deciding her future without any regard for her feelings.

Stumped by her answer, Jim decided to intervene. "Yes, we are!"

She turned on him. "No, we aren't!"

"Why not?"

Megan thought about a minute. "'Cause I'm not ready yet!"

Jim frowned, confused. "What do you mean you're not ready?"

"Just what I said. I'm not ready. You haven't even courted me proper yet."

His mouth fell open. Last night had far surpassed any courtin' he'd ever done. "What do you think I've been doin' these past months when I came out for a visit?"

She gave him a disbelieving glare. "You came out to see the boys!"

"I came to see you!"

"Well," she said and thought a minute. "You haven't even asked me to marry you!"

Silence, then, "All right. I'm askin' ya."

"Not that way." She huffed and plunked her hands on her hips.

Jim's face got red. He lifted his hands at his sides. "What the hell do you want?"

Megan poked her nose into the air. "Somethin' nice! I want you to ask me like you mean it."

Matthew interrupted their argument by saying, "You're gittin' hitched whether he means it or not. An'," he added, "we don't care whether you're ready or not!"

"Yeah!" Luke said, "'specially after what you been doin'!"

She turned on her brothers like a spooked rattler and decided to fix them good for their interference. "What the hell do you think we've been doin'?"

Both men blushed as red as the wool caps that hugged their heads. Embarrassed into silence, they shuffled their feet and hedged.

"I'll tell you what we've been doin'!" She arched an eyebrow, stalking them, enjoying their discomfort.

"Now, Meg . . ." Matthew began, lifting his palms, "nice women don't talk 'bout those things—"

"Oh, the hell they don't!" she interrupted him. "What do you know about what women talk about! I'm not talkin' 'bout them. I'm talkin' bout me and him and why he's here in the first place." She angled Jim a glance that said she thought him as brainless as her brothers. "I spent the first half of the night takin' buckshot outta his fool hide!" She carefully left out an explanation of what they'd done the other half of the night and said to Jim, "Show 'em!"

Dumbfounded, Jim's mouth dropped open. "No!" he finally managed.

"Go on." She waved a hand at him in an impatient circle. "Show 'em 'fore they break your bones and force me into marryin' a corpse!"

Jim's mouth snapped shut. He frowned. He wasn't baring his backside for them or anyone else! Even if they did try to break his bones! "No!" he shouted and crossed his arms over his chest.

"You show 'em, or I won't ever marry you!"

"Yes, you will!"

"The hell I will!" She snorted her disgust and huffed off to the table, where she'd placed the pan that held the buckshot. "Here!" she said, hauling it over to her brothers and shoving it under their noses. "See?"

The brothers exchanged confused glances once again.

"Now aren't you two ashamed of yourselves?"

They shuffled their feet again and lifted grins of chagrin to both her and Jim. "Sorry," they said as one.

Jim was so mad he could have throttled her. Her ability to manipulate her brothers was a well-known fact and went back to her days in the cradle. The only person she had never been able to pull one over on was Johnnie. It angered and hurt him that she had fooled her brothers into believing that they were wrong in their assumption of what had happened between them last night. He wasn't ashamed of what they'd done, but apparently she was.

He loved her.

And he was pretty sure she loved him.

That meant it was time for a wedding as far as he was concerned. But there she stood, sayin' she wasn't ready, that they hadn't even courted proper yet, when just last night she had been ready as could be. *Well, fine!* he thought, turning on his heel. *See if you'll ever get another offer from me!*

He stormed off to the bedroom, whipped his shirt from the bed, pulled it on, jammed his feet into his socks, hauled on his boots, then stomped back out to where the three siblings waited. He scowled his meanest at all of them, then grabbed his coat from the peg on the wall. Shrugging into it, he yanked the door open, turned to them, and barked, "Merry Christmas!" then slammed the door behind him.

He stalked across the porch and down the steps, only to spin around two seconds later and stomp back up to her door. He threw it open without knocking, his scowl murderous, and informed Meg, "An' I won't be back till you're ready to get married!" He whirled, leaving the door open, and clumped off toward the barn, his ass hurting, reminding him that he had more than one score to settle.

Flabbergasted, Megan stared at the open door, her jaw slack. After a few seconds her senses returned, and her temper followed right behind. She huffed after him, her arms swinging ferociously. Reaching the door, she stuck her head out and yelled, "Well, then, you'll never be back, 'cause I ain't never marryin' you, Gordie Lawson. I wouldn't marry you if you were the last man on this earth!"

"Fine!" he said, not bothering to turn around.

"Fine!" she returned and slammed the door so hard it vibrated. She spun and glowered at her brothers, then swept past them to go sulk in her bedroom.

"Well," Luke said, raising his eyebrows, offended by Jim's rude departure and Megan's bad temper. "What the hell do ya think got into them?"

Matthew picked up a day-old biscuit from a plate on the table. Taking careful aim, he pinged it off his brother's forehead.

"Ouch!" Luke flinched and sent Matt an injured look.

"Probably all riled up 'cause you accused him of ruinin' our Meg, and her of bein' ruined." Matthew's expression was one of total innocence.

"Me!" Luke slapped a palm to his chest, his forehead reddening. "You're the one who started all this shit—"

"The hell I did. . . ."

In the days after Christmas Megan stewed.

Jim didn't come back, and she didn't seek him out. Her brothers stayed on. Clarence had insisted they watch after Meg till time for spring planting, so they did, and gladly.

It irritated Megan that Jim, along with her brothers, had tried to bully her into a wedding. Yet, as she lay in her bed at night, alone and lonely, she knew a wedding was exactly what she wanted, even if she wasn't ready to admit it. She loved Jim Lawson, but she'd be damned if she'd admit it till he came back and apologized to her for walking out on her like he'd done.

But a week passed, then two, and he didn't come. She began to worry that maybe he was seeing someone else.

Megan knew it wasn't Clarissa. Clarissa had told her so herself, that she had a special feeling for someone else. Maybe, Megan thought, Jim was seeing someone at Merilee's.

Even though she liked Merilee and her girls, the thought of Jim with another made her blood boil.

January turned nasty. It rained, it sleeted, it snowed, and the days dragged on.

On one such dreary day, Henry Holloway brought out the pup he'd promised Megan. Anxious for company, she greeted Henry with a smile and snuggled the dog against her breast. He was a small, black, furry critter not bigger than the palm of her hand. He blinked and hiccuped often, and observed his surroundings calmly, as though he needed time to decide whether he liked his new home or not.

Megan loved him. She knew Danny would adore him. She could hardly wait to give him the dog.

Danny finally came to visit on a chilly Thursday afternoon during the third week of January.

She opened the door to find him and Theo standing on her porch. Romeo and Juliet were snorting noisily at the boys' feet. The pigs were getting big, and Megan let them have the run of the small farm. They'd taken to greeting all visitors and did a sight better job of watchdogging than Samson ever thought of doing.

"Well, howdy, boys!"

"Hello, Megan," Danny said.

"Hello, Doctor," Theo said.

"Come on in." She stepped back to let them enter. "You can call me Megan, too, if you want, Theo." She closed the door behind them.

Theo blushed, pleased by the offer, but decided he'd call her Doctor just the same.

"So . . ." She tipped her head and nailed Danny with a knowing gaze. "You been in school?"

"Yep." He nodded, fidgeting.

"How 'bout you, Theo?"

Theo nodded.

"Good." Megan approved. "School's important even though you don't think it is. Someday you'll understand." She changed the subject by asking Theo, "How's your new baby sister?"

"She's noisy." Theo wasn't impressed by babies.

Megan chuckled. "I imagine she is."

Danny wondered if it would be bad manners to remind her of the gift she'd promised him. He was so excited he could hardly contain himself. The collar she had given him had kept him awake more than one night in hopeful anticipation. At this very minute it was burning a hole in his pocket.

"Your pa and ma know where you are?" she asked both boys.

"Uh-huh," they said, their heads bobbing up and down.

Danny said, "I asked Mother if I could come out and visit. She said I could if I didn't stay too long. She said I could come fishing with you in the spring, too, as long as I didn't play hooky from school."

Well, Megan thought to herself, *how 'bout that.* She remembered the expression on Lucy Kincaid's face the night they'd taken Danny home. Lucy had wanted to take up for her son, but hadn't. Maybe she'd begun to do so in her own way.

A whimper came from the far corner of the room, drawing her attention. Each boy's head whipped toward the sound. Megan smiled. "What's this?" She walked across the room and bent over a small wooden box. She reached down and picked something up. It grunted noisily. She turned to the boys.

Danny's green eyes lit with expectation.

"Come here, Danny," Megan said.

He did.

She held out the dark furry ball. "I think this little fella belongs to you. He's the something else that goes with the collar."

Slowly Danny reached out to accept the pup. "Wow," he whispered reverently. He turned to his friend. "Look, Theo! A dog! A real dog!"

Theo smiled and patted the dog's silky head. "Yeah, he's great," he agreed politely. Theo had plenty of dogs, so he couldn't quite figure out Danny's excitement over one little ol' puppy. But he figured he'd pretend just the same.

"Wow!" Danny exclaimed again. "I just can't believe it! My own dog!"

"What are you gonna name him?" Theo asked.

Danny's face screwed up thoughtfully. After a short moment, his expression brightened, and his eyes got big. "I know. I'll call him Cody. After Buffalo Bill! I've read all about him!" He sobered and looked up at Megan. "Is that all right with you?"

Megan laughed. "He's yours. You can call him anything you want." Her expression sobered. "Now, you listen. If your folks don't want you to keep him at home, that's all right. You can keep him here with me."

Danny nodded. "All right."

She turned to Theo, not wanting to leave him out. "Mr. Holloway has plenty of pups, if you're thinkin' you might like one."

Theo shook his head and smiled. "No, thanks. My ma would skin me. She says we got too many critters to feed as it is."

"Wow!" Danny said again. "Wait till Amy sees him! She'll just shit!"

Megan blanched. "Why, Daniel!"

Daniel blushed hotly. "Whoops. Pardon me. I slipped."

"I guess you did!"

Matthew and Luke came down the hall. "Aw, take it easy on the boy, Meg," Matthew told her. "You said worse at his age."

The boys' faces brightened. They'd grown real fond of the Hawkins brothers. They were bawdy, brazen, and bold! Danny's parents said they were a couple of country bumpkins. Danny didn't exactly know what a "bumpkin" was, but after getting to know Matthew and Luke, he thought he'd like to be one.

Theo's folks said the Hawkins brothers were just a couple of good ol' boys, who were always ready to help out a neighbor, just like Megan was. They were farm folk, too. Practically kin.

Megan shot Matthew a look of disapproval. "You don't need to tell him that. It isn't proper to allow a young'un to take on so."

Luke grinned, remembering her younger days. "Come on, fellas," Luke said. "Let's go outside and do man stuff. I'll teach ya how to spit proper."

"Yeah!" Theo said, excited.

"Yeah!" Daniel repeated, still clutching his puppy.

Luke led them out the door and onto the porch. "Now, a real man oughta be able to spit from here to that outhouse." He pointed toward his destination. "Watch." He made a horrible sound from down deep in his throat, then expelled a powerful shot out toward the small building. It plopped in the snow just inches from the outhouse.

The two young boys whooped their approval.

Matthew joined them on the porch. "Oh, hell. That ain't nothin'. Watch this." Mimicking his brother's actions, Matthew sent a big glob catapulting off into the air, besting his brother's attempt by nearly two feet.

The boys whooped even louder.

Luke scowled. "That's jist a lucky shot!" He got ready to give it another go.

Megan watched from the window, unable to keep from smiling, especially when the boys started to practice hitting the outhouse on their own. She wondered what it would be like to have sons like Danny and Theo, and maybe even a pretty little girl like Amy Applegate. Would they look like her or Jim or both of them? She never stopped to think that the father of her children might be anyone other than Jim.

It wouldn't have seemed fitting.

February brought a brief respite from the cold temperatures, but it lasted only long enough to make folks wish for spring; then it turned cold again, and everyone complained and hurried back to their stoves to keep warm.

Still Jim stayed away. And Megan fumed. But every bit as stubborn as he, she refused to seek him out. She avoided sitting anywhere near him in church, and averted her eyes when she passed him in the street.

The boys said she had a head like a rock: hard.

Habel and Clarissa said she was just plain silly.

Both of her friends had figured out long ago that Jim and Megan belonged together. They just couldn't understand what all the fuss was about. In fact, most of Boonville had figured out there was something funny going on between the deputy and the lady veterinarian. The spark that existed between them had been obvious clear back on the day of the pie and box supper. They were courting, most folks said, but it was a strange sort of courtship, often bordering on battle.

Little did everyone know that the battle had been brewing between the two for quite some time. Jim refused to be Megan's obedient puppy for the rest of his life, and Megan had never been obedient for any of her life and didn't intend to begin now.

They were at a deadlock.

Things were about to change, however.

On one bright February morning, Megan rose and went out to the kitchen. She let Samson outside, then went about the house performing the tasks she did every morning. Quite suddenly her stomach roiled, and her head spun. She lowered herself into a chair at the kitchen table and waited for the dizziness to pass. She was still sitting there, looking whiter than a frog's belly, when the boys came in to join her.

Luke took one look at her and said, "Woo-ee, Meg, yew look sicker than a barn full of grass-gorgin' cows."

Matthew's brow knotted in concern. "What's wrong, Meggie? You eat somethin' bad?"

Megan took a deep breath, forced a smile, and dabbed the perspiration from her forehead. "No. Must be a touch of somethin' I picked up. I stopped at the schoolhouse the other day 'cause I saw Theo out in the yard, and I ended up playin' a game of tug-of-war. I got dragged through a pile of snow and got wet, clear through to my drawers. I must have taken a chill."

Luke took the coffeepot from the cookstove, poured her a cup, and placed it down on the table in front of her. "Well, if you don't feel better by tomorrow, you go on into town an' see the doctor."

"I'll be fine," Megan assured him, feeling better already. "Don't you two be frettin' after me, now."

And she did feel better—until she went out to the barn to feed Jesse later that morning. Her angry bellow could easily have reached Kansas City. Matthew came running from the house, shotgun in hand. Luke came running from the outhouse, his suspenders flopping in loops at his knees. Megan came storming from the barn, pitchfork in hand.

"What's wrong, Meg?" Matthew asked.

"Do I gotta bean somebody?" Luke asked. His eyes swept the area for the varmint who'd upset his sister.

"That goddamned, no-good peckerhead stole my pigs and my Jesse, too!" Megan brushed past them without giving them a glance. "I'm gonna run this pitchfork clear up his ass!" She ran for the house, grabbed her six-shooter, shoved it down into the front of her britches, and took off for the barn again, intent on saddling up one of her brothers' horses. "You wait till I get my hands on that Jim Lawson," Megan muttered to herself. "This is all his fault anyway."

Meanwhile, Matthew and Luke looked on, their faces twin masks of confusion.

"Who's the peckerhead?" Luke asked, blinking.

"Hell if I know," Matthew answered.

"Think we oughta stop 'er?"

Matthew shrugged. "Naw. I think we should have some vittles first. I'm hungry as a grizzly. Breakfast was kinda sparse, don't ya think?" He rubbed his stomach meaningfully.

Luke brightened immediately. "Yeah. Our Meg shore ain't much of a cook. I feel real sorry for Jim. He's liable to starve to death. He'll be skinnier than Hurley after a year o' living with her."

"Let's eat first," Matthew decided. "We can catch up with her later."

"Yeah. Let's eat first."

For once they were in agreement. They went back into the house.

Two seconds later, Megan, astride Matthew's big chestnut gelding, bolted out of the barn and rode down Rocheport Road, hell-bent past Mrs. Pribble's pretty house and on into Boonville, burning with the hunger for revenge, her pitchfork still clutched in one hand.

When she reached the jail, her feet were on the ground before her horse even came to a complete stop. She flew up the stairs, threw open the door, and stared, wild-eyed and winded, looking like some demented thing that had been caged for far too long.

Jim sat with his chair tipped back, the heels of his boots resting on the edge of his desk. He had been just about to nod off for his afternoon nap when the door banged open and his plans were obliterated.

Seeing her, he snapped right to, his feet hitting the floor with a thump.

She aimed the pitchfork at him and bellowed, "That goddamned polecat Fletcher stole my pigs and my horse!"

Jim stood. Understanding immediately dawned. He lifted his palms in an attempt to quiet her. "Now, Meg, calm down."

"Calm down!" Her chin jutted forward. "I'll calm down, all right!"

"If you give me a chance, I'll take care of this."

"The hell you will! If you had taken care of that varmint, he wouldn't've got Romeo and Juliet or Jesse."

"Will you give me a chance—"

"Did you get Tom's pigs back?" She fired the question at him and waited, her foot tapping.

"Well . . . no, not yet!"

"Ha! See!"

"I haven't hardly had the chance."

"Seems to me that's all you keep sayin'. You've had plenty of chances far as I'm concerned with just about everything." While she was at it, she thought she'd add, "I've given you a chance for nigh onto two months now, Deputy, an' you haven't even darkened my doorstep to see how I'm gettin' on! I coulda been robbed blind by now, and what would you know 'bout it?"

Jim's jaw stiffened. He knew how she was gettin' on. She was gettin' on just fine. He'd asked after her constantly—every time he saw her brothers or Clarissa or Habel.

But he'd have rather spent a day confessing his most corrupt sins to Preacher Mosely than confess his loneliness to this hard-hearted woman. "I told you I'd be back when you were ready to get married."

She narrowed her eyes and mashed her lips together flatter than two sheets of pressed paper. "Well, I ain't!"

"Fine!" His face heated, and he stabbed a finger in her direction. "Now, you get on home where you belong, Meg Hawkins. Don't you make me lock you up again. I will an' I mean it!"

She aimed the pitchfork at his belly. "I wouldn't try it if I were you! I'm gonna get that varmint, and when I do, he's gonna be wishin' he'd stolen anybody's animals but mine."

With that said, she whirled and stormed out the door.

Jim was right behind her. "Listen here. You can't go off crazy like this."

"I can do anything I goddamn well please, Jim Lawson!"

She stabbed her pitchfork into the hard ground and swung up onto her horse. "There. You can have the pitchfork," she said. "I think I'm gonna shoot him instead." She whipped out her six-shooter, spun it, and grinned wickedly.

Jim wanted to clobber her. Instead he scowled and said, "You'll have to find him first. He's mine, and I intend to get him." He knew where Fletcher spent most of his days and nights. Standing there, looking up into Megan's stubborn face, it never occurred to him that he'd given her that information, also.

"Oh, I can find 'im." She gave the gelding a sharp kick. "By damn, you can count on it!"

CHAPTER
16

"You can't be serious!" Habel's eyes nearly left her skull.

"Oh, yes I can," Megan answered, handing her a bright yellow dress decorated with a frilly trim of pale yellow feathers. She turned to Clarissa and tossed a short, ruffled, red dress in her direction. Clarissa caught the dress and stood staring at the garish garment, flabbergasted.

"Get dressed!" Megan ordered and whirled back toward the floor-length mirror that graced the bedroom she'd once let from Habel.

Baffled, Clarissa lifted her gaze to Megan's. "Where did you get these dresses?"

"At Merilee's," Megan answered easily.

Habel teetered and placed a palm above her heart. "Oh, sweet Jesus . . ."

Clarissa's usually sweet expression turned skeptical. "You can't tell me you just walked up to her door and asked for these dresses."

"Yep!" Megan met her eyes in the mirror and continued applying the paint to her face. "That's exactly what I did. We understand each other, me and Merilee. I like her, and she likes me. After I told her what I wanted the dresses for, she not only gave me the dresses, she gave me this face paint, too."

"Oh, dear Lord . . ." Habel wilted onto the bed, her heart palpitating.

Confused, Clarissa asked, "What do you expect us to do once we put them on?"

"I expect you to go with me to Merilee's. I got a polecat to trap, and I'm gonna need your help."

Habel blanched.

Clarissa's mouth bore a stubborn expression. "Ooooh no . . . I might tromp through fields looking for your dog, but I'm not going into that place. Friend or no friend, I'm not going, and that's all there is to it. I like Merilee, too. I always did think Mrs. Pribble and her ladies were too hard on her. But her place is still an immoral establishment for women like us to frequent!"

Habel's head bobbed in agreement. "Yes, immoral!"

"Oh, hell!" Megan spun and faced them in only her brief white undergarments. She plunked her hands on her hips and looked disgusted. "We're not frequentin' it. We're just visitin', sorta. An' prancin' around in these dresses isn't any more immoral than swappin' a few kisses with your favorite beau at a Sunday picnic. Besides, Merilee says she don't allow evil doin's in her place, other than gamblin' and dancin', and I believe her." She took the bright blue dress from where she'd draped it over the back of a chair and pulled it over her head, shimmying it down over her breasts. The skirt belled outward, stopping well above her knees. After smoothing everything into place, Megan shook out a pair of stockings and drew them up over her legs, securing them with garters mid-thigh. Both of the other women watched in silence, their jaws dropping open in astonishment. "Now, hurry up," Megan said, throwing them an impatient glance. "We still have to paint your faces."

*   *   *

In less than two hours they stood at the back door of Merilee's big yellow house, waiting for their knock to be answered. Dusk had fallen, and the moon glowed bright against the starry February sky.

Piano music, tempered with laughter and voices, seeped out from the house to greet them. Fighting the urge to turn tail and run, Habel and Clarissa exchanged worried glances behind Megan's back, while Megan tapped out an impatient rhythm with her high-heeled shoe.

They were quite a sight, these three women who had no experience frequenting such places. Megan looked determined, Clarissa wary, Habel terrified.

They'd stolen down the rear staircase of Habel's house like three shady thieves, slipping out the gate and cutting across backyards so no one could see them. They'd arrived at Merilee's without mishap. Now they stood waiting. . . .

Merilee answered the door on the second knock and gestured them in. "Hello, ladies. I've been expecting you."

"Is he here?" Megan asked hopefully.

Merilee smiled. "But of course. It's Saturday night, isn't it?"

It was late afternoon when Jim met Matthew and Luke on the road out to Megan's place. Seeing them riding toward him, he reined in his horse and waited. He'd stewed all afternoon before deciding to go after her, trying to figure out how to deal with her and Fletcher at the same time.

He didn't blame her for being riled about her horse and pigs. But he knew what Fletcher was doing. He was trying to force his hand by taking Megan's animals. Fletcher knew that the connection between him and Megan and her brothers was a powerful one, and he probably figured he'd play on it.

"Hey, Matt, Luke," Jim said when they drew abreast of him.

"Hey, Jim," both men returned.

"I was just on my way out to see you boys. And Megan," he added.

"We're lookin' for her ourselves," Matt said. "She lit out late this mornin', madder than a grizzly after her young, hollerin' somethin' about gittin' some peckerhead. We ain't seen 'er since. We figured we'd best git lookin' for her, 'fore she hurts herself or somebody else."

"She never came home?" Jim felt his gut tighten and knot.

Both men shook their heads.

Jim looked worried, then disgusted. "Well, I'd like to know where the hell she went, then."

Luke said, "Maybe she went to see Clarissa or Habel."

"Maybe," Jim said, but he looked doubtful. "Let's take a ride over and see."

They didn't find Megan at Clarissa's—they didn't even find Clarissa at Clarissa's. Her mother said she had left with Megan hours ago. The men went to Habel's next. Habel's boarders said the three had disappeared upstairs sometime during early afternoon. No one had seen them come back down.

Jim took the stairs two at a time. "Meg!" he called, rushing down the hall, fighting a stab of panic. "Meg, you come out here right now. I want to talk to you!"

Silence greeted him. Matt and Luke followed at his heels.

"Clarissa!" Luke yelled.

"Where ya at, Habel, honey?" Matthew called out, peeking in doors as he passed.

Jim passed by an open door at the end of the hallway. He stopped dead, then quickly backtracked, his attention drawn by the haphazard condition of the room. He stalked in and propped his hands on his hips, studying the mess around him. Matthew and Luke joined him, their brows drawn tight in bewilderment.

Jim recognized the britches and shirt that lay across the bed. They were Megan's. Also cast across the bed were two dresses, one especially tiny one. It couldn't have belonged to anyone other than Habel. He walked to the bureau, picked up a pot of bright red face paint, and turned it over in his hand. His mind churned out the possibilities.

A startling thought struck him. He spun to face the brothers. "They're at Merilee's."

"Merilee's?" Matt said, confused.

Luke sent Jim a look of bald surprise. "You mean that gamblin' house down by the river that has all them pretty dancin' girls?"

"That's the one," Jim said.

"How'd you know 'bout that?" Matthew asked.

Luke blushed guiltily.

Matthew's eyes got big. "You been there, ain't you? Without me!"

"Well, yeah," Luke said, then turned to Jim. "Clarissa wouldn't go in a place like that."

"Neither would Habel," Matthew put in.

"But Megan would," Jim told them. "And she could talk a horse into believing he was a donkey if she wanted to bad enough."

Her brothers couldn't argue with that statement.

"What would they be doin' there?" Matthew asked.

"Huntin'." Jim spun toward the door. Over his shoulder he said, "An' probably gettin' themselves into one heap of trouble."

Megan stood on the stage, searching the assemblage of male faces for Maxwell Fletcher's. It was a busy night at Merilee's, as most Saturday evenings were. Though most of her patrons were peaceable, nonviolent sorts, only wanting to feast their eyes on the ladies for a little while, drink a little whiskey, and play a few hands of cards, there were times such as tonight when some of the surlier sorts came in off the riverboats.

After a few minutes Megan found Fletcher. He was seated at a table with a small group of his cronies. She smiled and winked in his direction, hoping to catch his attention. She did. He perked and straightened in his chair, flattered. He smoothed his hair, preening like a cock courting a chicken. He lifted his glass in silent acknowledgment. She tipped her head coquettishly and wiggled her fingers, letting him know she was interested.

He didn't recognize her, and Megan knew it. Gussied up as she was, she hardly recognized herself or either of her two friends.

On Megan's right, looking quite seductive and beautiful in her scarlet dress, Clarissa eyed the crowd of men anxiously, while Habel, on Megan's left, quaked in her shoes, the feathers on her dress visibly trembling.

The three were flanked on each side by Merilee's girls, who'd already been instructed to show the ladies what to do. Megan looked over Habel's head to Libby Logan and said, "I guess we're ready."

Libby grinned. "Good. We're gonna do the cancan."

"What's the cancan?"

"A dance. A French dance."

Clarissa looked reluctant. "What if we can't do it?"

Libby smiled tolerantly and waved a hand. "Hell, anybody can do the cancan, honey. Just do what I do!"

"Oh, Meg," Habel groaned, "it sounds terribly wicked."

Amused, Libby winked. "It is."

Megan grinned. "Then we'll give it a go."

Libby nodded and sent the piano player a wordless message, and he launched into a lively tune. To Habel and Clarissa's horror, Libby and the other three girls immediately flipped up the fronts of their ruffled dresses and waved them in the air, back and forth, exposing their garters and ruffled undergarments to the men seated below.

The men applauded their approval. Some of the rowdier ones howled and whistled.

After several more stanzas of skirt-waving, Libby and the other dancers linked arms and kicked their stocking-clad legs high into the air, keeping time to the bawdy tune the piano player banged out on his piano.

Megan mimicked their actions as best she could.

Habel, however, froze stiffer than a mouse facing a pack of cats. She looked for all the world as if she'd swoon dead away at any moment.

Clarissa, too, balked, and stood stiff and staring.

With the front of her dress in the air, Megan looked at her two companions and yelled, "Come on, you two!"

Habel's cheeks flared.

"Come on!" Megan hollered again. "Habel, do you want to be invisible all your life?"

Habel cast her a glance that said yes. But her mouth whispered a silent, "No . . ."

"Well, then . . ."

Stung, Habel reluctantly lifted her dress a mere inch and tried to move her feet.

Watching her, Clarissa decided to give it a go, but she did little better. Her face was every bit as red as Habel's, her movements just as stiff.

"Oh, come on, Clarissa!" Megan begged. "Put some life into it! Mr. Shakespeare woulda never written a word about Romeo and Juliet if he'd went at it with as much spunk as you're doin'." She flashed the crowd a bright smile and kicked her legs higher.

The crowd roared. Some of the men stood and clapped.

The mention of Shakespeare's name got Clarissa's attention. Megan was right, she thought. One had to have spunk.

She swallowed her embarrassment and lifted her skirt.

The men applauded and cheered. Some whooped their approval.

From the back of the room Sam Sweeney, drunk as a traveling revivalist after a busy Sunday night, eyed the little yellow canary on the stage. "Gawd-dang, she's purty," he said to no one in particular. "Looks jist like a gal I know." He weaved his way through the tables toward the front of the room to get a better look.

Megan glanced over at Clarissa. Over the ribald laughter and the sounds of the piano music, she yelled, "Isn't this fun?"

Clarissa had begun to relax, but still she wouldn't have called what they were doing fun. Challenging, maybe. But fun? No. She was a performer at heart, however, and she realized she had the ability to pull off this fiasco if she really wanted to. She gave Megan a confident smile and put her best effort into showing Merilee's girls she was quite a kicker in her own right.

Megan shot Habel a worried glance. "Come on, Habel! Get with it! You can do it. It's just like cussin'. It gets easier the more you do it. It just takes practice!"

Habel thought about that, smiled weakly, and nearly tripped over her feet as she lifted them, one at a time, into the air.

Jim, Matthew, and Luke came through the gaping double doors. They swept the crowd with their eyes, then looked to the stage at the front of the room.

Luke saw them first. "There!" He pointed toward the stage, his eyes nearly bugging out of his skull. "If that don't beat all! Ain't that Meg up there with Clarissa and Habel?"

Each of the three women flipped up the front of her skirt. Matthew looked as if he'd been struck. "Gawddang! Look at 'em!"

Furious, Jim's face turned purple. "Meg!" he yelled so loud his voice could be heard over the din. "You get the hell down off that stage this minute, you hear me? Or I'm comin' up after you!"

Megan's steps faltered. She searched the room, trying to locate the voice. When she did, anger lit within her. What the hell did he want now? He was gonna mess up her plans, for sure. Vexed, she turned her back to him and flipped up her skirt, exposing her ruffled bottom. Mimicking every movement she made, Habel and Clarissa followed suit without giving it a second thought.

The men roared and applauded.

Jim, Matthew, and Luke turned redder than Clarissa's dress.

Jim's left eye took to twitching. He decided at that moment that drowning Megan was the only recourse he had if he wished to live out a peaceful life. He didn't think he'd wait till spring.

The brothers' mouths fell open. Their heads jutted forward.

Appalled, Luke blinked and pointed toward the stage. He glanced from Jim to Matthew. His mouth worked soundlessly for a moment. "Di-di-did you see what they did?"

"'Course we did," Matthew said, shocked by the indecent actions of his sister and her companions. "We're standin' right here next to ya, ain't we?" He went silent a second, his temper building. "We-e-l-l-l, they ain't gonna git away with showin' off their bottoms like that. Nosiree, by God!" He shot off toward the stage, barreling his way through the crowd, creating a path for the other two to follow. "Habel," he ordered, "you git down off that stage, goddammit! That ain't no place for a decent woman!"

Seeing Matthew's blond head and wide shoulders lumbering toward her, Habel moaned her mortification, and her eyes fluttered as she fought to retain consciousness.

"Yeah!" Luke bellowed, right behind him. "What in tarnation are ya doin' up there, Clarissa?"

Clarissa's eyes got big. Her heart lodged in her throat.

Merilee's girls' steps faltered. They frowned their annoyance at the interruption of their performance, while Megan, Clarissa, and Habel tried their hardest to ignore the three men.

A low rumble of irritation rippled through the crowd. The three newcomers were ruining the show and disturbing the ladies, and the riverboaters didn't like it one bit.

"Shut the hell up!" someone yelled and spit a long stream of tobacco juice in their direction. It hit Jim in the shoulder, leaving a dark, ugly stain on his shirt.

"Yeah, leave the ladies alone!" another barked.

"Go back where you came from!" someone else hollered.

Matthew turned on the crowd, his blue eyes bright with fury. His gaze swept the throng for the owners of the voices. "Ya watch who yer talkin' to! That's my sister up there. And that," he yelled and pointed toward Habel, "is my woman!"

My woman! The words hit Habel with force, nearly knocking her off the stage.

"Oh, yeah?" A big man, with a chest shaped like a barrel, rose from his chair. "Who the hell does that make you? King Shit?"

Matthew stopped.

Luke did, too.

The piano music tinkled into silence. The crowd hushed.

Jim felt a prickle of apprehension claw its way up the back of his neck, while tension enveloped the room like a storm cloud ready to release a torrent of lightning bolts. He decided he'd better calm things down and fast. "Now, wait a minute, fellas." He raised his palms in a gesture of peace. "We ain't here to disturb your fun. We just want the three ladies, that's all. Those three—" He pointed toward the stage but never finished his sentence. Someone grabbed his hand and bit his wrist, hard. Jim bellowed his pain and clobbered the offender over the head with his other fist, freeing himself.

The barrel-chested man howled his amusement. "Well, you ain't gittin' them girls. They're too purty fer the likes of you. You boys are 'bout as ugly as piles of cowshit covered with maggots. You look like a mess of farmers. Is that what yew boys are"—he tipped forward—"fahmers?" He sneered the word as though it were a profanity, purposely baiting the three. "They don't want some dirty ol' ignorant 'fahm' boys. They want some real men like us, don't ya, ladies?" He leered up at the stage and took a step in that direction.

Ignorant! Luke and Matthew saw beyond red. There was nothing in all the world they hated more than to be called ignorant. They were proud of being farmers. But being labeled ignorant! Now, that was something else.

Matt slugged the boatman hard, sending him sailing backward over the table, taking glasses and whiskey bottles with him.

The boatman's friends didn't take too kindly to Matt's treatment of their pal, so three of them jumped Matt from behind, trying hard to bring him down by choking him.

In Poplar Bluff there was a code of honor to fair fighting. There was no biting, choking, or spitting allowed. Other than that, the philosophy was anything goes. So far the boatmen had violated every rule. That meant war!

Luke roared and threw himself into the fracas like a wild man, meting out a flurry of punishing blows, dropping bodies right and left.

Having no choice, and a bit riled himself, Jim joined in, clearing a path of his own. He caught a blow to his left eye that made the entire room go fuzzy for a while. He shook his head to clear it and barreled his way back into the pandemonium.

Men cursed, clouted, and panted. Blows were delivered, blood spurted, bones crunched. Some of Boonville's boys joined in to help Jim and the Hawkins brothers, while the boatman's crew seemed to double like a batch of bread dough left out in the sun.

Megan saw Fletcher and his cronies rise from their chairs. Common activities like brawling were beneath them. She watched them as they carefully backed out of the confusion. Her heart hit her stomach. She'd hoped to get Fletcher alone and get the truth out of him, one way or the other. By torture if necessary. If he left, she'd lose her chance, and she doubted she'd ever get another one like this. She hopped down off the stage and lit out after him, dodging a swarm of flailing arms and legs.

From her place on the stage, Habel saw a man rise up behind Matthew and raise a bottle over his head. She screamed out a warning as the man brought it down, but Matthew didn't hear her in time. He went down. Frantic, Habel hobbled down off the stage. Sam Sweeney was on her in a flash. He grabbed for her. She swatted him away. He grabbed for her again. She slapped at his hands. But drunk as he was, he kept on grabbing and trying to get close enough to steal him a smooch.

Jim fought his way to Matthew's side. He helped him to his feet, while Luke held the revelers at bay. Matthew got his bearings just as Sam Sweeney slopped a big gushy slobber onto Habel's mouth. She shrieked her indignation, and instinct took over. She turned on Sam with the fury of a rabid dog. "Dammit! Git the hell outta my way, you god-damned peckerhead!" She drew back her fist and slugged him hard in the jaw. He went down like a felled tree.

Satisfied, she stepped over him, her nose in the air, her jaw set in determination.

Hearing her voice and what she'd said cost Matthew his concentration. Astounded, he stared open-mouthed, and took a blow to the right side of his temple that sent him reeling once again.

Jim came to his aid and buried his fist into the fleshy face of the man who'd struck his friend. Once the man had been fought down, Jim searched the room for Megan. He found her, charging toward the double doors, trying to catch up with Fletcher, who was attempting a hasty retreat from the brawl.

Merilee rushed through the door, knocking Fletcher aside, her broom raised high above her head, ready to land a blow where necessary. Her girls had armed themselves in similar fashion, wielding bottles and brandishing feather dusters.

Luke took off toward the stage, where a man had Clarissa cornered. Clarissa was not a hapless victim, however. She'd taken the hat pin from her headpiece, and when the man came close enough, the hat pin found a new home deep in the left cheek of his hide. He howled, and Luke came up behind him and beaned him a good one, then grabbed Clarissa's hand, dragging her off the stage.

Jim caught Megan before she could leave the room. He grabbed her from behind and yanked her backward into his arms. Her breath left her in a whoosh. She elbowed him hard in the ribs and bellowed her rage. He grunted in pain, but held fast to her waist. She turned her head up to get a look at her captor. "Jim Lawson! Let loose of me!" she ordered, her eyes sparking anger.

"I can't do that, Meg." He tightened his arms around her and held her clamped against his chest.

She wiggled and tried to break free, while she watched Fletcher slip out the door and into the night. As her hopes for the evening evaporated, her temper flared. "You let loose of me!" she hollered. "You're ruinin' everything, goddammit!"

"Too bad!"

She brought her high-heeled shoe down hard on his instep.

He yelped and grabbed his foot, hopping on one leg.

She spun to face him.

He grabbed for her again, and she poked him one in the nose.

His eyes flew wide with surprise. His eyebrows slowly dropped.

She froze, her gaze slowly lifting to his. Suddenly she wondered if maybe, just maybe, she'd gone too far this time. She had. Before she knew what was happening, he had her over his shoulder, her backside pointed toward the ceiling, her legs flailing helplessly in the air.

Furious, his nose stinging, he swatted her on her tail. "Keep still, goddammit!"

"You put me down, Jim Lawson!"

"I will, but not till you're outta here. No wife of mine is gonna show her backside to anyone but me!"

"Ooooooo! You put me down! I'll show my backside to anyone I damn well please. An' I ain't never marryin' you anyway! I already told you that!"

"Oh, yes you are!"

Merilee picked her way across the layer of limp bodies that littered her floor. "You all right, Megan?" she asked, tipping her head, looking into Megan's upside-down eyes.

"I will be when you make this baboon put me down!"

Merilee fought hard to hide her grin. Things were getting mighty interesting between the deputy and the lady veterinarian. "Sorry things didn't work out. Fletcher left."

"I know." Megan sobered. "Sorry 'bout your place."

Merilee shrugged. "Come by Monday morning. You can help us clean up."

"She will," Jim answered for her and stomped his way through the double doors and out into the night.

Megan's brothers were waiting outside with Clarissa and Habel and a rig. Jim flipped Megan off his shoulder and deposited her into the dirty snow at Matthew's feet.

"Goddamn you, Jim!" she shrieked.

He pretended not to hear her. To her brothers he said, "Take her home, or I'll lock her up, and this time I'll gag her first!" He glared his meanest at all of them, then stalked off into the night, ignoring the snowball that hit him in the shoulder a few seconds later.

CHAPTER
17

The next morning found them all in church.

The news of the ruckus over at Merilee's had made the rounds all over Boonville and the surrounding farms long before the Reverend Dunmire led his congregation in the morning's first prayer.

The story had many variations. Most of the townspeople were shocked, though there were a scant few who were amused. Tongues twittered. Stares were openly curious, some openly condemning. Gossip and opinions ran rampant.

Edith Pribble's ladies said, "Humph! I told you that girl was nothing but trouble!" And later, when Flora Fletcher passed by Megan's pew, she jerked her nose so high into the air she almost tipped herself over backward.

The farmers shrugged and bragged, "The deputy and those Hawkins boys shore gave those boatmen something to think about, now, didn't they!"

When Megan entered the church, Lucy and Stuart Kincaid were standing near the door. Without a word of greeting, they steered Danny in the opposite direction. That more than anything cut her. She didn't care what others thought of her, but she'd developed a real affection for Danny and the local children, and she knew the sentiment was returned. It hurt her to think they would not be allowed to associate with her.

Unaffected by such gossipy nonsense, Matthew and Luke proudly sported their black eyes, knowing their friends back home would suffer great fits of jealousy if they could see the severity of their injuries, while Jim, not so proudly, sported a bump the size of a large plum on the left side of his temple.

Clarissa sat beside Luke, equally unaffected by the stares and whispers around her. Her hand was clasped safely in his. He glanced down at her, and through his swollen eyelids, his gaze told her, as his lips had done last night, that he loved her—that he'd never loved anyone but her, and that he wanted her for his own. She'd lain awake long into the morning hours contemplating their future and the children they would have, determined to make him a good wife. He was kind and honest, and he liked William Shakespeare. How could she have known on the day of the pie and box supper that the one who'd won her company for the day would be the one who'd win her heart for eternity? But he had. And she was very, very glad that he had.

Her mother had been mortified by Clarissa's actions at Merilee's—much more so than she was at the announcement of Luke's intentions toward her daughter. That she was rather pleased with. But when Clarissa explained the situation at Merilee's in its entirety—telling her how Megan suspected Fletcher of stealing animals from the townsfolk, how she figured he had stolen Megan's, and that they had gone to Merilee's together to try to trick him into exposing his guilt, Mrs. Westfield just shook her head and said, "Oh, my. When is this town going to do something about that man?"

Habel sat beside Matthew, steeped in a lasting glow of newfound happiness. Like Clarissa, surprisingly enough, she was not in the least bit embarrassed or ashamed of her actions last night, though she'd pretended to be quite vexed and chagrined for Matthew's sake. Last night had opened a whole new world to her, and if prancing around on a stage in a feathered yellow dress had brought it about, then she'd gladly do it all over again. She stole a glance up at the big handsome man at her side and remembered his words: *My woman!* She, Habel Habershaw, who'd long ago given up all hope of ever being anyone's woman, was Matthew Hawkins's woman. Now, wasn't that something. . . .

Megan sat at the opposite end of the bench, as far away from Jim as she could get. Every now and then she attempted to skewer him with a hateful glare, but he ignored her, refusing to look her way, robbing her of the chance to vent her anger.

So the morning passed, and the Reverend Dunmire preached on. He delivered a message of tolerance and love that morning, and did so with a much firmer voice than usual. His gaze fell often on Edith Pribble and her ladies, and every now and then lingered thoughtfully on Flora Fletcher and her husband, and before he ended his sermon, his gaze sought out Jim Lawson and Megan Hawkins.

Monday morning found all three women—Megan, Clarissa, and Habel—at Merilee's door once again, dressed much differently from how they'd been dressed two evenings ago. They spent the entire morning cleaning the main room—sweeping up glass, righting tables and chairs, and scrubbing floors. Matthew and Luke joined them and did most of the heavy work. Merilee and her girls helped, too, saying they couldn't remember when they'd last had such an exciting Saturday night. And wasn't it wonderful to see those boatmen put in their place for a change?

Jim didn't show up to help his friends, however.

Before Megan left, Libby Logan approached her. She pressed forward eagerly and asked, "You got any plans for you and that pretty preacher man?"

Megan smiled. "Not in the least."

Libby grinned and straightened. "Well now . . ." she said thoughtfully.

When the group had finished their work, they agreed to meet over at Big John and Beulah's for the noontime meal. Megan said she'd meet them there, but first she had business to attend to. She washed up and went over to the jail to find Jim. There was still the matter of a horse and two pigs—hers. Without her pigs to keep watch, any varmint could get to her door. Without her horse, she would have to borrow Matt's or Luke's gelding every time she needed to go somewhere. That simply wouldn't do.

On her way over to the jailhouse, she saw Danny. He was walking toward her on the other side of the street, carrying his puppy. Behind him trailed Amy Applegate. Amy tapped his shoulder and pointed at Megan. Seeing Megan, Danny's face brightened. "Megan!" he called out and ran to greet her. Amy was right at his heels. "Where ya goin'?"

She smiled and waved. "Over to see the deputy."

"You all right?" he asked, the smile dropping from his young face.

" 'Course. Why do you ask?"

"Father said you were tarnished."

Stumped, Megan's feet stopped. Her gaze met Danny's. "He did, did he?"

"Yeah. Is that bad? Can ya die from it or anything?"

Touched by his concern, she smiled once again. "No, sugar. You can't die from it." She started walking once again. "How's Cody?"

Danny held him out for her to see. "Gettin' big."

"Isn't he, though?" She patted the dog's head and smiled at Amy. "What do you think of this little fella?"

"I like him fine." Amy smiled, then made a face. "I got a new pony, and I'd share him with Danny if he wanted, but Danny won't let me hold his dog."

"Why, Danny," Megan scolded gently, "you oughta let Amy hold him."

Danny looked disgusted. Reluctantly he held the pup out to Amy. "All right. But just for a minute. He don't like girls much."

"Is that a fact?" Megan said and arched an eyebrow.

Daniel nodded. He eyed Megan meaningfully. " 'Less they're full-grown."

"Ah, I see." Megan bent down and whispered into Amy's ear, "You just hang on, honey. You'll be full-grown 'fore you know it."

Megan found Jim as he was leaving the jailhouse. She walked right up to him and, hands on hips, nailed him with a determined gaze. "You ruined my plans to get my horse and pigs back. I'd like to know what you're gonna do 'bout that."

He fixed his eyes squarely on hers. "I told you I'd take care of it. I'll get Jesse and your pigs back for you."

"An' what if he sells 'em 'fore you can?"

"He won't."

"You don't know that."

"Yes, I do." His voice was quiet and patient, and something about his tone hit a vulnerable spot within her, making her want to believe him.

The events of the last few days had worn her out, and she was tired of fighting. "Jim, I love that horse. I love my pigs, too."

"Meg," he said softly, "don't you think I know that?"

She balked. His eyes stayed on her. She had the fleeting suspicion that he knew more about what was going on than she did—that maybe she should trust him, that maybe he was on her side, that maybe he had always been on her side. . . .

While she was considering that possibility, a low rumble of noise drew her attention. At first she thought it was thunder. But then she realized it couldn't possibly be. It was February. The air was cold and dry, the earth frozen—hardly appropriate weather for thunderstorms.

The ground vibrated beneath her feet.

The passersby stopped in their tracks. Some fled through the doors of some of the shops lining Morgan Street.

"My lands! What's that?" one lady asked Jim on her way past him.

Jim's eyes met Megan's. Confused, they stared at each other, thinking, remembering. . . . There was only one critter that could shake the ground like that. Only one. His name had been Beauregard!

Their heads swung in the direction of the rumble.

At the same time, on their way over to Big John's, Luke, Clarissa, Matthew, and Habel were making their way toward the jail.

Behind them strolled Danny and Amy. Danny had reclaimed his puppy from Amy. He stooped and set him down on the road. "Come on, boy. Come on," he said, slapping his thigh, urging the puppy to follow.

The rumble grew louder. The birds left the trees. A fat dog lounging on a porch crawled under a chair.

The Hawkins brothers exchanged worried glances and took their ladies' arms, steering them to the side of the road. "Come on," Luke ordered over his shoulder to the children, expecting them to follow.

Amy did. Danny did not. "Here, Cody!" Danny called, trying to catch his puppy, who'd wandered into the middle of the street.

A wide, dark hulk came into view. It bore down on the boy. People screamed and scattered. Megan's heart shot into her throat. Jim's stomach clenched. All movement seemed to shift into a hazy slowness.

"Get off the road, Danny!" Megan's voice was shrill with panic. "Get off the road!"

Thunderous hooves beat the frozen earth with a relentless fury.

"Now!" Jim yelled and started after him. Megan lurched in front of Jim, her thoughts focused on the little boy she'd grown so fond of during these past many months. Jim caught her arm, jerking her to a halt.

The brothers ran into the road, staring at the approaching beast. "Get your shirt off, Matt," Luke said, his voice clear and authoritative. The brothers knew well what form of beast they had to contend with. "The color will distract him."

Matthew never thought to argue. He shrugged off his coat, then ripped his shirt off, ready to draw the bull's attention away from the boy and the dog, to himself.

Frightened, the townsfolk huddled in their homes and on their porches. This was not the first time Beauregard had run his fence and gone on a rampage, cutting a reckless path through town.

Down the street, Lucy and Stuart Kincaid stood in front of their lovely ornate gate, staring down Morgan Street, wondering at the commotion. From where they stood, it was hard to see exactly what was happening. They saw their son and his dog. . . .

And then they saw him. He appeared like some giant, bloodthirsty warrior, thundering his way toward the child and the dog.

Lucy screamed. The colonel froze in terror. Megan broke Jim's hold and ran for Danny; Jim ran for her. He knocked her to the ground. Luke launched himself at the boy. They hit the ground as one, and Luke covered the boy's body with his own, while Matthew flapped his shirt wildly, hoping to draw the bull's attention his way.

Beauregard stomped over the puppy. It yipped and went as still as the earth beneath it. Danny's scream rent the air.

The bull stopped dead in his tracks.

He pawed the ground with one hoof, then the other, and snorted his fury in a white puff of air that dripped moisture. He was a frightening being, his horns bowed and pointed, his eyes burning with an unholy rage.

Slowly Megan got to her feet. She looked from Luke to Matthew, then to Jim, who rose beside her.

"My dog, my dog . . ." Danny wept, while Luke hushed him, hoping Matthew could divert the bull.

"Yee-haw!" Matthew said and jiggled the shirt enticingly. "Come on, you big ugly bastard." He stepped in front of Luke and the boy. "Come an' git me."

Beauregard snorted, and his eyes bulged. He pawed the ground some more, kicking up snow and dirt.

"We need a rope, Jim," Megan said, her eyes wide with fear.

"We need more than one rope to stop that son of a bitch," he said and edged his way to the jailhouse door. He slipped inside and grabbed his rifle from the rack on the wall. He was back outside within seconds. He lifted the gun to his shoulder and took careful aim. "Matt," he said, "if he charges, you get the hell outta the way. This is no time to play hero. I'm gonna shoot him."

Matthew threw him a skeptical grin. "I shore hope you can shoot better'n you used to."

"I can," Jim said and squinted down the barrel of the gun.

Everyone quieted.

Another rumble of hooves broke the silence. Fletcher and several of his men bore down on the group. Seeing Jim with his gun aimed at his beloved bull, Fletcher hollered, "Noooo!"

All hell broke loose.

Beauregard rushed Matt. Matthew dodged to the right, but the bull gored him in his thigh. He went down. "Matt!" Megan yelled and ran to him, putting herself between him and the bull. Jim's heart thumped up into his throat. Clarissa and Habel screamed. Jim fired, aiming low. His bullet found its mark, winging the bull in his front leg, dropping him to his knees, only a fraction of an instant before he would have trampled Megan. Megan threw herself at Matthew, and the bull lifted his nose to the sky and bellowed his rage. He struggled to rise, while Matthew and Megan inched away from him.

Fletcher yelled his distress and swung down off his horse, running for the bull. His men leapt to the ground, taking their ropes from their saddle horns and following him.

Jim kept the gun ready at his shoulder. "Fletcher. Have your men tie him up and get him home, or I swear by God I'll kill him and be done with it!"

Fletcher turned on him in a fury. He stabbed a finger in Jim's direction. "I'll have your badge for this! You can count on it! That bull is my property. You had no right—"

Jim lowered the gun, turning it toward Fletcher. "I had every right. It's my job to uphold the peace and protect these people. That animal," he said, pointing to the trussed and bellowing beast, "is a menace." Jim stared at Fletcher as though he couldn't quite figure out what kind of being he was looking at. "Good God, man! That animal almost ran down a little boy. He did run over his dog. He gored my friend." He pointed at Matthew, who lay wounded with Megan tending him.

"He's still my property!"

Jim's jaw got tight. "Then take your property and get him off the street." He dismissed Fletcher and strode to Megan's side. "You all right, Meg?" he asked, dropping to his knees before her. He touched his hand to her sunny hair and felt his chest get tight.

She lifted her blue eyes to him, her expression one of calm purpose. "I'm fine." Turning back to Matthew, she ripped the sleeve of her shirt off and tied it firmly around his leg to stop the bleeding. "I never knew you could shoot like that, Jim Lawson."

He grinned and honestly told her, "Neither did I."

"Oh, Gawd," Matthew groaned and collapsed onto his back.

"Jim," Meg said without looking at him.

"Yeah?"

"Come and get me when you go for Jesse?" It was a request, spoken softly, almost humbly.

He looked at her, at Matt, at Fletcher. There wasn't a woman alive who had more spunk than Meg. She deserved to have a part in getting her animals back. "All right," he said. "I'll come for you."

"Promise?" She turned to him and held him captive with her gaze.

He nodded. "I promise."

The crowd grew as folks gathered to discuss the incident. They were downright angry at Fletcher for allowing such a terrible thing to happen again. Wasn't Frank Bozeman's boy enough?

Incensed, Fletcher ordered his men about, still chafing at the young deputy's rebuke. He wasn't used to anyone giving him orders except for Flora, and he had no choice but to put up with her. After all, he might own the important family name, but her family had the money and practically owned the town. He glared at Jim's back, hatred oozing from every one of his pores. Then he spun on his heel and went to instruct his men on how to handle his precious animal.

Meanwhile, Lucy and Colonel Kincaid rushed to their son. Danny was huddled over his dog, crying. "Oh, Daniel," Lucy said. "Oh, darling . . ." She swept her child up into her arms and sobbed his name over and over. The colonel dropped to his knees and embraced the two, his eyes burning, his throat working silently. He realized how foolish he'd been. His wife had tried to tell him, but he hadn't listened. He hadn't listened to anyone in quite a long time. It didn't matter whether Daniel went to Kemper or the school in town. It didn't matter whether he was a soldier or a farmer. What mattered was that he was their son, their only son, and they loved him, and would continue to love him no matter who or what he turned out to be. Kincaid's eyes found Luke. "Thank you," he said gruffly, seeing him not as a country bumpkin, but as the man who'd saved his child's life.

Luke nodded, embarrassed. He turned to find Clarissa at his shoulder. They joined hands and walked away.

Colonel Kincaid searched the crowd for Jim and the rest of Luke's family. Locating them, he left his wife and son and went to them. He stopped before Jim, Megan, and Matt and cleared his throat. "I don't know what to say. I've been a pompous ass for most of my life. I'm pretty good at it. I'm afraid I'm not very good at anything else right now."

Megan wiped her hands on her britches and stood. "Oh, I don't know. You're doin' a fine job of apologizin'."

Stuart Kincaid forced a shaky smile and extended his hand to her. She took his hand and squeezed hard. "Danny is a wonderful boy."

The colonel nodded. "Yes, he is."

Habel elbowed her way to Matthew and fluttered over him, driving everyone else away.

Megan spotted Danny's pup where it lay on the ground. She felt a rush of sadness. While she watched, she saw him twitch and raise his head. She took off through the throng and, reaching the pup, went down on one knee.

Very carefully, she pressed her fingers to his chest. She found a thready heartbeat. She watched him lift his head and blink, focusing on her. "He's alive, Danny!"

"He is?" Danny was beside her in an instant.

Very carefully, Megan lifted the dog in her hands. He whimpered, but did a fine job of holding his head up. She sighed her relief. "He has a mess of broken bones, but his neck isn't one of 'em. He just might make it. Let me take him home. I'll do what I can."

And she did. She did it so well her professors back east would have been proud of her. Cody would live. He'd have one helluva limp for the rest of his life, but at least he'd have a life. He was lucky—Beauregard had kicked him more than he'd trampled him.

March stormed the county, bringing half a foot of snow and a wind that could turn a man's sweat to ice crystals. In the days that followed Megan thought about that February day. She thought about Jim—about how he'd said he'd get her horse back, about how solid he'd looked when he faced Fletcher, about how he rushed to her, worried over her and Matt, about how he could shoot a gun, by damn!

She was crazy in love with him. She was so in love with him that every day she was away from him seemed long and pointless. She wanted to tell him how proud she was of him. She wanted to tell him that she loved him— had always loved him. And there was something else she wanted to tell him: She was carrying his baby.

She knew it for certain. She had suspected for quite some time, but after missing her third monthly, she was sure. She figured the baby would come sometime in early fall. The thought of that baby, that precious little life, hers and Jim's, growing within her body, filled her with joy. She wanted to tell everybody—her family, her brothers. But she knew that if she told Matthew and Luke, they'd have her and

Jim before Steven by nightfall, forcing them to take their vows whether they were willing to or not. She wanted to be willing, and she wanted Jim that way, too. . . .

Flora Fletcher pulled her rig up in front of Colonel Kincaid's impressive wrought-iron gate. She got out of her rig, then very carefully patted everything into place before making her way up the walk to the equally impressive door. Once there, she knocked and waited.

Lucy answered the door. Surprised to find Flora on her doorstep, she ushered her in. "Flora. What a surprise!"

"Morning, Lucy," Flora said primly.

Lucy was one of Mrs. Pribble's ladies, but little by little she had distanced herself, finding the ladies' lofty expectations of one another stifling and foolish. "What can I do for you?" Lucy asked, genuinely concerned. Flora was not likely to favor anyone with her presence without a purpose.

"I've come to visit Daniel if I may."

"Of course. He's in his room," Lucy said, still puzzled. Flora and Maxwell had not been blessed with children of their own, and it was common knowledge that Flora abhorred the noisy young beings.

What was not common knowledge, however, was that for many years Flora had yearned for a child of her own. It had been a great source of sadness for her to find that she would never bear a child. She sometimes wondered if she and Maxwell would have found a way to love each other if they'd had children.

She'd heard about the upheaval Beauregard had caused in town. She'd also heard how the damned bull had trampled the boy's dog. The dog would live, she'd been told, but only because the lady veterinarian had nursed it back to health. The boy, she'd learned, had suffered nothing more than a sprained ankle, which he'd received when Luke

Hawkins had fallen on him in an effort to protect him.

Still, Flora felt singly responsible for the boy's and the dog's injuries. She should have butchered that bull long ago, despite her husband's ridiculous affection for him.

She found Danny sitting on his bed, petting his dog. She marched across the room, holding her head stiff and erect. "Daniel," she said in quiet greeting, her expression one of somber purpose.

Alarmed, Daniel's heart thudded, and his expression grew grim. He paled, and his freckles stood out sharply on his face. "Hello, Mrs. Fletcher," he whispered, his mind clicking furiously. She'd found out about that pumpkin he and Theo had mashed upside her barn last November! His life was over!

"I've come to apologize, Daniel."

"Ma'am?" Daniel looked confused. He held his breath, afraid to accept the shaky smidgen of relief that hovered.

"I came to apologize for what my husband's bull did to your puppy, and for what happened to your ankle."

Relieved beyond words, Daniel let out his breath. He stuck out his leg and wiggled his foot in one direction, then circled it in the other. He smiled. "It don't hurt much anymore. See? And Cody's doing just fine. Aren't ya, Cody?" He patted the dog, carefully avoiding the splints that were taped to three of Cody's legs. The dog was wrapped from neck to tail like a mummy, but he didn't seem to mind or be too terribly uncomfortable.

"Well," Flora said and sniffed. "I'm glad to hear that. I truly am." Feeling incredibly awkward, she reached out and patted the boy's flaming head of hair. "You're an admirable young man, Daniel. It's most charitable of you to be so forgiving." She paused a moment, struggling for the right words. They were hard for her to say, yet she wanted to say them. She felt them. She meant them. "If you should ever need anything, Daniel, please let me know."

Lucy had been waiting outside her son's door. Hearing Flora's words, she felt a stirring of sympathy in her breast and entered the room, slowly crossing the floor to stand beside the older woman. She reached out and touched Flora's arm. "Thank you for coming, Flora. It was very kind of you."

Kind? Flora had been accused of many things, but kind was never one of them. It was an interesting notion. "Yes, well, it was necessary," she said, embarrassed. She turned to the door. "Remember what I said, young man. I meant it."

Jim and Zach came for Megan one evening in early spring.

March was drawing to a close. It was barely dusk, yet the moon was fully visible, shadowed only by a few thin, wispy clouds threading by its face every now and then.

Megan was home, sitting by the potbellied stove, petting Willy, wondering when she would feel the baby move within her. Matthew had gone into town to visit Habel. Luke had gone to visit Clarissa.

When she heard the knock, she rose and went to the door. Opening it, she was surprised to see the two men, looking determined and ready.

"It's time," Jim said and held out his hand.

CHAPTER
18

Fletcher had finally forced his hand.

Jim received word that morning that Fletcher was shipping a load of animals over to St. Louis for an auction next week. They were moving them tonight by barge.

Jim's instincts told him he'd come by the information too easily, that this, also, was a trap, another ploy to draw him out. But he couldn't take the chance of losing Megan's horse and pigs, or the many other animals that belonged to his neighbors and friends. He'd promised himself he'd get them back. He'd promised himself he'd get Fletcher.

He hadn't wanted to come for her tonight. But he'd promised her that, too. And though much had passed between them over the course of their lives, he had never yet broken a promise to her. He wasn't about to start now.

He was worried about her, though. Fletcher had shot at him and Zach. He would not hesitate to shoot at Meg, too, Jim was certain.

So he and Zach had formed a plan.

They'd found Fletcher's latest camp several weeks ago. He'd abandoned his old haunts, knowing Zach and Jim were raiding him at will. The new camp was several miles north of Boonville. Jim would go in alone. If Fletcher was there, Jim planned to arrest him. He believed the town would support him. Word had it that the townsfolk were coming around to his way of thinking. Suspicions had escalated. Tempers had flared. Even Fletcher's cronies were ready to listen to charges against him—especially since Beauregard's rampage. The fact that he owed them substantial sums for unpaid gambling debts only boosted their growing indifference toward him.

Zach and Jim had agreed that if Maxwell wasn't at the camp, Jim would slip as many animals as he could out to Zach and Megan, who would herd them back into town. If they couldn't get Fletcher, at least they would reclaim some of the animals.

Zach was to keep Meg with him at all times, even if he had to tie her up to do it. And if anything should go wrong, if anything should happen to Jim, Zach was to get Meg to safety, no matter what.

Zach had promised he would, and Jim believed him.

As they rode on through the twilit night, Jim stole a glance over at Megan. He felt his heart quicken. It amazed him that after all these years, just looking at her could still make his insides quiver.

She felt his gaze on her and turned to him. "You kept your promise. You came for me." The words were spoken softly, appreciatively.

"I said I would."

"Yes, you did."

He grinned at her. "One of these days you're gonna learn to trust me, Meg."

She dropped her gaze a minute and wondered if she should trust him now, if she should tell him about the baby. A man had a right to know about his own baby. Somehow she knew he would be glad. . . .

Her thoughts were interrupted when Zach and Jim slowed their horses, and Jim pointed toward a rise in the distance. "Fletcher's camp is just over that ridge." He turned to her and guided his horse close to hers. "You wait here with Zach."

She nodded.

"You do what he says, no matter what."

"I will."

"Promise me." The night was dark, the moonlight dim, but his eyes were clearly visible as they found her face.

She nodded again.

He waited. They both knew her nod was not the affirmation he wanted.

Finally she huffed and said, "All right. I promise."

"Zach," Jim said, "you're my witness." He grinned and leaned toward Megan. "You break that promise, Meg, an' you'll have to marry me the first Sunday in May, whether I ask you nice or not. Deal?" He arched one dark eyebrow and waited.

Her faced flushed with anger. So, he fully expected her to disobey his orders, did he? Damn him anyway for knowing her so well!

He grasped the back of her neck and pulled her face close to his. She resisted stubbornly, but he persisted, and with Zach looking on, he kissed her—slowly, thoroughly, possessively. When finally he drew away, he whispered into her ear, "If you try to get outta this one, I'll tell your brothers exactly what we did Christmas Eve. In fact, I might even write a letter home to your pa and Johnnie."

Megan's eyes opened wide. "Jim Lawson, you wouldn't!" She pictured all of Poplar Bluff holding shotguns at her wedding.

His grin grew wicked. " 'Course I would." He chuckled, dug his heels into his horse, and cantered off toward the hill in the distance.

Zach and Megan watched his dark form disappear over the ridge. They waited. The moon rose fully over them, and the stars stood out sharply against the onyx sky. An hour passed before Jim came back. When he did, he was on foot, leading a horse. The horse was Jesse. Megan jumped down off her mount and went to Jim. She threw her arms around him, hugging his neck, then turned and did the same to her horse. "Oh, Jesse, you varmint, you. I've missed you somethin' fierce."

Zach swung down off his horse. He looked worried and more than a little nervous. "Everything all right?"

"So far," Jim said. "I got close enough to catch part of their conversation. Seems Fletcher is s'posed to show up and give the boys their pay sometime tonight. I figure I'll get a few more animals out to you 'fore he comes, just in case I don't get a chance later. Then you can take Meg and get outta here. I'll meet you in town once I get Fletcher."

"What happens if he shoots you again?" Megan asked, trying to keep the worry out of her voice.

"I don't plan to let him get the chance. I'm gonna keep my hide to myself this time," Jim answered, unconcerned. "You just do what Zach tells you. I'll be all right."

She gave him a doubtful look, but she held her tongue.

He brought the pigs next. Romeo and Juliet had grown quite a bit, and Jim had a hell of a time convincing them to cooperate with the ropes he'd tied around their necks. It took him twice as long to get them over the ridge to Zach and Megan as it had to get Jesse over. Once he delivered them, he left once more. Zach and Megan tied the animals to a couple of trees and continued to wait.

It was quiet. Too quiet. The night stretched on. Zach got down off his horse, took a short walk into the woods, then came back and swung back up into his saddle. Megan tried to get comfortable in hers, but her neck and shoulders had begun to ache terribly. The two looked at each other. They looked at the moon, then back at each other. Finally Megan asked, "So, you gonna marry Anna?"

Zach nodded, and his white teeth flashed in the darkness. "Yep. I asked her father last week. I guess he likes me enough after all. The wedding'll be in June."

"That's wonderful, Zach," Megan said sincerely. "I'm happy for you."

They fell silent once more. The minutes ticked by.

"You think he's all right?" Megan asked quietly.

" 'Course he is," Zach said to comfort her. "Jim knows what he's doing."

Silence. A rabbit hopped across the road. Seeing them, it went still for a few seconds, then shot off across the field. Megan's nerves seemed strung to the limit.

Suddenly the silence was punctured by several loud rounds of gunfire.

"Holy Moses," Zach said, knowing the time had come for him to keep his promise. "We'd better get out of here!"

Megan looked from Zach to the hill, then back to Zach. "Zach!" she hollered, making a decision, turning her horse away from him. "I guess you're gonna be attendin' a weddin' the first Sunday in May, 'cause I'm goin' after that fool!"

Zach lurched forward in his saddle, trying to catch hold of her reins, but she kicked her horse sharply, sending him bolting out of Zach's reach.

"Dammit, Doc!" he yelled, taking off after her. "Jim's gonna kill me!"

"He can't kill anyone if he's dead himself! I intend to see that he doesn't get that way."

She leaned low over the neck of her horse and rode hard, as though possessed by the spirit of one of the outlaws she'd once pretended to be. She galloped up the hill and over the ridge, and barreled her way smack-dab into the center of Fletcher's camp, drawing the attention of at least two dozen men. Jim stood in the center of the men, near a smoldering campfire, holding them all at bay, his gun aimed at Fletcher's heart.

Diverted by Megan's arrival, he lost his concentration for one flicker of an instant. And that flicker cost him greatly.

He didn't see it coming. Someone knocked his gun barrel up. A shot rang out into the night, ricocheting off a tree branch overhead. The blow that caught him was fast and decisive, snapping his head backward. He went down, seeing stars. He dropped his gun. Zach rode into the camp, wild-eyed and winded. Within seconds, he and Megan were surrounded by a group of surly men.

"Shit!" Zach said, feeling helpless and inept. His gaze found Jim and spoke his apology. "I guess you're getting married."

Jim sat up, rubbing his jaw. His gaze found Megan. He glowered.

"I'm afraid not," Fletcher said and walked to stand before Zach's horse. "It looks to me like we have horse thieves among us. What do you boys think?"

A hearty rumble of agreement answered his question.

"Well, then," Fletcher smiled coldly. "Looks like a hanging would suit the occasion much better than a wedding."

The Cooper County Jail barn had served its purpose over the years. It stood next to the jail, beside a brick privy, a cistern, and a smokehouse.

It was here in the "Hanging Barn," as most folks called it, that all public hangings took place. The building had originally been designed to house the horses of the local sheriff, so that they'd be on hand should a posse ever be needed. The fact that it served as a place to carry out executions, however, had added to its importance.

Jim, Megan, and Zach were led into town by Fletcher's

men. They were seated on their horses, gagged and bound, unable to alert anyone to their predicament. Dawn had begun to seep its way across the sky in a peachy swirl of color, while a golden sun slowly crested the distant hills.

Fletcher knew he had to work fast. The townsfolk would fight him on this, he knew. But if the lynching had already taken place—well, not much could be done. He would have to explain, of course: how he'd caught them red-handed, stealing the animals he'd planned to ship to the auction; how they'd been stealing their neighbors animals, too, and for quite some time. Of course, certain details would be added, others omitted. . . .

He was determined to carry out his plan. He had gambled away most of his wife's money and dug himself deeply into debt. The only way out of his predicament was to recoup what he'd lost, and fast. He would be able to do that by delivering this latest shipment of animals to his associates in St. Louis.

He really had no choice in the matter.

If he failed to deliver the shipment, those same associates, to whom he owed a substantial sum of money, had threatened to go to Flora with the truth about his debts, and about Fay, the longtime ladyfriend he kept quite comfortably in silks and chocolates in Kansas City—with Flora's money, of course.

Fletcher knew that if Flora ever found out about his debts and the loss of her money, he'd have himself a peck of trouble.

But if she ever found out about Fay, he might as well be dead.

So he figured if he could get the deputy and the blacksmith out of the way, he'd be able to take care of all his problems with one rope, all in one morning. And he had to admit, things were working out rather nicely. He hadn't planned on getting the outspoken lady veterinarian, too.

*   *   *

It was barely dawn when Danny was awakened by Cody. The dog lapped at his face and pushed his wet nose into Daniel's closed eyelid. Gently Danny shoved him away and turned over, but back the pup came, crawling on his belly, licking at Danny's face again.

Danny sat up in bed and rubbed the sleep from his eyes. "You need to go out, boy?"

The puppy whimpered and wagged his taped tail.

"Okay," Danny said and got out of his bed. He picked up the dog and very quietly made his way out of his room, down the hall and steps, and out the front door to the yard. He stood on the cold ground, in the dim light of early morning, dressed in only a red-and-white-striped nightshirt. A movement down the street caught his eye and, curious little boy that he was, he walked down the walkway to the gate, to see what was happening. Puzzled, he wrapped his fingers around the cold iron bars and stared at the group of riders. Three of the riders' horses were being led by their reins. One of the riders had long blond hair.

He ran back to fetch Cody, picked him up, and put him in the house. Then he shot down the walkway and out into the road, following the riders.

He caught up with them at the Hanging Barn. He stole around to the back of the building and peeked in through a window. His eyes widened with shock. Deputy Jim was standing between Zach and Megan. All three were bound and gagged. Danny's breath quickened as he strained to hear what the men were saying.

"Get the rope ready," Fletcher said to one of his men.

Frightened, Danny went still as death. He'd never liked Mr. Fletcher. His father had said Mr. Fletcher was unscrupulous, that he had no conscience. Danny wasn't sure what "unscrupulous" was, but the way his father said it meant it was a lot worse than mashing pumpkins, or even worse than playing hooky. His young mind worked frantically, trying to make sense of the situation. He didn't know why, but he knew they were gonna hang his friends. He knew he had to tell someone. He had to tell Matt and Luke. He had to find Theo. Theo would know what to do. But how could he get to Theo? He couldn't run there fast enough. He backed away from the window, scared and confused. Amy! Amy had a pony. He spun and broke into a run, heading for Amy's house. Amy would get him to Theo, and Theo would get to Matt and Luke.

From somewhere in the back of his eight-year-old brain Mrs. Fletcher's words called to him: "If you should ever need anything, Daniel, please let me know."

He would go get Mrs. Fletcher! If anyone could make Mr. Fletcher be good, it was Mrs. Fletcher.

The rock hit Amy's window. Within seconds another followed. She came to the window, peered out, and, seeing Daniel on the ground below her, opened the window and stuck her head out. Her pigtails flapped out in front of her face.

"Psst! Hey, Amy!" Daniel called out.

Flabbergasted, Amy rubbed her eyes and blinked. "What are you doing down there?" He had never, not even once, sought her out, let alone come to her house.

"I need you, Amy!"

A slow, triumphant smile spread across her face, exposing the empty space between her front teeth. She didn't bother to change her nightgown, or even get her shoes. She climbed out of her window, onto the nearby tree limb, and shimmied down the tree to where he waited for her on the ground.

Jim climbed the thirteen steps to the loft, then waited while one of Fletcher's men threw a rope over a beam, readying it.

Megan stood on the hay-dusted floor below him, her eyes pained, her expression sad.

Zach stared up at him and shook his head.

"I'm sorry, Zach," Jim said, able to do so now that Fletcher had allowed his men to remove their gags. The three had held silent until now. They had had no choice. Fletcher had told his men to shoot the first one who tried to yell for help.

Zach forced a smile. "Well, at least I don't have a back-side full of buckshot."

Jim tried to smile, but couldn't. He could have accepted his own hanging, but knowing Megan and Zach would follow him was almost more than he could bear. His eyes found Fletcher. His only chance was to stall him, to try to buy some time. If he could get him to talk . . . everyone knew how Fletcher loved to talk. His arrogance was his weakness. "You're gonna have a lot of explainin' to do," Jim said, looking down at Fletcher.

Fletcher nodded. "Yes. I suppose I will. But I'm very good at it."

"I always wondered why you'd do this. Stealin' and such . . ." He let the sentence hang. Jim had already guessed Fletcher's motivations, but he could try to get Fletcher to tell him. He eyed the lightening sky through the open barn doors hopefully and asked, "Why would a man who has everything need to take from others?"

"Because I want to keep everything," Fletcher said easily and fulfilled Jim's hope by launching into a lengthy explanation of his actions, unable to resist the urge to expound on his cleverness.

When he was done, Jim smiled and said, "Well, I guess you got me first, after all."

Fletcher nodded and preened. He smoothed back his meticulously combed hair. "Yes, I did. I always knew I would."

Jim's expression sobered. "Let Zach and Megan go, Maxwell."

"I'm afraid I can't do that. I have no choice but to hang them, too. They know too much."

"Mr. Fletcher," one of his men interrupted, eyeing the ever lightening sky, "if we don't do this now, we ain't gonna get to."

Fletcher suddenly realized he'd been manipulated. His eyes went cold. He nodded to the man beside Jim. "Do it."

"Wait!" Megan turned to Fletcher. "Please. I want to tell him something."

Fletcher eyed the rising sun through the open barn doors. Sweat beaded on his forehead. His palms felt damp. He was growing nervous. Soon the entire town would be stirring. Yet it seemed sinful, almost sacrilegious, to refuse a last request. Oddly enough, he wondered what such an action might cost him on Judgment Day. "All right. Hurry up!" he barked.

One of the men untied her hands, and Megan climbed the steps to the loft. When she reached Jim's side, she stood for a moment, silent and uncertain, searching her mind for the right words. "I'm sorry," she whispered, fighting back tears. "Jim, I'm so sorry. If I'd only listened to you . . ." She walked up against him, hugged his waist, and laid her head against his shoulder. They stood, belly to belly, head to shoulder, heart to heart.

"Aw, Meg," he said, "don't cry." He longed to put his arms around her, to hold her close one last time. He felt cheated of the lifetime they would have had together, cheated of his last chance to embrace her. He blamed no one but himself for having led her into danger. He should have known she wouldn't listen. She never had.

"Did I ever tell you that I love you?" she asked out of the blue, her head still on his shoulder.

"No," he whispered into her hair. His eyes slid shut. "You never did."

"Well, I do."

"Ain't that somethin'," he said and smiled.

"You wanna know somethin' else?" She raised her head and looked up into his beautiful brown eyes.

"What?"

"I always have."

"You wanna know somethin'?" Jim asked.

"What?"

"I think I always knew that."

"Yeah?"

"Yeah."

"Criminy," she said softly and laid her head back down on his shoulder.

"Yeah, criminy," he repeated, laying his cheek against her hair.

They stood pressed together like two leaves, taking all they could from this one last moment—two lovers, once children who'd romanticized the fantasy of growing up to become outlaws. How could they have known their childhood fantasy would foreshadow this impasse? She felt his heart thud in tempo with hers; she felt the warmth of his body reach out and wrap around her. She wanted to tell him about the baby, but she felt his knowing would only sadden him further. It was better he didn't know. It was enough that she had finally admitted the truth about her love for him. She should have done so long ago.

"I would have married you," she said at last, her voice thick with unshed tears.

"I know." He grinned, sealing each memory of her deep within his heart. "I would have married you, too."

"Yeah?" she said softly.

"Yeah," he returned.

Sunlight blazed across the sky, and day broke fully. "All

right!" Fletcher called up to them. "That's enough! Let's get this over with."

Fletcher's man put the rope around Jim's neck and guided Megan back out of the way.

Then quite suddenly the silence was punctured by "What the hell's goin' on here?" Sheriff Jasper Johnson came through the barn doors, surprising them all. He blinked his confusion, while his gaze swept the faces of all present. His mouth dropped open in surprise. His big ears twitched. When finally he found his voice, he looked at Fletcher and asked, "Maxwell, what the hell do you think you're doing?"

"Now, Jasper," Fletcher said, "you stay out of this. These folks are outlaws, horse thieves. Bad ones, too! The ones we been looking for. I caught them last night, red-handed."

Jasper looked disgusted and propped his hands on his hips. "Like hell you did!" He pointed at Zach. "Zach here wouldn't steal a nickel from anyone, and you damn well know it. And Jim." He jabbed a finger up at where Jim stood, hands tied, noose around his neck. "Hell, there ain't a more decent fella around. As for the doctor," he said, gesturing toward Megan, "she's been a help to this community from the day she came." He looked at Fletcher and asked, "What's the matter with you, Maxwell? You tetched or somethin'?"

Fletcher's nerves were frayed. The weight of his debts pressed down on him. He pinned Jasper with a meaningful stare. "You interfere with this, Jasper, and your days as this town's sheriff are numbered."

Jasper gazed at him for several seconds. Slowly his jaw hardened, and his face turned red. He plucked the badge from his chest and pitched it into the dirt at Fletcher's feet. "Fine! Jim's more sheriff than I am or ever will be. He can have the job! I quit! I'm sick and tired of you and Gladys and her mother tryin' to run my life! The hell with this! The hell with all of you! I don't even like the goddamn job!"

Fletcher blinked his surprise. No one in town had ever seen Jasper mad, not even his wife. It hadn't occurred to Fletcher, or anyone else for that matter, that Jasper wouldn't want to be sheriff of Boonville. Damn! Fletcher felt cornered. He'd have to hang Jasper, too. Making the decision, he turned to his men and said, "Tie him up, boys."

They were about to do just that when the thunder of hooves rumbled down upon them. Fletcher's men didn't have time to think or scatter or prepare themselves in any way. Matthew and Luke Hawkins burst through the open barn doors, horses and all, looking meaner than two provoked grizzly bears. Behind them rode Theo Skeets. When the boys saw their sister, Zach, and Jim, their expressions got really mean. As one, they brought their shotguns up to their shoulders. "Which one you wanna shoot, Luke?" Matthew asked, aiming the shotgun dead center at Fletcher's chest.

"Well, I kinda wanted him, but since you have him, I'll take me a couple of his men."

Fletcher felt sweat flood his fancy suit. "Now, wait just a minute, boys." He forced a conciliatory smile and raised his palms in supplication. "This isn't what it looks like—"

"Looks like a hangin' to me. What's it look like to you, Luke?" Matthew asked, his eyes still focused on Fletcher.

"A hangin'," Luke said simply. "A lynchin', more like."

Colonel Kincaid rushed through the door, rifle in hand. His wife followed, still in her nightdress and nightcap. "Amy stopped to tell us where Daniel went," the colonel huffed, winded. "We aren't too late, I hope?" His eyes found Zach, then rose to the loft to find Jim and Megan. Relieved, he closed his eyes and hugged his wife's waist.

Edith Pribble, her hair still pinned into the short, fat sausage ringlets she'd worn to bed, elbowed her way into the barn. She'd heard the Hawkins boys thunder by her house, whooping. Curious, and not about to miss something, she'd set off for town herself, leaving her husband to follow.

Pandemonium broke loose as a slew of townsfolk burst into the barn. Amy had done her part. After giving Daniel her pony, she'd awakened as many of the children as she could, and they in turn had run through town, alerting everyone they could to the plight of their friends. Many came: Silas Goldman, Mr. Barton, Big John and Beulah, the Reverend Dunmire, Clarissa and Habel—even Merilee and her girls crowded into the barn and around the open doors. Everyone talked at once.

Then, very slowly, the crowd parted and went stone silent.

To Fletcher's horror, Flora, with Daniel Kincaid at her side, marched toward him, her expression one of grim determination. "Maxwell!" she barked. "What is going on here?"

"Now, dear," Fletcher began, quaking in his shoes.

"Don't you dear me, you old fool!" She stopped before him. Without a second thought, she reached out and snatched his toupee from his head and flung it into a pile of horse dung over in the corner of the barn.

The crowd gasped, then grew silent again.

Shocked, Fletcher stared at her wordlessly. He turned scarlet clear up to his shiny bald head. No one in town had ever seen him without his toupee. Not ever.

"Maxwell," she said quietly, her gaze unyielding, "it seems we have a lot to talk about." She shoved an envelope under his nose. "I've been waiting for you to come home all night. I received this bill yesterday. It seems you've been purchasing an extensive amount of silk and chocolates." She pierced him with her gaze, then turned to Jasper. "When I'm done with him, you can have him."

Jasper held up his palms. "You'll have to give him to

Jim. I quit this morning!" He looked up at Jim. The noose had been removed from his neck. Megan was pressed to his side, as though she were a part of him. "I'm gonna buy me a piece of land and farm it," Jasper went on. "And if Gladys don't like it, she can move back in with her meddling mother!"

Hearing him, Edith gasped and huffed, "Well, I never!"

Flora turned to her. "I'm sure you don't, Edith. It seems many of us have the same problem."

Edith blanched, then turned redder than a ripe tomato.

Flora spun back around to face her husband. "Come, Maxwell!" she ordered. "It's almost time for breakfast." She pivoted on her heel and marched back through the crowd. Reaching the doors, she whirled and gave him a secret, almost evil smile, "We're having steak and eggs. Prime beefsteak to be exact. Fresh off the hoof!"

CHAPTER
—◆◆ *19* ◆◆—

The first Sunday in May was a splendid day for a wedding.

The sun applauded the day, shining its brilliance down on Cooper County. The air was light and sweet, warm and ripe with the heady promise of summer.

Most of Boonville attended the ceremony, as did many from Poplar Bluff: Uncle Chester and Megan's father, Clarence, Mark and Ellie, Johnnie and Adam, Maude and Hurley—they all came, family and friends, to see these two, the new sheriff of Boonville and his lady veterinarian, joined together in matrimony.

There had been little talk of anything else lately. Though for weeks the folks of Boonville had talked of nothing but Maxwell and Flora Fletcher and how nature had put things right at last. Flora had put him aside, or as modern women would put it: she'd divorced him. Maxwell was in prison now, where he belonged, reflecting on his sins, while Flora seemed different these days, smiling often and spending many afternoons down at the local schoolhouse, helping the children work their sums. Danny Kincaid, having no grandmother of his own, had grown quite fond of Flora and often took Cody out to visit. He still attended Kemper Military Academy, but his parents were much different with him—more tolerant, much more accepting of his whimsical nature.

There was other news afoot: Luke Hawkins and Clarissa Westfield were getting married this fall. They planned to make their home in Boonville. Matthew Hawkins and Habel Habershaw were wedding up, also. But he was taking her home to Poplar Bluff.

For a while, however, the talk was of Megan Hawkins and Jim Lawson. Today was their day, theirs alone, and a happy day it was, indeed.

The stood face-to-face, the young bride and groom, in the presence of their friends, families, and neighbors, bathed in the sublime glow of tinted lights, which threaded down through the stained prisms of the pretty Presbyterian church windows.

The bride was beautiful, dressed in an elegant but simple white wedding dress that Mrs. Westfield had made for her. Her sunny hair was swept up into a puffy nest upon her head and interwoven with a crown of white daisies. Her cheeks were flushed a lovely rosy pink; her mouth was softly stained with color Merilee had applied most carefully. She looked up at her groom and felt a jolt of pride in his appearance.

He was indeed handsome, dressed in his best Sunday suit. His cheeks were ruddy with excitement, his mustache freshly trimmed. His dark hair fell onto one side of his forehead in a careless, boyish manner that only added to his appeal.

His gaze met his bride's. They thought themselves luckier than most. All of their lives they'd been heading toward this moment, and now the moment had finally come.

Her eyes still locked with his, the years swept back for Megan. She saw him as he'd once been—a homely little boy, following her about, mimicking her every word—and her throat got tight at the memory. He was no longer a homely little boy, but a fine, strong man, hers, the man she would call husband till the day she died. She blinked back the tears and thought, *Criminy, Meg, to think you almost let him get away.*

As he gazed down at her, the years melted away for him, also. He remembered her as a pretty little girl, stubborn and outspoken, yet kind and caring, unable to stand the suffering of any being. He'd adored her then. He adored her even more now. She was no longer a child, but a woman, his, the one he would call wife till the day he drew his final breath. The realization rocked him.

The Reverend Steven Dunmire took his place before them, smiling. He, too, wore his best suit this day. He was happy to have the honor of joining them. Despite his affection for Megan, he truly believed that she and Jim were destined to spend their lives together, as only those blessed by God could do.

He took their hands and placed them together, large over small, rough over smooth, and the room quieted. "Dearly beloved," he began and looked from Jim to Megan, "we are gathered here today . . ."

All listened, hushed, steeped in emotion, moved to see two of their own becoming one. Sniffles sounded. Throats were cleared. But when he came to the words "Do you, Jim, take this woman to be your wife?" all present went still and held their breath.

A short silence ensued. "I do," Jim said softly.

An audible sigh of relief reverberated around the room.

"And do you, Megan, take this man to be your husband?"

Once again, they all held their breath and waited, wondering. . . .

Many of the folks from both towns remembered Megan's words—words she'd spoken many times over the years: "I wouldn't marry you, Gordie Lawson. I wouldn't marry you if you were the last man left on earth!"

But those words were part of the past and were not spoken this day.

Instead she smiled up into Jim's eyes and softly said, "He's the only one I'd ever take."

A whoosh of relief rushed out among the crowd, and everyone breathed again.

Matthew and Luke blinked suspicious glints from their eyes. They avoided looking at each other and loosened their grips on their guns. They'd brought them just in case either of these two needed persuading at the last moment.

When the final words were spoken, and Jim and Megan were joined as one, all of Poplar Bluff's and Boonville's residents exchanged misty glances, sighed with relief, and said things like "There now. That wasn't so bad."

And it wasn't, because both were ready and willing at last.

Later, when all the feasting was over and all the dancing had ended, Jim and Megan rode home in the buggy. Jesse led the way, with the bright Missouri moon shining overhead. They sat side by side, hip to hip, pressed close, in silent anticipation of the night to come. She looped her arm in his and laid her head on his shoulder. "Do you think Habel will be happy in Poplar Bluff?"

"Yes," Jim answered. "Habel will be happy anywhere Matthew takes her."

Megan nodded, realizing the truth of that statement. "Of course she will. I'll miss her, though."

"They'll come visit. And we'll visit them."

"I'm glad Luke is staying here with Clarissa."

Jim smiled into the night. "Yeah, me, too."

In the semidarkness of twilight, Jim bent his head and looked down at her. She tipped her chin up to meet his gaze. His eyes were dark and ardent, rife with desire. She sent him a slow smile, a smile full of promises, full of love.

"You got out of asking me nice, didn't you?"

"You broke your promise."

"I did, didn't I?" she conceded and laid her head back down on his shoulder.

"I knew you would."

He laughed; she did, too.

When they reached their home, the home Megan had purchased from Mr. Barton those many months ago, Samson bounded off the porch to greet them. The pigs came, too, snorting out a howdy-do of their own. Jim got out of the buggy and walked around to Megan. He held out his hand and she took it. She got down and turned, starting for the house, but he surprised her by tugging her into his arms.

Her palms against his chest, she looked up at him. Her eyes spoke a silent question.

He dropped to one knee and smiled up at her. He gave her that lopsided grin—the one that sent arrows straight to her heart. "Megan Hawkins," he said quietly, earnestly, "will you marry me?"

She stared down at him, touched, unable to respond. She placed her hand against his cheek and tipped her head to the side.

"Meg," he said softly, his expression somber. "I've loved you for as long as I can remember."

"Yeah?" she asked just as softly.

"Yeah," he answered.

"Honest?"

"Honest." He stood and pulled her into his arms, then dropped a light kiss upon her forehead. He trailed his lips over her temple, down her cheek, finally finding her mouth. It was a long, slow, mellow kiss, that grew and deepened, leaving them both anxious for more.

When they parted, she looked up at him and simply said,

"Who else would I have married?" She grinned. "You're the only one I've ever loved, even though it took me a while to figure that out." She left him and walked through the yard.

He watched her move, willowy wanton that she was, and thought to himself, *I'm the luckiest man alive. She's mine. The prettiest girl in Missouri. Isn't that somethin'?*

The moon beamed down on her, flooding her in a thin wash of silvery light. When she reached the porch, she turned to him and lifted the crown of daisies from her hair. Smiling, she tossed it to him. He caught it deftly and returned her smile.

"Hey, Sheriff," she said, sliding him a secret glance out of the corner of her eye.

"Yeah?"

"Wanna know somethin'?"

"What?" He started toward her.

"We're gonna have a baby."

Staggered, he stopped. His expression sobered, and his mouth dropped open. "A baby?" He said the words so softly he barely heard them himself.

"Yeah. Isn't that somethin'?"

He could not have loved her more at that moment. His legs broke loose, and he ran to her. He swept her up into his arms and whirled her about, howling his joy to the moon. She hugged his neck and laughed, while he threw open the door and carried her into the house. The light from the moon was dim, barely lighting his way. He stumbled over a pair of boots left by the doorway and caught his foot on a chair by the hall entrance. He righted his footing and hauled her through the kitchen and down the hall, to the bedroom they'd shared that one cold Christmas Eve night.

He lowered her onto the bed and gently lay down on top of her, flooding her with a volley of questions: "Are you sure? When will it come? What do you think it'll be?"

She laughed at his eagerness and answered as best she could: "Yes, I'm sure. Sometime in early fall. A boy or a girl." She rolled him over till she lay on top of him. "Jim Lawson," she said, her voice soft with emotion. "I love you more than snow on Christmas morning."

"Aw, Meg." He clutched her to him. "I love you, too." He shook his head. "Gawd almighty. A baby! Ours!" He cupped both sides of her face and pulled her head down. He kissed her lovingly, easily, tracing her lips slowly, then darting his tongue inward to sweep the interior of her mouth. She returned his kiss eagerly, tangling her tongue with his, learning the feel, the smell, the taste of him all over again. Their kiss grew heated, heady, seasoned. His hands moved down her back, over her curves, over her waist, to cup her buttocks firmly, pulling her in toward him, letting her feel the hardness of his arousal. She pressed down into him, giving herself up to his touch, letting him mold her, shape her to his will.

He found the long row of buttons on the back of her dress, and he worked his way down them, undoing each one, then he peeled the dress apart, and spread his hands over her back, over the thin material of her chemise.

She rolled to her side and lay beside him. Slowly she undid the buttons on his shirt, then helped him slip off his coat and his shirt, while he propped himself up on one elbow. He cast the garments aside, and she touched his chest, pressing her palms to his body. Her hands roved over him, and in awe she quietly told him, "I never imagined you'd grow up like this."

"Disappointed?" he asked and took her hands, kissing each palm.

She teased him with a smile and said, "What do you think?"

He chuckled and got off the bed. He pulled her up to stand before him. "Wait here," he instructed and went to the bureau and lit the lamp. The room came to life in a soft spill of light. He sat down on a spindle-backed chair by the bureau and removed his shoes. Then he rose and returned to her, his gaze heated. "No britches under there today, huh, Meggie?" A grin caught at his mouth.

"Not today," she said, returning his grin. She eased the dress down.

His eyes left hers and followed her dress down over her shoulders, to her waist, to her feet, exposing her pretty white undergarments. His breath caught in his throat. Their eyes met. "Ah, Meg . . ." he whispered, his expression one of somber reverence. "You're so beautiful. Sometimes I just can't believe it." He stooped to his haunches and helped her lose her shoes and stockings, then rose once again and untied the ribbon between her breasts that held her chemise closed. He pushed the garment off her shoulders, letting it, too, fall to the floor.

She stood before him in only her lace-trimmed drawers, her breasts bare. They were fuller than they'd been several months ago. Slowly he reached out and gently brushed his palms across her taut nipples. He closed his eyes and cupped her breasts fully in his hands.

The heat of his palms radiated out from him and into her, and her eyes slid shut, also. His touch was intimate, possessive, splendid. His hands left her breasts and rode her ribs downward. He opened his eyes and slipped his thumbs into the waistband of her drawers, sending them sailing on a ride down over her hips, to join her dress on the floor.

Watching his face, she manipulated the buttons free on his trousers. Impatient, he helped her and with one sweep was free of the confining garment. He stood before her naked, a beautiful man.

From the parlor down the hall, her mother's clock chimed out the hour, while he lowered himself to the bed, drawing her down beside him. He kissed her gently, breaking away only long enough to murmur her name over and over again. They melted into each other, rolling from side to side, tangling arms, legs, and tongues. She threaded her fingers through his hair, while he found the pins in hers and cast them aside. He loosened her hair, fanning it out on the bed beside her.

He kissed a heated path over her face, neck, breasts, and stomach, then stopped and went still as a shadow. His hands found her warm belly. It was slightly puffed and rounded, though the puffiness had not been noticeable beneath her dress. He spread his fingers and laid his palms against her, molding his hands over her shape. "He's in there," he said, his voice full of wonder. "Our baby . . ."

"Yes," she whispered, stroking his head gently.

"Imagine that . . ." He laid his cheek against her stomach and, for several seconds, pondered the awesome prospect of fatherhood. "Ain't that somethin'?" he said at last and kissed his way back up to her mouth, his mustache prickling, his tongue warming. When he reached her mouth, she hauled him down and they exchanged a hot, wild, impatient kiss, while his turgid body pressed down into hers. Their caresses grew intimate, as they rediscovered each other all over again. And when kisses and touches could satisfy no longer, he poised himself above her.

Suddenly his expression grew worried. "Will this hurt him?"

"Him?" Megan asked, smiling, amused he had already decided the gender of their unborn child.

"Our baby?"

She laughed and tightened her arms around his neck. "No, not at all." She kissed him briefly, then drew him down, opening for him, ushering him in, welcoming him home as she would so many times in the coming years. His entrance was slow and blessed, pure and perfect, locking them as one, as they'd always been destined to be.

She marveled anew at the sense of wonder, of joy, of holding him deep within, and when he moved, she moved also, and their lovemaking became a beautiful thing, a beginning of their lives together, an end to their journey toward finding each other.

His strokes were silken, his words lovely. When at last he tensed over her, a frisson of feeling swept them into a magical world of their own, and everything billowed and spilled over, holding them captive for a precious moment, until they sank contented and sated back to reality.

In the minutes that followed, she lay sleepy and replete in his arms, his leg thrown over hers. She kissed his neck and snuggled against his shoulder, while he stroked the hair back from her temple. "I love you, Gordie Lawson," she said softly, using his nickname, coating its syllables in love.

"I love you, too, Meggie."

"Do you think it'll always be this way for us?" she asked, drifting in and out of her own little piece of heaven. She threaded her fingers through the curly hair on his chest.

He tipped his face on the pillow and looked down into her eyes. "What do you think?" he teased, his mouth wearing a lazy half-grin.

"I think," she said softly, drawing him down for another kiss, "it's always been this way for us. We just didn't know it."

"Ain't that somethin'?" he whispered.

"Yeah, ain't that somethin'?" she mimicked.

EPILOGUE

August 1908, Boonville, Missouri

"Hey, Ma!" the dark-haired boy yelled. He sent his older brother an injured look and rubbed the purpling bump on his temple. "Hey, Ma!" he hollered again, even louder.

Megan came through the kitchen door and out onto the porch. She wiped her hands on the backside of her britches and frowned. "Bob, what are you hollering about now?"

Bob stabbed an accusing finger at his ten-year-old brother. "Cole hit me in the head with that dad-burned squash over yonder!"

Megan's eyes found the older boy just as he was kicking the remnants of a broken squash behind him, trying to hide the evidence. She sent the blond-haired boy a disapproving glance. "Cole! What in tarnation do you think you're doin' hittin' your brother with a squash? Wastin' good food is a sin, and you know it!"

Cole made a face and looked at his feet. "He was lookin' at me funny."

"I wasn't!" Bob said in defense, still rubbing his temple.

"You was so!"

"I wasn't!"

"Bugger-brain!" Cole said.

At that insult Bob's sleepy brown eyes got bigger than walnuts. Uncle Luke had told him he wasn't sure what a bugger-brain was. Only Uncle Matthew knew for sure. But Uncle Luke said he was sure it was somethin' no one wanted to be.

"You take that back, Cole Lawson!" Bob hollered.

"Make me!" Cole stuck out his chest and balled his fists.

"Oh, for criminy's sake!" Megan exploded. "You two are gonna be the death of me!" She shook her head in disgust. "When are you gonna quit your squabblin' and start actin' like brothers?"

The brothers exchanged petulant glances and fidgeted, their faces reddening at their mother's rebuke.

"Now, make up," she ordered.

Reluctantly they lifted their eyes and found each other, then quickly looked away.

"Boys . . ." Megan crossed her arms over her chest and waited.

A soft summer breeze whispered through the trees. Out in the pasture Samson barked and chased a groundhog down into his hole. A little girl came out onto the porch and hugged her mother's leg. Megan reached down and stroked the little girl's chestnut curls. "What's the matter, Belle, darlin'?"

"Missed you, Mama." The four-year-old popped her thumb into her mouth and eyed her two brothers with silent adoration.

The boys looked to their feet again and secretly plotted revenge on each other.

"Bo-o-y-ys . . ." She drew the word out meaningfully. "I'd hate to have to tell your pa 'bout this." Her gaze found the oldest son again. "Cole, tell your brother you're sorry for beanin' him with the squash."

"Aw, Ma." The oldest boy looked up at her with eyes as blue as her own. "Do I have to?"

"Now, Cole, what do you think?"

Aw, shit! He sent a venomous glance his brother's way. He fidgeted, stalling until the very last moment.

"Cole," his mother warned.

"Sorry," he mumbled, refusing to lift his gaze.

"Now, Bob. Tell your brother you forgive him."

Bob sent his brother a venomous glance of his own. "But I don't."

"Bob!"

Bob kicked at a stone and sent it flying up over Cole's head. "I forgive ya," he murmured begrudgingly.

"All right, then," Megan said approvingly. "I'm gonna take your pa out some supper. You two look after Belle for a minute." She went back into the kitchen to fetch the plate she'd prepared for her husband. She grabbed a fork and the plate of food and went back out onto the porch. "You mind what I said now. You look after Belle. I'll be right back."

She left the children and went out behind the barn, where her husband was mending one of the fences their new cow, Dixie, had pushed through.

Jim wiped the sweat from his forehead. He straightened, forcing the kink out of his back, then went back to hammering the post into the ground. He sensed her presence even before he saw her. He always did. He stopped his hammering to watch her approach. Laying his hammer aside, he rested his boot on the bottom rung of the fence and tipped back his hat. He smiled, watching her move toward him. She was as graceful as ever. Her figure was still willowy, and her hair was every bit as sunny as it had been that first day he'd kissed her, on the banks of the Black River those many years ago. Today she wore a clean, homespun shirt, open at the throat, and a faded pair of britches. Unlike on that long ago day, she wore no skirt over her britches. And he thought, as he had so many times in the past ten years, that he was indeed the luckiest man alive.

"Howdy, Sheriff," she said, stopping before him.

His sleepy eyes raked her, and his mustache twitched with humor. "Howdy, Doctor."

"Today's Sunday. You're s'posed to be restin'."

"An' I will. Soon as I make sure Dixie won't get loose and get bred by some varmint bull."

Megan set the plate down on the wagon bed beside them and walked up against her husband, hugging his middle. "There's varmints, and there's varmints."

"I s'pose," he said and embraced her close to his heart.

She tipped back her head and gazed up at him. There were lines around his eyes now, lines that had not been present ten years ago. But she loved those lines, every one of them. His hair was still dark, but if she looked hard enough, she could find a thread of gray here and there, and she often teased him about it. But each hair on his head was dear to her, every single one, gray or otherwise. She smiled up at him and said, "The boys are fightin'."

"I heard them." He chuckled. "Namin' them after the Younger brothers might not have been such a good idea after all." He went silent a minute, then said, "I can't help but wonder what Belle will turn out to be like."

Megan grinned. "Scary thought, huh?"

"Sometimes."

"I'm afraid our children are gonna murder each other 'ventually."

"I suppose they will."

"Then what'll we do?"

He wiggled his eyebrows suggestively. "Make a couple more."

She laughed and kissed his Adam's apple. "You always were a randy sort."

"You never seemed to mind."

"I don't."

"You wanna know somethin'?" he asked, gazing down at her.

"What?" She tipped her head to one side, waiting.

His expression sobered, and his eyes grew earnest. "You're still the prettiest girl in Missouri."

She shook her head and blushed. At twenty-nine, she hardly thought of herself as a girl, and there were times she all but forgot about being pretty. "Humph! My sister always did say you told the tallest tales, Gordie Lawson."

"Is that a fact?"

"Yes."

"I love you, Meggie." He kissed the tip of her nose. "That ain't no tale, and you'll always be the prettiest girl in Missouri to me."

Her throat got tight. She blinked and felt the bright Missouri sun beat down on her, reminding her of the blessing they had in this land, their home, their children, each other. "I love you, too, Jim Lawson. More than I can ever say."

They kissed, their bodies flush, their arms wrapped around each other. When finally they broke apart, Megan cleared her throat and said, "Well, you'd best eat your dinner 'fore it gets cold. I'll sit with you a spell."

Hand in hand, they turned and slid up onto the wagon bed. They sat like two children, their legs dangling over the edge of the bed. Jim was just about to take his first bite when they looked up to see Cole storming around the barn, coming toward them, holding his bloodied nose.

"Hey, Ma!" he hollered.